Destroyed and Detained

The Sara Martin Mystery Series:
Lost and Found
Found and Destroyed

Destroyed and Detained

Danelle Helget

North Star Press of St. Cloud, Inc.
Saint Cloud, Minnesota

Copyright © 2013 Danelle Helget

ISBN: 978-0-87839-662-7

All rights reserved.

First Edition: June 2013

This is a work of fiction. Names, characters, places, and incidents are the products of the author's imagination or are used fictitiously. Any resemblance to actual events or persons, living or dead, is entirely coincidental.

Printed in the United States of America

Published by
North Star Press of St. Cloud, Inc.
P.O. Box 451
St. Cloud, Minnesota 56302

www.northstarpress.com   Facebook - North Star Press   Twitter - North Star Press

For my daughters, Brooke and Taylor. You two bring me so much joy, and I am so very proud of who you've become. I love you both with all my heart.

Love, Mom

A special thanks to:

My husband Jared—for holding down the fort while I got this done.
Michelle Kremers—for suggesting the title for this book.
My writers group—for the opinions, encouragement and support.
Beta Readers: Milissa Nelson, Kristin Alderink—for edits and suggestions.
North Star Press—for all the help in making this a successful book.

1

Sure as shit, there it was! My mouth was hanging wide open as I stood there and looked out the window at it. I blinked quickly a bunch of times and shook my head violently to make sure I was actually awake. I was.

Derek, my boyfriend, a detective for the St. Paul Police Department, had just yelled for me to come into the dining room. I yelled back, "Why?" annoyed I was being interrupted while curling my hair.

He insisted I hurry. "You'll really want to see this!"

"See what?" I'd asked, setting my curling iron down, and leaving the bathroom.

"Ah, there's a big pirate ship out here," were his exact words. *What?* I'd mumbled to myself. *Did he say pirate ship?* I'd walked down the hall into the dining room and joined him at the sliding glass door that faced my back yard, which includes a patio, some grass and a medium-sized lake.

As clear as day, I could see a pirate ship. Not a boat. A ship! A ship much too large for this lake. "What . . . the . . . fuck . . . is . . . that?" I quietly gasped when I finally found my voice. I was suddenly very scared . . . or excited . . . or scared. I was in shock! I didn't really know what I felt.

"That's . . . a pirate ship?" Derek answered, completely dumbfounded. He lifted his coffee cup and took a drink.

"I . . . ah . . . Yeah, but what's it doing in my lake?" I asked, my mouth still hanging open between sentences. Neither of us had peeled our eyes from it since we'd noticed it. We stood there, shoulder to shoulder, riveted. Pepper, the Great Dane, was sitting next to Derek's leg on the other side, staring too. Pepper was my temporary dog.

Derek finally moved. He swigged the last of his coffee from his cup, turned to the sink and placed the cup in. "Not sure what it's doing there, but this is definitely not my jurisdiction, or my department, or my issue. You have a great day, honey. I gotta get to work. Long drive, ya know?" He gave me a quick peck on the cheek and scooted out the front door.

I ran to the front door after him and protested, "Wait! What am I supposed to do about this?"

"Sweetness, you're a much better detective than I am! Get your girls on it! I'm sure Tannya knows something!" he yelled back, still walking, then stepped up into his Jeep and shut the door.

Great, now what? I quickly closed the door to the house and went back to the window. It was still there. The ship was huge. The sails were up and sported a skull-and-crossbones flag. I was simply dumbfounded. Why the hell would someone put a ship on this lake? And now that I thought of it, how in Sam Hill did anyone get that thing in it?

Only three other houses were on this lake besides mine, and we all had our own little private boat launches. There was no public launch. This made absolutely no sense! Were there real pirates on the ship? The only ones I heard of on the news were killing people and taking hostages in other parts of the world's oceans. I recall hearing at least a couple pirate stories over the last few years. None ended well.

I needed binoculars! I looked at the time. I needed to get to work, too. I had to open the store today. I mentally made a plan to go to work, stop by the diner and talk to Tannya to see if she knew anything, and then go to Miss Kitty's house and borrow binoculars from her place. I was able to use equipment whenever I wanted. She and I have kind of a history that involved some . . . . . . surveillance, if you will. She kept all the supplies from that venture at her house, but I knew she'd let me use anything I needed.

And so went my life. I was starting to get used to it. I try, and *want* to live a quiet life, but it never quite works out that way. Right now I was living in a remote "North Country" town in Minnesota.

Nisswa hadn't been the same since I came to town and everyone knew it. Sometimes when I walked down the street and smiled at the older crowd, I felt like they hated me. It seemed some folks loved that I found the remains of a longtime missing girl, and helped her family put her to rest. Others felt I had psychic abilities and I was scary.

And then there were the haters. It didn't help that I moved here, to Nisswa, from the Cities shortly after that initial incident. A couple of months later I was involved in the shooting of a very rich, very bad man from this town. I didn't shoot him, but I made the paper again, and around here that was all it took to get the stink eye from everyone.

My boyfriend, Derek, had been offered a job here as chief of police but hadn't taken the offer. I think he wanted to, but he was waiting to see where our relationship went. Right now it was pretty good. But there had been bumps in the road, one of those bumps being Jodi.

Derek and I saw each other as much as possible but it was sometimes hard with him working in the Cities and me working here. I owned Lost and Found, a boutique on the small main street in Nisswa. We sold home décor, clothes, candles, handmade jewelry, and other small items. The store came as a package deal with the cabin I bought and lived in, along with the land surrounding most of the lake. The three other houses on the other side of the lake all had been situated near each other. I had this whole side to myself. I owned three-quarters of the land surrounding the lake. Very nice, at least until a few moments ago when a pirate ship showed up.

I guess I would worry about that after work, when I had binoculars. I poured the last cup of coffee into a travel mug and grabbed my purse. I rushed into work and got all set up for the morning, turning lights and specialty lamps on and lighting a few candles. Then I took a quick bathroom break before opening the doors for the day. While washing up, I glanced up in the mirror. Holy hell! I'd forgotten to finish curling my hair! Oh, my gosh, what was I going to do? My hair was shoulder length, and one side was in a bunch of tight ringlet curls, while the other totally straight! I had been so completely distracted by the ship I'd forgotten to finish. I ran across the store to my office and dug through my purse hoping, praying, I'd at least find a ponytail holder in it. Nope. Nada. Nothing.

I grabbed my keys and ran out to my Jeep and searched it. Nothing on the stick shift, nothing in the storage areas. After contemplating my options, which were slim, I decided to gift myself a new t-shirt and hat with my own store logo on it. Back in the bathroom, I wetted down the curly side of my hair and blew it for a moment under the hand dryer in an effort to straighten it a little. It helped, but the hat was the best choice. I was just glad I was in jeans and not a skirt or dress pants. Hopefully no one would come in, and I wouldn't run into anyone I knew. Ginger was scheduled at 11:00, and Monday mornings were usually pretty slow.

With paperwork caught up and most of the new inventory unpacked, I left the pricing and shelf stocking for Ginger and left promptly at 11:00. I went straight over to Morning Glory, the diner two doors down, to see Tannya.

Tannya was a fr . . . fri . . . acquaintance. I guess I could call her a friend, but it seemed weird. She was a bit unorthodox. She was heavy-set, but wore really tight clothes that did *not* flatter her shape. She wore heavy make-up, too, with really bright pink blush, and always wore her hair in a pony. This past winter my best friend, Kat, took her shopping to get her hair done and made her buy some nice, good-fitting jeans and a nice shirt, and then dyed her hair from a half black root-half blonde, fried frizzy tail into a shorter, softer darker blonde. The cut was great, and she was talked into a good conditioner, which she'd been using. She has come a long ways but was still a sight most days.

In the friend department though, she'd been great. She liked to hang with me as much as possible and had been there for me when I needed help. And a bonus: she loved to cat-sit for me. She watched Faith for me a while back, and I was glad to have her.

I opened the doors to Morning Glory and found a booth. I slid in and took a quick peek at the "special" board. Two eggs, two bacon, caramel roll, and a coffee for $5.00. That sounded perfect to me. I looked around and saw Tannya behind the counter plating up some toast. BING! "Order up," Marv yelled from the kitchen window.

Morning Glory was the only restaurant in town open early for breakfast. They had their regulars, a few men bellied up to the counter and stool area and a few older couples in booths. The restaurant was older-themed but well-maintained. The tables and chairs were shiny chrome with red vinyl seats. It was bright and cheery and tastefully decorated. Tannya had worked there a long time and mostly worked the day shift. She was newly single. She'd recently thrown out her drug-addicted husband after one year of marriage. She got the house and was taking some online classes to try to get a degree.

She was fun, had tons of energy, and was ready for anything at any time. Tannya was also my primary source for information. Working at the diner and being a social butterfly came in handy. She got all the gossip every day at work. She was great at getting people to tell all. Trust me.

Walking by with two plates in her hand, she noticed me and smiled. "Hey, girl!" she yelled as she passed. This was normal. Tannya was loud and had conversations from across the room sometimes. "I'll be right there!" I wondered if she'd heard anything yet about the pirate ship. The lake was small, with only four houses on it, so unless someone called the police, I doubted the story had broken yet.

"What's up, girl? You want breakfast? Caramel rolls are on special for one more hour!" Tannya informed me, when she returned.

"That sounds good. I'll have the special and coffee. And when you get a second, I want to ask you something," I told her quietly.

"Oooh, what? What is it?" She asked eagerly as she slid into the booth across from me.

"Order up!" Marv yelled again.

"Crap," she said. "Hold that thought!" She scrambled over to the window, grabbed the plate and put it in front of one of the men at the counter. She topped off everyone's coffee and then came over with a cup and the pot for me. She filled me up, put the pot on the table and leaned forward. She was staring at me with anticipation and a big grin. "What is it?"

I mentally shook my head and took a sip. "Well, I had a strange morning and wanted to know if there was any buzz around here lately about the lake I live on." Letting that sit for a moment, I continued when I didn't get a response. I leaned forward and lowered my voice. "There was a ship on the lake this morning," I said frankly.

Tannya pressed her eyebrows together and tipped her head. "A ship? Did you say a *ship?*" she asked raising her voice.

I nodded and glanced around. Then leaned even closer and whispered, "A *pirate* ship." Then I nodded again.

Tannya stared at me hard for a long moment. Then she smiled and started looking around. "Ah hah! I'm on one of those hidden camera shows, ain't I?"

I could see she was getting worked up. I grabbed her arm to calm her down. I didn't want a scene. "Shhhh, I'm not sure what it's about, but I don't think we want the whole town to know."

"Are you shitting me? Are you serious?" she whispered. "There's a pirate ship on your lake? Like a *Pirates of the Caribbean* pirate ship?" she asked. Then she smiled huge. "Are there are pirates on it? Like Johnny Depp? I mean I know Johnny's not on your ship, but what if there's a cute pirate like him?"

I shook my head and put my face in my hands. I'd just opened a can of worms. "First off," I warned, "it's not my ship or my lake. Secondly, I'm not sure what's up with it. I was hoping you knew something."

"No, girl! I haven't heard anything. I want to, though. This is great! Can I come over and see it? I'm off at 2:00." She was very excited.

"Um, yeah. I guess."

"Do you think it's still there?" she asked, concerned.

"It couldn't have gone far. I mean, really, how would you get that in and out of a lake that small? It's not like there's a boat launch. I don't get it," I said, still in shock. "I'm going to go to Miss Kitty's and pick up some binoculars. I'll meet you at my place when you're done with work," I told her.

"Okay, but promise me you two won't go explore it without me. You *have* to wait for me!"

"Whoa! There'll be no exploring of anything. I just want to look at it closer. We're staying in the house with the shades drawn and the doors and windows locked."

Tannya faced changed to serious. "Oh, yeah. I never thought none about that. Pirates are dangerous. They steal people's stuff and kill 'em! Holy cow! Are you going to stay living there?" she asked. "You can stay at my house if you'd like. I got plenty of room!"

"Well, they don't *always* kill people. I mean, how much do we really know? Maybe they're just lost." As I said it out loud I knew that made no sense.

"Yeah," Tannya said sarcastically, "they're lost . . . on a small lake with no inlets or outlets, in the middle of a continent, more than a thousand miles from an ocean. Riiiight!"

I shrugged. I was too proud to admit to Tannya Potter that I was wrong. "Well, then you tell me!"

"Order up!" Marv yelled from the kitchen. "Woman, get off your butt and work!"

"Marv, I *am* working! We got much bigger business over here than your eggs!" Tannya yelled back. She was standing now, shaking her head like an angry hen, with her hand on her hip and a finger pointing while she spoke.

She turned back to me. "Those are probably your eggs, so I'll go get them," she said in a pleasant voice with a smile.

I watched the continued, quieter conversation between Tannya and Marv. Those two were always yelling at each other. I think they got along, but yelling was just the way they showed their love. I shook my head and smiled as Tannya took the plate, and Marv stuck out his tongue at her back. "I saw that!" she said without looking back.

"Here, you eat up. You're going to need your strength for our next adventure. I'm so excited. We haven't been on a big adventure in a while. Not since Jodi, anyway."

"There's no adventure, and keep it down. I don't want a bunch of people hanging around the lake. Let's just go see what we can see later and take it from there. In the meantime, if you hear anything about this ship, let me know. And get details!" I started eating and she left.

Great, now I had Jodi on my mind again. I hated that woman! Jodi was Derek's ex. His almost fiancée, the girl he had dated for almost two years and had been living with and ring shopping with.

He came home on a lunch break from work one night, as a surprise, and caught her half-dressed on top of the guy who lived across the hall. He threw her out, and that was the last he saw of her. She tried to fix things, but he walked away. That was five and a half years ago. Now, all of a sudden she wants him back.

Last winter she had been calling his phone. He was ignoring it, but when he went home to his apartment one night, she was leaned up again his door waiting. He talked to her for a while and then left to meet me. He never told me why he was late that night, but I knew something was off.

I saw the number of times she tried to call him in a day, and it was ridiculous. So I asked him about it. Derek told me she wanted him back. Things were over with the guy from across the hall, and the two after him, and now she was lonely and knew she'd made a huge mistake when she cheated on Derek and wanted to try again.

He told her that he wasn't interested, but she kept bothering him. So one day when the phone rang and Derek was outside, I answered it. I told her I was his new girlfriend and that he was sick of the calls and to stop. Well, she didn't. So I followed her one night. Not just me, me and Tannya and Miss Kitty. We did what we do and spied on her. We all went out for a drink or two and after talking about it and feeding each other's imaginations we decided to take care of it.

We loaded up in Miss Kitty's Mercedes Benz and went to Jodi's apartment. Miss Kitty and Tannya were down for the weekend visiting me because I hadn't been to Nisswa in a while. It was winter and the Cities are much more fun than the cabin in the winter time, so they drove down together, and we made a weekend of it.

I did a little investigating and got her address, and we went for a visit. We really didn't have a plan, but we parked in the lot and watched her apartment windows. I had never met her before, but I found her picture on facebook so I knew her when I saw her. She looked to be getting ready, so we waited. When she came down at 9:00 p.m., we followed her to a club that was kind of skanky. I was pretty sure she didn't know me, and so we just walked right in and sat down at the bar near her. Slowly Tannya started making conversation with her. She ended up hanging out and drinking a bunch of martinis with us. Miss Kitty asked her if she had a boyfriend and she said, "Umm, kind of."

"What does kind of mean?" Miss Kitty asked.

"Well, I'm working on it. You see, we were an item years ago and he caught me making out with another man and left me. But I've given it some time, and I mean, I, like, never slept with the guy, so I didn't really cheat, but he was pretty upset about it, so I gave him his space. And now, well . . . I'm ready for marriage and children, and I want him back. He'll be a great husband and father, and I can't wait to start my life with him again."

Tannya shot me a look. I took a big gulp of air, then downed the rest of my coconut martini. Then I turned to her and said, "Wow, and you think he'll want you back? I mean you did kiss another man . . ."

"Yeah, but he'll want me back. I just have to get him alone for a few minutes. I know his weaknesses. He'll come around. He'll come back to me. I just need a few moments to convince him I'm the only one for him. He said he has a girlfriend and doesn't want me to call, but I can hear in his voice that he's still in love with me."

"So, why doesn't he just break up with the other girl then?" Tannya asked.

"I don't know. But it won't take too long. I saw him face-to-face a while back, and I could tell I took his breath away. He still loves me."

"You're delusional!" I said.

"What?" Jodi asked. *Shit! I'd said that out loud. Oh, well, may as well get this over with,* I thought. "Look, JODI—yeah I know your name," I said in my "bad girl's" voice. "I know who you are, and I know exactly what Derek, your 'kind of boyfriend' thinks about you." I was standing up, in her face, pointing my finger and talking loud. "You cheated on him, and he threw your ass out. FIVE YEARS AGO! Move on! He doesn't want you. He hasn't looked back since that day. He's my boyfriend now! Stay away from him and stop calling him! Got it?"

Her eyes went from shocked, to scared, to pissed off, rather quickly. She'd figured out I was the woman standing in her way, and her anger looked hard. Now I was a bit scared.

She stood too and yelled back at me. "So it's you! Listen here, bitch, Derek and I have hit some rough patches, but we have always loved each other. You think he's yours? Well, guess again! I'm back, and I always get what I want. An ugly thing like you isn't going to get between me and him," she yelled at me.

Tannya and Miss Kitty were both on their feet now. "Ugly? Who you calling ugly?" Tannya said. "No one calls my friends ugly! Girl, you're a fake, from your bleach job to your lop-sided, silicone boobs. All that work and you still don't come close to a class act like Sara! She's beautiful inside and out, and she ain't had no work done!" She quickly turned to Miss Kitty, "No offense."

"None taken," Miss Kitty nodded in agreement.

"You're living in fantasy land, child. Ain't no way Derek's ever leaving Sara for you. They're in love. You had your chance and blew it," Tannya told her.

"Yeah, give it up! Derek and Sara are a wonderful couple and will be together forever," Miss Kitty added.

Okay, now it was getting thick and a bit scarier for me.

"Puuuulease! She has no idea how to please him!" Jodi told Miss Kitty. "Derek and I had tricks and games that'd make Hugh Heffner blush. We're hot together!"

And well, I guess that's all I could take of the skank, because I hauled off and punched her straight in the face. She came back at me scratching and biting, and it instantly turned into a huge bar brawl. Yup, not my proudest moment.

All four of us were going at it pretty hard until the bartender turned the hose from the drink station on us, and we stopped. We were soaked in water, eyeliner running, hair a mess. We all stood there looking at each other.

"Yeah, you're real classy, bitch. What would Derek ever do without you?" Jodi spat at me. I lunged at her again, but Miss Kitty and Tannya held me back.

"Stay away from me and stay away from Derek!" I yelled trying to get free.

"Never, bitch! I ALWAYS get what I want!" She turned and strutted into the bathroom.

I apologized to the bartender and gave him a one-hundred-dollar bill, and we left.

When I got home, Derek called to see what I was up to. He never said so, but I had a feeling he'd gotten a call from Jodi. The next time I saw him things seemed funny between us, and so I brought her up. That opened a dam, and it all came pouring out. He had been talking to her, ran into her at the apartment that night, and had met her for a drink. He told me he just needed to talk to her face-to-face and make sure there weren't any feelings there and to tell her once and for all it was over. I didn't believe him and threw him out.

I didn't see him or take his calls for two weeks. Then he showed up on my doorstep in Nisswa, looking like a lost puppy, tears in his eyes and, well, I let him in.

It took a while, but I think we're okay again. That was a few months ago. We are moving at a snail's pace in our relationship, which was fine with me. We now have an official on again-off again relationship, and those don't usually work out well. I wasn't getting my hopes up. I loved Derek, but he lied to me and went behind my back to meet her. And I'd had my fair share of deception lately. I knew he loved me, but I didn't want to be hurt again. So what could I say, my walls were up!

I finished my breakfast or lunch rather, and left enough money on the table for the tab and Tannya's tip.

I drove out to Miss Kitty's, which was out on a dirt road, and slowly pulled up the drive. I called ahead and told her I was coming. When I got there, I put the car in park and reached down to grab my purse. Then I heard the passenger side door open.

2

Miss Kitty jumped in the passenger seat and shut the door. She was wearing black head-to-toe with a black-and-rhinestone baseball hat to boot. I looked at her, surprised.

"Hey! Oh, my gosh! I'm so excited to see this pirate ship! What do you think is going on? Tannya called and told me all about it. She said not to start without her. I got everything here for us," she said holding up one of the big bags she'd brought with her. Then she set it on the floor in front of her next to the purse she always brought, which I knew contained a small dog named Smoochy Poo. She reached for her seat belt.

"I . . . ah . . ." I started to argue, but then I remembered this was Miss Kitty, and there was no point in arguing with her. She always got her way. She was rich and thought she was powerful, which she wasn't, but she had a way of getting people to cooperate, and if they didn't, she bought her way. She was divorced now. With the divorce, she received a large settlement and the enormous house. Miss Kitty also believed I could either see the future or that I was psychic. Neither was true but she wouldn't listen to me. She was tall, thin, blonde, and everything that could be fake, was. She was a total diva, even down to the small dog in the purse. From a distance, she looked twenty-five, but I bet she was more like fifty. I'd ask but she'd probably have me killed.

"Okay, then, let's roll," I said as I reluctantly turned the key. As I turned back down the drive, I wondered if I should call Rex. I'd been avoiding him as much as possible lately because there was a lot of chemistry between us, and I wasn't sure what would happen if we were in the same room together, and Derek and I were on again. Actually, I knew what would happen . . . and, well, it couldn't right now.

Rex, a police officer here in Nisswa, had been very helpful in the shooting I was involved in. And he helped me get my pontoon out of the lake, and taught me to make a Mexican dish and so on . . . I had him on speed dial and I knew he would help me with anything if I asked. He was in his late twenties, very fit, and looked great in a uniform. He was tan, dark-haired, and had a perfectly white set of teeth and a dimple on one cheek. Seriously, he made my knees weak.

I decided to call him, just to see if he knew anything about the ship.

"S'up, stranger?" he answered in his velvety voice.

"Ah, nothing, just calling to check in," I said with a smile.

"Oh, yeah? I haven't heard from you in a while. Almost like you've been avoiding me," he said.

"Nah, just not much going on."

"I bet. How's that detective treating you?" *There he goes with the "are you single yet?" comment, fishing for information.*

"Good. He's fine. I'm fine. I was just wondering if you heard anything about anything strange goings on in town?" *Geez, there I go again, stumbling over my words and sounding dumb.*

"Nooooo, why? Is there something I should know?"

"Nope, everything's fine. Like I said, just checking in," I said trying to sound chipper. I didn't want him to send the 5-0 over and make a ruckus. If I was the cause of any more drama in this little town they were going to run me out.

"You'd tell me if I needed to know something, right, Sara?" he scolded.

"Yes, if I ever need your assistance, I'll definitely call you right away," I told him.

"Or if you see anything or anyone suspicious?" he added.

"Of course. Well, you have a great rest of your day, and I hope to see you soon. Okay?" I said in closing.

"Yeah, sure," he said suspiciously. "Stay out of trouble, Ms. Martin," he added and disconnected.

"Oh, Sara, Sara, Sara," Miss Kitty said with a head shake. "You have the hots for Officer McHottie!"

"Pffft! I do not!" I argued.

"Sure do. I can see it in your eyes and hear it in your voice. And, honey, it ain't fair! There are plenty of us single women in this town, and the only one he ever looks at is you. You got a sexy cop already. Leave some for the rest of us!"

I made a right turn onto my county road and shook my head. "He's all yours. I don't want him. I was just checking to see if he knew anything."

"Sure ya were, darling. Sure."

"Well, he didn't know anything, so I guess we'll just take a look and see if it's even still there, and if there's anyone on board."

When I got to my driveway, I couldn't see the lake well so I parked and we got out.

Miss Kitty walked the best she could, carrying the dog in one purse and the equipment in the other. I threw my purse on the front step and took the equipment bag from her and set it there too. "Let's go around and check quick to see if it's there," I said.

When we rounded the corner we could see the ship right away.

"Hooooooleeeeeyy Shit!" Miss Kitty said. "That really is a pirate ship!"

"Yup," was all I could manage, I mean really, what could I say?

"It's huge! What the hell is it doing on THIS lake?" she asked.

"I don't have a clue," I said, staring in shock at it once again.

After a few minutes passed, I suggested we go inside and wait for Tannya. We grabbed the stuff from the front step and went in.

It was almost two o'clock already so we wouldn't have to wait for long. When we got in, Pepper casually greeted us at the door and sniffed the vented side of Miss Kitty's purse.

"Why is Pepper still here?" Miss Kitty asked.

"Well, I talked to Kerry the other day, and she's been over to visit a couple times, but she has an apartment now that won't take dogs."

"So are you keeping him?"

"I said he could stay as long as he needed to. He travels well and is a really easy going, gentle dog. And I don't mind the company."

"Do you think that Smoochy Poo with get along with him?" She asked me.

"Pepper gets along with everyone. It's Faith I wonder about."

Faith, my nine-month-old cat, was lying on the back of the couch and now that she was older she didn't seem to care if we were there or not. Miss Kitty removed her dog from the bag and held her up nice and high in her pink collar with rhinestones and a pink and white skirt that looked like a tutu. Smoochy Poo always looked her best.

Pepper sniffed her and walked away. For a little dog, Smoochy Poo was very quiet. She followed Pepper around, but he wasn't interested in her at all. That's how he was. He didn't care that other animals were around him. Pepper was more of an people lover. Faith perked her head up and stared wide-eyed at Smoochy Poo and quickly switched into pounce posture. She was unpredictable.

"Oh, here we go!" I warned, but it was too late. In a split second, Faith was on her. Faith leapt from the couch and scampered after Smoochy and dove onto her back. Smoochy didn't have a chance. Smoochy Poo screeched and dropped like a fly. I rushed over, but they were already going at it.

Miss Kitty screamed, "Oh, no, my baby!"

"I reached down and tried to separate them, yeling, "Stop!" but it wasn't working. They were rolling around like crazy—small yips coming from Smoochy and yowling from Faith. I was trying to reach in, but I didn't want to get bit or scratched so I didn't. Pepper walked over to the brawl and barked once. He had a huge, loud bark. They both stopped in shock, and when they did, I grabbed Smoochy Poo and picked her up quick. Faith shot her eyes at me and jumped at my leg. She dug her claws in and climbed me like a tree!

"Yeeeooowwww!" I yelled. Miss Kitty stood there with her hand over her mouth.

"Ahhhhh!" She yelled, horrified at the sight of a cat climbing a human.

"Here!" I yelled and threw Smoochy into her arms. Then I reached down and grabbed Faith by the back of the neck and peeled her off. I held her in the air face to face with me and pointed at her. "NO! NO! THAT'S A BAD KITTY!" I screamed and dropped her on the floor. She sat down right there and groomed herself like it was just another day.

"Are you okay? Oh, my gosh, that must hurt so bad!" Miss Kitty said.

I looked down and my pants were filling with blood spots. They looked polka-dotted.

"Ah, awwww . . . yeeees," I stuttered. "That hurt bad! I'm going to go clean up," I said and excused myself.

I washed off the blood, and made sure each little puncture had stopped bleeding, then changed into some clean jeans and a sweatshirt. It was late April and chilly out. For the most part it had been a mild winter and temps had been nice for Minnesota. Today was in the mid-fifties and sunny. All the ice had gone off the lake weeks ago. Once in a while there were thin sheets in the morning, but they melted very shortly after sunrise.

I pulled the blinds open on the deck door and stared out at the lake again. The pirate ship hadn't moved since it had appeared.

"That's exactly where it was this morning," I told Miss Kitty.

"Unreal!" she said. "Maybe it's an April fool's joke."

I let out a snort. "That would've been a pretty big joke. But it's a bit late for that. Who would the joke be on?"

We each helped ourselves to a pair of binoculars from the bag of goodies Miss Kitty had brought and headed to the window for a close-up look at the pirate ship. I heard a noise from the front yard and knew it must be Tannya's car door. A moment later there was a knock. I opened the door and barely got a hello out before Tannya pushed right past me and darted to the patio door.

"Holy moly, you weren't kidding. There is a freaking pirate ship on your lake!" Tannya exclaimed. "How in Sam Hill did that get there?" They both looked at me.

"Hell if I know! I woke up and there it was. It wasn't there last night when I went to bed!"

"It's new," Miss Kitty said.

"Well, that's what I said. It's only been there today. Must have appeared overnight," I told them.

"No, I mean it's *new*. It's not old. Look at it! The paint's shiny and fresh. The wood looks strong and new, even the sails are clean and new. Most pirate ships look old and ragged. This one's new."

She was right. It was new. I took the third pair of binoculars out the bag, since Tannya had claimed mine from the table. I scanned the ship. It was definitely new. "Can you see anyone on board?" I asked.

"No," Tannya said.

"Nope," Miss Kitty added. "But I do see something at the house to the right behind it. There's a big guy in a rowboat over by the dock."

"Maybe he's going to go check it out!" Tannya said.

I swung my binoculars over to the right. The trees had been cut down!

Across the lake, the area had been covered in thick, tall, mature white pines so one house couldn't see to the next. Where the last house on the right was, a large swath of trees looked like they'd been clear cut. I hadn't noticed that this morning. I was so shocked at the sight of the ship that I hadn't even looked beyond it. I had just stared at the ship.

On the ground in front of the opening were piles of two-by-fours, and a few sets of saw horses were set up near a small shed.

In front of the opening to the left of the dock were what looked like railroad tracks. It appeared that the ship had been built there and then rolled into the water on the tracks.

"What . . . the . . . heck?" I stammered. "Do you think the neighbors built it?"

"Who lives there?" Miss Kitty asked. We both looked at Tannya.

"I don't know," she said.

I thought about it. I didn't know either. I knew the Sanders lived in the first house to the left, but I hadn't met the people in the other two houses yet. The one in the middle I could barely see. The one with the tracks was on the far right.

We all raised our binoculars back up and watched as the man in the old wooden rowboat rowed from the dock near the tracks over to the ship. We could see he had a large wooden crate in the boat with him. As he approached, a rope came spiraling down from the top of the ship's deck and landed in his boat. I looked back up to the ship and could see another man up on deck. He was dressed like a pirate, hat and all. The man in the boat tied the rope around the crate and up it went into the ship. Then the man rowed back to the dock, tied up the boat and walked up to the house.

"Strange . . ." Tannya said slowly. "Did you see the guy on the ship dressed like a pirate?"

"Yes, do you think they're real pirates?" Miss Kitty asked. "Are they going to steal stuff and burn other boats and take hostages, raid and pillage the town?"

"I doubt it!" I said with an attitude. "This lake's private. There's no access. Who would they steal from? And what would they want that a boater on Lake Hawsawneekee would have? It's not like we're transporting treasures," I laughed.

"Well, then, darling, what are they doing?" Miss Kitty sassed back.

"That's what we are here to find out! We need a plan!" Tannya said with excitement in her voice. *Oh boy!*

"Why don't we just go to the edge of the lake, yell to them and ask what they are doing?" Miss Kitty suggested.

"Better yet, we could put your pontoon in the water and ride out there and ask for a tour! I ain't never been on a real pirate ship before!" Tannya suggested. "I bet they'd give us a tour. It's new, and people always like to show off their new stuff."

"I don't have my dock in yet. It's too early, isn't it? The dock has to be in to put the boat in. Otherwise where would I park it? And no, we're not just going over there and ask for a tour. What if they're bad guys?"

I saw movement on the ship deck again, and we put our binoculars back up. It looked like there were two men on board now.

"How many people do you think are on it?" Miss Kitty asked.

"I don't know," I admitted.

My phone rang and scared the bejeebers out of all of us. We laughed at how hard we jumped as I answered. The caller ID showed Derek.

"Hey!" I answered with a giggle.

"What's so funny?"

"I'm standing here at my patio door with Miss Kitty and Tannya looking out at the ship and the phone startled us."

"So it's still there, huh?"

"Yes, it's so strange. And there are two men dressed like pirates on it and another just rowed over from the dock of the house on the right and dropped a crate off to it. There's a bunch of big trees down and a railroad track looking thing leading to the lake. It must be how they got it in there."

"Really? So the neighbors built it?" he asked.

"It looks that way."

Tannya said loudly, "Ask Derek if it's too early to put the boat and the dock in the water."

"Was that Tannya?" he asked.

"Yes."

"You want to put the pontoon and dock in?" he asked me.

"No, not really. Is it too early?"

"Not really. You should be fine, but someone has to get in the freezing water to do it."

"Tannya wants to boat over and ask for a tour," I told him.

"Ha ha ha! Let her. Tell her to bring treasure with, though, just in case they don't like her company. I better get back to work. Stay safe and out of trouble, Matey! Arrr!" he said and hung up.

I set the phone down and looked out again. Over at the house, the boat man was loading more stuff into the little boat—smaller boxes and containers this time. He seemed to wave goodbye to someone still in the house as he left. I couldn't see anyone through the window, though.

"So, did Derek say we could put the dock in?" Tannya eagerly asked.

"He said it should be fine, but we're not doing that right now. It takes a few men and time."

My phone rang again. I reached over and checked the ID. The number was "Blocked." I answered and it was Aunt Val.

My aunt Val, my Dad's younger sister, was one of my Dad's four siblings. To sum her up would be to say she's a wild one, always ready for adventure. Kind of like Tannya, a jump-now-think-later type of gal. Aunt Val had been married and divorced three times, no kids, no pets—she hates both and doesn't like responsibility. She liked to drink and liked to be involved in crazy things. She didn't have a job. She'd had many, but she usually jumped a bus after a few months and moved to a different town. She made just enough to eat and depended on the government and men for everything else. She wasn't homeless—there usually was someone to lend her a couch or take her home for the night when she needed it. She had been in town this past winter and came to the cabin to visit and stay for a couple weeks, which reminded me, she had started running to get back into shape, at age fifty-four. She had mentioned she'd met a nice older man at a mailbox on the lake. I wonder if she'd remember who it was or which house it was.

I quickly answered. "Hello?"

"Hi, love!" she said in a sweet high voice. Her tone made me laugh. She was probably drunk already.

"Hi, Aunt Val. How are you?" I said with a smile.

"Oh, ya know me. I'm always good."

"That's great to hear," I quickly responded. "Hey, do you remember when you stayed here for a few weeks and you went running every day?"

"Yes . . . but, Sara, I . . . ah," she stammered.

"No," I interrupted. "I have to ask you something quick. You said you meet a nice man who lived on the lake and spoke with him at the mail box. Which house did he live in? Do you remember?"

"Hah!" she shouted and then giggled. "Funny you should ask!"

3

I arrived at the police station in Nisswa at about 3:30 p.m. Tannya was smiling ear to ear as we all exited my Jeep.

"Bailing your Aunt Val out? I can't believe this! This is gonna be great. I wonder what she did," Tannya said to me as she walked quickly to the entry.

"I have no clue! She only had a minute on the phone. She said she'd tell me in the car."

Miss Kitty was looking around the lot. "I hope no one I know is here. I didn't even get to check the mirror before we left. Are you sure my hair and lipstick are still good?" she asked us.

"Yes!" we answered again.

"We have to hurry. I don't want Smoochy Poo to worry about me. She doesn't like to be alone, and I'm not sure how she'll do with your cat."

"She's in her kennel, or purse, or whatever! Faith can't hurt her when she's in there. And she won't, anyway," I tried to assure her.

"She attacked her the moment we arrived!" Miss Kitty snapped.

"Yeah, but she's used to big dogs. She probably didn't know that your dog was even a dog."

Tannya chimed in, "Well, then it's good. Your dog needs to step up and start acting like a dog! You're confusing her by putting clothes on her and carrying her around in a bag. Dogs got four legs for a reason. Let her be a dog for a while and chase the cat, not run crying from it!"

"Ahh!" Miss Kitty gasped. She was offended, and I was holding back my laughter. Leave it to Tannya to tell it straight out exactly how it is. "She knows she's a dog . . ." From the look on Miss Kitty's face I could tell she was wondering if what Tannya said was true.

"Just sayin'," Tannya said and reached for the door.

When we stepped into the police station door Tannya led the way. She seemed to know exactly where to go. I supposed so since her ex-husband had been in trouble with the law a lot, and she'd filed a restraining order on him a year and a half ago.

We went down a hallway and took a left, which put us in a large open lobby area with chairs. Along the back wall was an opening in the wall that had a glass panel and a small vent for conversation—like an old-fashioned ticket booth for a movie theater. I could see a woman at a desk beyond the glass. She looked up when we came in. She was in her fifties, chubby, and looked angry and underpaid.

As we crossed the room, she said, "Can I help you?" in such a way I was sure she didn't really mean it. I could tell by her wrinkled brows and judgmental eyes. She was done scanning me, so while I answered her she scanned Tannya and then Miss Kitty.

"I had a call from someone who needs to be bailed out . . ." I told her.

"Mmm hmm. And?" She tipped one eyebrow up.

"And . . . I'm here to bail her out," I sheepishly replied.

"Does she have a name?" she sassed at me.

"Yes, her name is Valeida Lewis, Val for short."

"Have a seat."

We all moved to seats and Miss Kitty started right in with her no-one-tells-me-what-to-do attitude. "Well she's a rude one. There are plenty of people in this town who could do better at that job than her. Who does she think she is? Did you see the way she looked at us?"

"Yes! I feel violated!" said Tannya. "She'd better chipper up and treat us nice or Sara's gonna tell Rex he needs a new secretary. Right, Sara? He'd fire her in a second if you asked him to."

I dropped my jaw. "No, he wouldn't. Rex isn't my puppy. He doesn't do everything I ask him to. I barely know him. In fact, I haven't talked to him in quite a while." *Well, except for earlier. Oops.*

"Yeah, but he still talks about you, and I see the look in his eyes when he does," Tannya said. "He'd castrate a bull with his bare hands and a rubber band if *you* asked him to."

"Rex's a hot, sexy man. Every girl in this town wants a piece of him. He has to know if he wants some, he can get it from any girl in this town . . . or the next town, for that matter," I told them with a smile.

"Maybe he likes a challenge," a familiar voice said. I nearly jumped out of my socks. The male voice came from right behind me and judging by the looks on Tannya and Miss Kitty's faces, it was Rex. OH, MY GOD! Open mouth, insert foot. My face was instantly red hot. Oh, this was humiliating. How long had he been standing there?

"Hey! Officer Dalton!" Tannya said in a loud, silly voice with a huge smile and wave.

I turned around slowly and grinned. "Oh, hey! I didn't know you were working today."

"Been here all day," he said, smirking. *Shit! I knew he'd heard me.* "So, you're here for Val?"

"Yes?" I squirmed. I still didn't even know what she'd done.

"And Val's your aunt?" he asked with his beautiful, quizzing eyes.

"She is."

"Yeah . . . I can see that," he said. *What's that supposed to mean?* "Come on up to the counter, and we'll get the forms signed and payment processed. Then she's all yours. Although I'll say that we're going to miss her around here. She adds a little sparkle to the place."

I smiled. "I can only imagine." I followed Rex up to the desk and signed some forms and paid her bond. "Do I get to know what she's in here for?" I asked, not wanting to know the answer.

"Possession of stolen goods," Rex said with a head shake. "I'll leave the details of that to her."

What? I can't believe she'd steal stuff! Would she? Maybe she was worse off than I thought.

"I'll go get her. Be right back," he said and walked through the secure door.

"Your aunt's a thief?" Miss Kitty asked.

"No. I'm sure it's a big misunderstanding," I said hopefully. She was a wild one, though.

After a few minutes Aunt Val and Rex came through the door. "She's all yours, Sara. Keep an eye on her for us." He winked and turned towards the door. Val reached out and slapped him on the ass.

"Rex," Val said to his back, "it's like I told you before, your lips are moving, but your ass is doing all the talking." He kept walking, all the while shaking his head until he was through the door.

The lady at the window tisked.

"Yeah you're perfect, ain't ya?" Tannya said in a snappy voice. "I'm sure you ain't never done no wrong! Well, keep your tisks to yourself, lady, and we don't need your stink eye, either!"

I shot a look at Tannya, surprised by her attitude. "I don't like her! Never have!" she whispered to me as she turned away.

"Sara, dear, how are you?" Val asked as she wrapped her arms around me. She wiggled me from side to side, moaning, "Oooh, so good to see you. Thanks for coming. I owe ya one." She jabbed my shoulder and gave me a wink.

"Oh, sweet," Miss Kitty said. "Like in Monopoly, Sara's got a get out of jail free card!"

"Yes, she does," Val agreed.

"Well, we best get moving back to Sara's. My Smoochy Poo is there all alone."

"She isn't there alone! Faith and Pepper are with her," I said.

"Yes, let's go. I can't wait to hear the story behind this!" Tannya said and slung an arm around Val's shoulder, leading her out to the hall. We all loaded into the car and drove back to my place. On the way, I asked Val about the arrest.

"So, Auntie Val . . . possession of stolen goods?" I asked as I turned out of the lot.

"Ha, ha, it's a funny story," she started. I could tell she was embarrassed, but she turned towards me in her seat and started right in.

"First off, thanks for bailing me out. I didn't know who else to ask. Your dad wouldn't understand, and everyone else is too far away."

"What are you still doing here, anyway? I thought you left two months ago."

Val looked to the back seat and smiled at Tannya and Miss Kitty. They were unbuckled and leaning forward, awaiting the details. "I did, but I only went to Brainerd, and then I met someone."

"You met someone? Like a guy?"

"Ohhhh, this is gonna be good!" Tannya chimed in and scooted closer to the front seat, her head literally next to my shoulder.

"Yes, a guy," she said hesitantly.

"Who? When do we get to meet him? What's his name?" Miss Kitty asked. I felt like she'd stolen my question.

"Soon, probably sooner than you think," she said, acting very mysteriously.

"Well, where is he from?" I asked.

"Nisswa," she said and looked out the window. She had a painful look on her face. She looked like a three-year-old about to fess up to breaking a crystal vase.

"Well, that's good! So he's why you stayed? Are you staying with him? I asked.

"Yes," she said.

"For the love of everything good and holy, tell us about the stolen goods!" Tannya yelled.

We all shot a look at her.

"Okay, ladies, brace yourself . . . here it is."

4

We all prepared for the entertainment as Aunt Val began the story of her arrest.

"So a couple months ago, after you were kidnapped, when I came out to stay with you for a couple weeks, remember in the mornings I'd get up and go for a run, which was actually a walk because God didn't supply me with endurance or lung capacity when he was handing out parts? Well, on my walk, on the second day I stayed with you, I went around the lake, towards the left when you leave your driveway. There's a dirt road on that side that dead ends at the three houses across the lake. I went all the way to the last house and turned around and came back—every day the same path. Well, on the second day when I was walking by the first house I noticed a lot of noise behind me. It was a huge semi with a load of wood and other stuff. The truck was from Menards. They stopped to ask if I knew the address of the guy on the order. 'Mr. Captain Caesar Wayde.'"

GASP! "Captain?" I asked. Tannya slapped her hand over her mouth and Miss Kitty moved closer to the front.

Val nodded. She was very calm. "I asked the guy in the truck if he'd repeat it and he did with a giggle. At that moment a man came walking down the driveway. He was middle-aged, maybe a couple years younger than me—I'd say around fifty, and dressed in a pirate costume. Head-to-toe, like it was Halloween. It took me by surprise. I watched him as he came closer, then talked to the driver and told him to back in and unload next to the ship.

"At this point my curiosity got the better of me, and I stuck my hand out and introduced myself. "Hi," I told him. "I'm Val. I'm staying with a relative on the lake here."

"He smiled behind his full mustache and beard and shook my hand. He had a great smile, except for the tooth he'd tried to black out with makeup. His eyes were black with liner and shadow and the best part . . . a fake parrot on his shoulder!"

I was just pulling into my driveway. "Hold that thought," I said. "Look out there!" I pointed to the lake. "Does that have anything to do with you?"

Miss Kitty gasped from the back seat, "Oh, my God! You stole a pirate ship and hid it here?"

We all shot her a look. She shrugged.

"Not exactly . . ." Val trailed off as she exited the Jeep and ran towards the lake. "Wow! Look at it! Isn't it beautiful? He did it, he actually did it!"

We all ran after her and stood at the edge of the water looking at the ship.

There was no one on board as far as we could tell. So Tannya demanded we go inside and finish the story. Miss Kitty had already gone in to check on Smoochy.

When we opened the door, Pepper slowly walked over and greeted us. Miss Kitty set Smoochy Poo on the floor and joined us at the dining room table. We all sat down and continued to look out the window.

"So what the hell is up with the ship?" I asked.

"Okay, so he introduces himself and kisses my hand and tells me I've got to be the most beautiful treasure in all the sea."

Oh, boy! I could tell by the look in her eyes that she'd fallen for that.

"And, well, we got to talking, and he was there again the next day when I went out for a run." I tipped my head. "I mean walk," she corrected.

"Go on!" Tannya demanded.

"The second day he was again dressed like a pirate but in different clothes. The parrot was still there, and we talked for a bit, and then he invited me to see his project. So I followed him back to his yard, and there this was," she said gesturing to the patio window. "It was built from a kit and then set on a track so getting it into the lake would be easy."

"Why?" I was dumbfounded.

"Well, because Caesar takes his LARPing seriously."

"Huh?" Miss Kitty said. She was usually so well-spoken that it was a funny sound coming from her.

"Caesar's the man I met. Captain Caesar Wayde. He's the pirate. The ship belongs to him and his crew."

"His crew? How many are we talking?" I asked.

"There are three of us."

"So this is *your* ship?" Tannya asked.

We were all staring at her, hanging on her every word, when my phone rang. I gave her the wait-a-minute finger and answered the phone. Derek.

"Hello."

"Hey, I'm on my way up. I have to work this weekend so I have Tuesday and Wednesday off."

"Great. I'll see you in a bit."

"Is the ship still there?"

"Yup."

"Know anything about it yet?"

"I'm just getting some details on that now," I told him. "I'll tell you all about it when you get here."

"Great, I can't wait to hear this!" he said and disconnected.

I hung up. "Continue!" I demanded.

Val looked towards the kitchen, "Ya'll might want a drink or two first."

I, for one, totally agreed and got up to mix them. I blended four margaritas faster than I ever had in my life, carried them to the table and slid back in to my chair.

"Go on," I said and took a long sip.

Val continued. "So I got to know him pretty well. He's a nice guy, strange maybe, but really nice. I really like him." She smiled at me and I smiled back and took another long sip.

"Captain Caesar's mother died three years ago. He'd lived with her for two years before that. He's divorced and recently lost his job. He had a lot of time on his hands. After his mother passed, he inherited the lake house and some money. The house is paid for, and he has enough money to live off for the rest of his life. He also had spent lot of time on the Internet and came across a thing called LARPing."

"Larping?" Miss Kitty asked. We all had confused looks on our face. Phew, I was glad I wasn't the only one at the table who had never heard of it.

"Yes, it's an acronym. It stands for Live Action Role-Playing."

Tannya rolled her eyes for me.

"It seemed kind of strange to me too at first, but then I kind of got into it, and now I kind of like it." She smiled an unsure grin.

I just stared at her. "So what the hell?" I said. I was so confused I couldn't even come up with a question for her.

"There's this whole society out there that does this. Some are pirate LARPs, others are ninjas. There's medieval . . . there's really . . . well, tons of themes."

"Oh, so like at the Renaissance Festival in the Cities. The whole place is themed, and the staff are dressed up and stay in character the whole time," Miss Kitty said.

"Yes, except way more organized. There are different levels to which one can be involved. Captain Caesar is very involved and operating at a very high level.

Obviously.

"So what's the point?" I asked.

"Well in this LARP, we built a ship to go out and sink our treasure into the deep blue sea." Val looked at us and we all picked up our glasses and drank from them. She continued on. "There's another crew and they have declared war on us. They have seen our treasure and are coming after it in three days. So we were preparing to launch and readying our treasure, at least we were until I got arrested."

She paused. She seemed ashamed to go on. "Sara, I really got into this, and now I'm fully involved and possibly in love with a pirate, and I really don't want to lose our treasure."

"So someone's really coming to take it? For real?" I wanted to know.

"Yes, and if they do, then they'll have the biggest treasure. We can't let that happen. We'll automatically slip a level and no longer be in the lead. Right now *Poseidon's Zebra Mussel* is the biggest ship on LARP record. And by last week's count, it'll soon hold the biggest gold treasure on record. If they take our treasure and add it to theirs, which is just trailing ours, it'll be years before we'd catch up again."

She was really worried about this. I squished my eyebrows together.

"I know it sounds crazy, but this is the most fun I've had in a long time, Sara!"

I looked around, and Miss Kitty and Tannya were looking sympathetic. I was feeling it, too. This was obviously very important to her. I just could NOT wrap my mind around it. It seemed really silly.

"And these are all adults? How did they know about this? Who's in charge?" I had so many questions I didn't know what to ask first.

"You have to be twenty-one in this one, but different LARPs have different ages, rules, and themes. They find each other on the Internet. There's tons of information on it out there. They are all over the world."

"This is awesome!" Tannya yelled, and shot her fist in the air. We all snapped our heads towards her. "Come on, this is huge. We have a frickin' pirate ship right outside this door and people who think they're pirates are on it." She laughed and slammed her drink. "Where do I sign up?"

Val smiled at her. "You're more than welcome to join us, Tannya! All of you can. The more the merrier!"

"No. NO! We are not becoming pirates and LARPING!" I shot Tannya a look. Miss Kitty just shrugged.

"We're not pirates all the time. We 'game off' once in a while," Val informed us. "Like the other night Captain Caesar, I mean Wayde, that's his real name, Wayde Johnson, took me out for a nice dinner. We took his car, and he dressed up nice—not pirate nice—and didn't talk in pirate the whole time. I really like him!"

"So, you talk in pirate too?" Miss Kitty asked.

"Yes."

"So do it. Talk in pirate to us."

"Ye asking too many questions fer me. I be makin' believers out of yous yet," Val said freakishly. It was too easy for her. She sounded good. Too good.

I got up and grabbed the pitcher and made another round. I needed it.

When I turned the blender off, Tannya asked again, "So how did you get arrested?"

"Yes, how?" I repeated with an annoyed tone.

5

"Well, that's the part that's a little above and beyond what most LARPs allow. Ya see, Captain Caesar and his arch enemy, Captain Morgan, have upped the ante. They decided all treasure must be *stolen* goods, *and* must be painted gold."

"Ha! Ha! Ha!" Tannya belted out a laugh. "Sorry. It's funny!" she said and quieted back down.

"So you stole from someone?" Miss Kitty asked as she played with the diamond bracelet on her wrist.

"No, well . . . not exactly. It's hard to get treasure if it has to be stolen, and Caesar and I are good people and so is his first mate, Willy. So we had to get creative. We steal things that people don't really want, or *know* they want . . . it's tricky."

"Explain," I said thinking about the money I'd just put up for her bail.

"I got arrested because of the suitcase I had in my car when I got pulled over for speeding. Rex pulled me over on my way back from Brainerd, and when he ran the plates apparently the airport had reported my license plate as suspicious. Ya see, I took a suitcase from the airport and someone must have seen me and reported it."

"You steal people's luggage?" I scolded.

"No, it's more like *stalk* people's luggage, well, *lost* luggage. I go to baggage claim and look for the few suitcases that are always back against the wall. And then I check the flight times, if the case is by a carousel that had arrived at least two hours ago, then I take one and bring it home. I mean, come on, even if someone goes for a bite to eat after their plane arrives, they'd have picked up their bags in two hours, if they really wanted them."

"Oh, so it's the *lost* luggage you steal?" Tannya said, okaying her.

"It all gets donated anyway," Val said defending her actions.

"Still, it's wrong," I said.

"Yes, it is, but people can claim insurance on it, and I always take the most expensive-looking bag. You know if they can afford that suitcase they can easily replace what's inside. And if it were really important to them they would have went to baggage claim right away."

"So, then what?" Miss Kitty asked.

"So, then I take it home and unload it in the yard and spray paint everything gold, except fabric stuff—that I dye gold with Rit in the washing machine."

"HAAAA!" Tannya let out another snort of laughter. "Even the good stuff, like cameras and iPods?"

"Oh, yes, all of it! We don't keep anything. It all goes in to the treasure."

"So how often do you do this?" I asked.

"A couple times a week. I can't go too often. I don't want any staff to recognize me, although I do wear wigs and stuff to disguise myself."

"Wow, I can't believe this," I said.

"Please don't think badly of me. There're not many ways to steal stuff without hurting someone, and we don't want anyone to be sad that we're doing this."

"So, is this the only way you build your treasure?" Tannya asked her.

"No, we also sneak into the Goodwill loading dock and wheel out a big cart when no one's looking. We have an extra, so when one is full, we wait until there are no employees or cars around and wheel out the full cart and replace it with the empty one. Then we bring it home, empty it and bring it back for the next time."

"Wow," Miss Kitty said.

"So how long has this been going on?" I asked.

"LARPing, or our team?"

"Both, I guess."

"Well, LARPing's been around a long time. It goes way back, but since the popularity of the Internet and social networks has grown rapidly over the last ten years, it's taking on a much bigger audience. Anyone can start a group or join an already existing group at any time."

"Really? So I could just sign up and join? Does it cost money?" Tannya asked as she leaned forward with excitement.

I shot a look at her. The look in her eyes scared me. This was not good. I could totally see her signing up.

"My group," Val continued, "is free and was started about four years ago. We have a small group right now, but we hope to grow bigger. We have some more intense rules and push the lines of legality. We are selective of who we let in because, for one, they could turn us in to the cops for stealing, and two, they could be a spy for Captain Morgan."

Val looked at me again and sympathetically added, "I joined a few months ago, while staying here. As I said, I started going for a run—"

"Walk!" I corrected.

Val smiled and agreed, "Walk, every day and ended up spending more and more time over there. I was really having fun and wished I could be part of this big plan, and that's when Captain Caesar invited me in."

"And you said yes?" Miss Kitty asked.

"I thought about it. I had nothing else planned. He lets me live with him in return for helping build the ship and the track, and for collecting treasure. We need to get all the treasure onto the ship and then we're going to sink the treasure so it'll stay hidden from other pirates who may try to steal it. We've already received threats."

"So, are you and Caesar dating?" Tannya wanted to know.

"No, we aren't really there yet. I have my own room, and we haven't been intimate or anything . . . yet. I really like him, but he's very focused on the ship project. During game off hours he's usually really tired. We've only been out a couple of times on game off time."

Miss Kitty made a grunting noise, "Game off time?"

"That's what it's called when you're not in character. As soon as Caesar's dressed and ready in the morning, it's game on. It stays that way for most of the day. Basically he dresses like a pirate, walks like a pirate, talks like a pirate and behaves as a pirate would until the costume comes off at night, unless he or anyone else says 'game off.'"

"What happens when someone says 'game off?'" Miss Kitty chimed in, with sass in her voice.

"The game is paused, and people can talk in regular voices and act normally. It's usually for an emergency or something really important, like a cell phone call from your boss, or a medical emergency—things of that sort," Val told us.

I let out a quick exhale. I was completely flabbergasted. *People actually do this! There's a fucking ship on my lake!* I slammed the rest of my drink and stood up. Miss Kitty and Tannya held up their empty glasses to me. They needed more too, I guess. I looked to Aunt Val. Her glass was still full. She took a sip while looking at me over the top of her glass with her eyebrows up.

No one said a word as I mixed the third pitcher. I looked at the clock while I waited for the blender. It was after five already.

"So, is the boat going to stay out there?" Tannya asked.

"Yes, for a while."

"Is that legal?" I asked.

"As far as we could tell Minnesota doesn't have any rules as to boat sizes on lakes as long as they're licensed. It's over forty feet in length so it cost ninety dollars. The stickers are on it. It's just hard to see from here. If we're breaking any laws, they weren't posted on the internet under Minnesota Water Restrictions. The lawyer we asked said he thought even if we were charged, he could get the charges dropped pretty easily."

"It's still crazy!" Miss Kitty said. "Can you get us a tour?"

Aunt Val looked quizzically at her. "I'm not sure. Wayde is nice when he's game off, but he's all business when it's game on. I'm not sure how he'd feel about civilians on board the pirate ship for a tour."

"So his real name is Wayde?" Miss Kitty asked. "Waaay dah?" she said again with wrinkled brows.

We all turned to her. Tannya caught her laugh in her throat. I shook my head slightly.

Aunt Val tipped her head and put her hand on her hip. "Yes, Wayde Johnson. Miss Kitty, is it? And just how did you get that name?" she snapped.

"That's really no business of yours. It's a nickname anyway. And I like it better than my real name. I was named after my grandmother and it's not flattering in any way to me, so I dropped it," she responded defensively.

BOOM!

We all jumped, and the house literally shook. Aunt Val knocked her glass over, which was almost empty anyway. We all turned toward the lake, where the sound came from. Tannya ran over and opened the patio door, and we all rushed out.

"What the hell was that?" I asked.

There was smoke coming from the back side of the ship. "Captain must be trying out the cannon," Val said with an amused, approving smile.

"Holy cow! You guys have a cannon, too? I seriously want in!" Tannya exclaimed. "I love this! I tell you, those pirate movies that Disney made with Johnny Depp are some of my favorites. He's so sexy as a pirate. I tell you if I ever saw him in real life dressed as a pirate, his body guards better be on high alert. I'd jump him right then and there!"

Miss Kitty and Val laughed. I could totally see that. I had to admit, Johnny did a great job in those movies.

"Well, then I'll have to introduce you to captain's first mate, Willy. He truly looks a lot like Johnny, just younger. He's twenty-six years old and built with solid muscles, and looks great in a pirate bandana and two-day-old beard," Val told her. "He lives in the area, too."

"Yes! Yes, you'll have to introduce us! The sooner the better!" Tannya's eyes lit up.

There was some movement on the ship, and we could see the two men on the deck looking over the other side. They didn't seem to notice us. I ran back in and grabbed my binoculars, and hurried back out. I could see the men better, but I couldn't really tell what they looked like. One was definitely older than the other, and the younger one looked strong and lean, but that was about all I could tell.

A dog was barking, and it took me a second to realize it was Pepper. He was standing at the door. I shook my finger at him, and he quieted down and sat. We pulled up the patio chairs and sat around the outside table.

"Do they know you're over here?" I asked Val.

"No. I told Wayde if I ever got arrested I'd figure things out and not give up any information on him or his LARP. He probably thinks that I'm still on my way home from the airport. I'll leave in a few minutes and walk home."

"Home?" I asked.

"For now!" Val said with a smile. She never stayed anywhere too long, so I wondered how she really felt about this guy. She was very defensive about his name so she must have cared. And stealing unclaimed luggage for him was probably a good sign of a serious relationship. My father would be happy she'd finally settled down, although I don't think he'll like the idea that the guy's a pirate.

We were sitting there discussing where one would get a cannon, cannonballs, and cannon fuses, when I heard a BANG! BANG! on the glass door behind me.

Startled, we all looked. Pepper was sitting in the same spot, with the plastic blender pitcher in his mouth. He was biting on the handle and shaking his head to bang it on the door. BANG! BANG!.

"Looks like the dog wants a margarita, too!" Aunt Val said.

"What the . . . how'd . . . he get . . ."

Tannya was laughing so hard she was bent over in her chair, and Miss Kitty wanted to know where Smoochy Poo was. She got up and went in to check on her. We all followed her in.

"Well, I'm going to head over to Wayde's and settle in for the night," Val told us. She reached out to hug me. I hugged her back and offered her a ride, but she said she wanted the exercise. I told her to stay close to her phone and keep me posted.

Miss Kitty said that Smoochy Poo was very upset about the bomb and she needed to get her home to rest. Sheesh!

I reached down and grabbed the pitcher out of Pepper's mouth and set it in the sink. He followed me and jumped up, his paws on the counter, and looked in. He was so tall his head was a good two feet above the counter. It occurred to me that between his height and leg length, he could reach anything from even the farthest corner of the counter. He had done some quirky things over the last few months, but getting the blender down and bringing it to me was a new one! I giggled and told him, "Off!"

Tannya gave me a hug and said she'd be back soon and to let her know if anything strange went on. She said she had some work to get done at home and followed the others out the door.

After they left, I asked Pepper if he wanted a margarita, and he wagged his tail and walked to the kitchen. Just for shits and giggles, I made him a non-alcoholic one and poured it in his dish. He lapped it up and then plopped down in his bed by the fireplace. I wondered if he often placed orders for drinks. It seemed too normal. The other night Derek was over and had meat ready to go on the grill. Pepper brought his dish over to the grill and set it down. Derek was so impressed he grilled him up half a steak and put it in his dish.

I started making lasagna for supper. Derek would be here in about a half-hour and would be staying for a couple days. The cannon went off again and shook the house. It was pretty annoying. I didn't want things falling off my walls and breaking. *This better not be happening daily,* I grumbled to myself.

My phone rang just as I put the lasagna in the oven. I looked at the caller ID. Rex.

"Hello?"

"Hey, there, Speedy," he said. He had pulled me over for speeding when I first came to town and that had been my nickname since then.

"Hey," I said with a smile.

"Your Aunt Val is quite the character! It's boring around here without her," he told me.

"I bet," I said truthfully.

"So, I was looking over paperwork, and she put her address down as yours. Is she living with you?"

I didn't want to lie to Rex, but at the same time, I didn't really know an address for her. For the last couple months it'd been Wayde's, but who knew where it would be next month.

"She comes and goes. She's kind of a gypsy, so to speak. But it's fine with me if her mail comes here."

"Okay." He paused and I could hear him typing on a computer. "Also, I just had a report come in from your lake area. Someone complained about the, and I quote, 'pirate ship's cannon noise.'"

I laughed quietly. "Yeah, it is pretty loud."

"So there *is* a pirate ship on the lake?" he sounded shocked.

"Yup, I woke up to it this morning."

There was a long silence. "I'll be right over," he said and disconnected.

6

I set the timer on the oven for the lasagna and went to the bathroom to check my hair and make-up. Then I changed into a cozy sweatshirt and laced up my tennis shoes. I was ready for anything.

I checked my email and paid a couple bills through my computer while I waited. I heard a car door, and Pepper got up from the fireplace and went to the window. He was tall enough to see out the large window facing the driveway. He then sauntered over to the door and waited.

A moment later the doorbell rang. *It must be Rex. Derek would have let himself in.* The oven buzzer went off, so I went to the take the lasagna out. After I set it on the stove top I hurried to the door and opened it.

Rex was looking fine, as always. He was in plain clothes, and smelled freshly showered. "Hello," I said, stepping back with the door and making room for him to enter.

"Hey! Wow, it smells great in here."

"Thanks, I made lasagna for dinner," I said. "I'm expecting Derek very soon," I added for informational purposes. "Come here," I said, beckoning him with a finger. "Leave your shoes on." We walked to the patio door and looked out.

"Holy shit!" Rex said.

"I know, right?"

"How . . . where . . . ah . . . why? Shit, it's huge. It's a ship! Not a boat." It was kind of fun to see him so confused. He's usually so smooth and confident.

"So, is this illegal in any way?" I asked.

"Ahh, I . . . don't know. I don't think you can shoot cannons, though. I mean, I guess I need to look into that, but I don't think the ship itself is breaking any rules by being on the water." I handed him the binoculars from the table. He took them and looked again. "It's licensed!" He said this with a laugh. "I don't get it. Why would someone put a ship on this lake?"

I didn't know how much I should share and I didn't want to get my aunt into any more trouble.

"Oh, I can see where it came from!" Rex said.

"Yeah, they cut a few trees down and put in that track. I noticed that, too. And the few people I've seen on deck are dressed like pirates, too," I told him.

"Do you know who lives there?" He asked me.

"No. I mean, I know his name. But I've never met him."

"What's his name?"

"Wayde Johnson."

I was standing next to him looking out at the ship when the front door opened.

Derek walked in carrying an overnight bag. He was still in his work polo and dress pants. Rex and I turned around and met his eyes. Derek set his bag down by the door and greeted us as he gave Pepper a quick back rub.

"Hey, Derek," Rex said. He walked towards him and shook his hand.

"Hey," Derek said back. "So, you've seen the ship?"

Those two talked about it while I went to the kitchen. They were analyzing the who, why, when and where of it. I didn't say anything.

"Rex, will you join us for dinner?" I asked. "I have more than enough."

"Umm, sure, but I can't stay long. I'm supposed to be off work and just checking on this situation quick on my way home. I have an extra-long overnight tomorrow. We've got a guy gone on vacation this week, so we all have extra hours to cover."

"How many men do you have on in Nisswa?" Derek wanted to know.

"Two full-time and two part-time officers right now," Rex answered. "I'm not exactly sure what to do about this call," Rex admitted.

Derek chuckled. "Yeah, I was here this morning and saw it. I don't think there's a protocol on this. And it *is* licensed."

"Yes, it is," Rex agreed, "but the complaint regarding the cannon needs to be addressed."

Derek about choked. "Cannon? Really? They're firing a cannon?"

I nodded, "Yup, a few times. It shakes the whole house. Kind of annoying," I added as I was got the salad ready and the French bread out. "I thought my pictures were going to fall off the wall."

Pepper walked over by Derek and sat down.

"What were they firing at?" Derek asked.

"I don't know. It shot out of the opposite side, in the direction of his own house. All I saw was smoke."

I didn't give them any information on LARPing. I mean, they were both police officers. They'd figure it out, right? It was none of my business.

"Food's ready!" I announced.

We loaded up buffet-style and sat at the table, all with a view of the lake. As we started, Derek asked Rex, "So, are you going to go out to the ship and talk to them about the cannon? How are you going to get out there?"

Rex stared off to the lake, contemplating while he chewed. "I don't know," he said with a half-laugh. "I guess I'll drive over to the property first and see if I find anyone there. I doubt they sleep on the ship, right?"

They both looked at me. "How should I know?" I said.

After we ate, Rex left and headed over to Wayde's. He said he'd let us know what he found out. Derek and I cleaned up the dishes, and then he went and changed into lounge pants and an old t-shirt. I put in one of the movies he had rented from the Cities.

"I'm ready for a break from work stress, and the public in general," he said as walked past me to the kitchen and grabbed two beers out of the fridge. "Sweetness, I just want to veg out for the next two days and think about nothing but us, and enjoy some peace and quiet," he said, joining me on the couch. He took a long pull on his beer and sat back against the cushion and put his feet up on the end table. "I've had a real shitty week dealing with the stupid people that roam this earth."

BANG! The cannon fired again, and we both jumped. Derek's foot moved so far that he kicked his beer over on the coffee table.

"Holy shit!" he yelled and ran to the window. I got a towel from the kitchen and cleaned up the mess, then joined him at the window.

"There's Rex," I said. I had my binoculars up and was looking in the direction of the house. Rex was out on the dock. He walked back towards the house and out of site. A few moments later he returned with a bullhorn.

"Uh oh," Derek said as he opened the door so we could step out and listen.

We couldn't make out what Rex was saying, but it was short and sweet. I watched with my binoculars and saw two men come to the edge of the ship and yell something back. Then one climbed down the built-in ladder near the back of the ship and got into the old wooden boat tied up there.

"Good grief! I can't believe I'm seeing this," Derek said. "And they're still in costume!"

I looked back over to the lake and noticed that Val was standing on the dock now with Rex. They continued speaking until the boat got to the dock. And then out climbed who I assumed was the first mate, Willy, a.k.a. Johnny Depp lookalike.

"There's a woman over there now, too," Derek said and took my binoculars. "What the . . ." he whispered.

I bit my lip and stared at the ground. Craaaap! Now I had to come clean. He would recognize her for sure.

"Sara?" Derek said in a tone I had never heard. He was not happy.

"Yeah?" I asked innocently.

He shot me a look. "Why is your Aunt Val over at the pirate's house?" There was a pause and heavy exhale. "And why am I not surprised?"

"Ha ha ha . . . funny story," I said with an unsure grin.

"Wait!" he said. Then he stepped past me back into the house. I watched as he went to the coffee table, picked up his bottle and slammed what was left of his beer and tossed it in the trash. Then he grabbed another out of the fridge and returned to the patio. "Okay," he sighed. "I'm ready."

7

"It's kind of a long story. I think we should wait for Rex. Then I can tell you both at the same time," I told Derek. He looked long and hard at me. I wondered if he thought I was too high maintenance. Maybe I wasn't worth all the trouble. Since I'd met him, my life had been kind of crazy. Come to think of it, it had always been kind of crazy, but never at this level. Some days I wished I had no friends or family and just a house on a lake, with a garden and a cat and dog. No drama, just peace and quiet.

We sat back down on the couch and talked about the couple of months that Aunt Val stayed with us. She had been so quiet while she stayed here. And thinking back, she was gone a lot.

"Soooo, since you're here tomorrow with the day off, and I will be too, what do ya say we put the dock in? Then I can have the pontoon in, too." I waited patiently for his answer.

"Why?"

"Well, now is as good as time as any! We both have off and the ice has been off even during the last few nights."

"And you want to have access to the water . . . to the pirate ship?" he inquired.

I was at a loss for words. He was right but I didn't want to admit it. I just locked eyes with him.

"Yes. Well, not *access*, but I want to see it closer. Come on, you got to admit it. It's pretty cool. I want to see it! Actually, I kind of want to talk to the crazy pirate neighbor too." Derek tipped his head at me. "Don't get me wrong, I think the whole thing is a bit insane, but it's kind of fun to look out at a pirate ship from your patio in Nisswa, Minnesota," I admitted.

Derek frowned. "This dude built a ship! In his yard! A ship! Not a boat! He's a bit beyond insane. And the guy is dressed like a friggin' pirate! Who does that? I mean, think about it, this is not a model car, or modular home, or ship in a bottle . . . it's a real, huge, floating ship. He had to have been working on this for years, and for what?" he asked, with a head shake.

Okay, so Derek was not very excited about this. He was annoyed. It's probably a good thing for Wayde that this was not Derek's jurisdiction. "I'll help you put the dock and boat in, but, Sara, do not get too close. They're crazy!"

"Okay, I promise to be careful. But for the record, I think that they are just having fun, maybe living out a childhood dream. I don't think they're crazy. Too much time on their hands? Yes. Too much time on the internet? Clearly. But I don't think they're . . . certifiably crazy."

Derek squinted at me and took another long pull on his beer.

My phone buzzed, indicating I had a text. I got up and checked it. "That was Rex," I told Derek. "He's on his way back here."

"Great." I detected some sarcasm in his tone.

Rex pulled into the driveway five minutes later. I met him at the door and ushered him in.

He took a seat on the couch across from Derek. I sat down by Derek and smiled. This was so awkward. Suddenly I had all these emotions rushing through me. My boyfriend, who was amazing in every way possible, Officer McHottie sitting on my couch, a visit and bail out of my favorite aunt, a dog that was way too smart, crazy friends Tannya and Miss Kitty, and a pirate ship on my lake . . . .with grown men dressed as pirates aboard who licensed it and were now launching cannonballs from it at their own property.

It was all too much. Way too much for one day! Way too much beer and margaritas mixed in, and I couldn't take it anymore. I looked at Rex and Derek, and my shoulders started shaking. I got the giggles. I couldn't control it. I just started laughing. Hard. Tears rolled down my face, and I couldn't catch my breath. I could hardly see Derek and

Rex through my tears, but they were exchanging glances and shaking their heads at me.

"What's so funny?" Derek asked with a smile.

I just kept laughing. Every time I tried to talk, it got worse. Everything got funnier the more I thought about it. I would get a word out and then couldn't finish my sentence. Rex and Derek were laughing at me now, too.

"I . . . ha ha ha . . . it's just that . . . ha ha ha . . ." I took a deep breath and wiped my eyes. I tried to calm myself, but it wasn't working. I finally stood up and walked to the fireplace. After a few more breaths I sat back down, my shoulders still shaking once in a while. Good grief, I hadn't had a good case of the giggles like that in a long time.

"Sorry," I said and took another deep breath. "Please, officer, tell us what you found out." I tried to sit still and listen.

"Well, your aunt Val was there!" Rex started. He looked at me with tightly squeezed eyes. "But you knew that, didn't you?"

"I, um. Yes. But I just found out, right before you did. I didn't even know she was still in town until I bailed her out earlier."

"What?" Derek said with angry eyes. "She was in jail?"

They both looked at me. I turned to Derek and told him, "I got a call a few hours ago from her asking me to bail her out. She was at the Nisswa police station and needed money and a ride. What was I going to do?"

"What was she detained for?" Derek asked Rex.

"Possession of stolen property," he told him.

Derek turned back to me, and I continued. "So I went with Tannya and Miss Kitty and bailed her out. Then we came back here and she told me why she was arrested."

"Yes, she mentioned that you might be willing to share more with me. She was pretty tight-lipped over there. Apparently Wayde was on the ship and not leaving it, so he sent Willy over to talk to me. When Willy got closer to the dock, she said she didn't want to talk in front of him in case he got mad for sharing too much information."

"When he got up to the dock, he said 'game off.' Val nodded at him. Any idea what that was all about?" he asked me.

I shrugged. "Is Willy his real name?" I asked.

"I asked him for ID. He said he didn't have any on him. He was dressed like a pirate, too. I asked him if they were firing a cannon. He said they were, that they'd keep it down. He said they just got it in and needed to make sure it worked before the thirty-day trial was up."

Derek shook his head and took a drink.

Rex turned his glance back at me and continued. "He asked if they were breaking any laws, and I told him none I knew of right now, but I asked him not to fire the cannon, because the neighbors were complaining. He agreed and got back in the boat. He looked at Val, said 'game on' and headed to the ship."

"What the hell does that mean? Game off. Game on." Derek asked. Then they both looked at me.

"Ha . . . ha . . . funny story." I said leaning back on the couch.

"Yeah, you mentioned that before," Derek said and finished his second beer.

I started at the beginning and told them everything Val had told me. Their faces were priceless. It must have been exactly how Miss Kitty, Tannya, and I looked as we were being told. When I was done with the story, Derek let out a long sigh and stood up. Rex leaned back deeper into the couch, stunned.

Returning from the kitchen with three more beers, Derek handed one to Rex and opened one for me and set it on the table.

"Sweetness, I don't know how you do it," Derek said.

"Do what?" I asked.

"Meet such crazy characters. It's as if you're a magnet for morons. Crazy people flock to you."

"Hey, not all of the people I know are crazy!" I said defensively.

"Yeah, name two!" he snidely shot back.

I thought for a second. "You and Rex."

Rex gave me half-smile and winked. Derek shut up.

We sat there discussing Derek's day and all the crazies he'd run into this week on the job. "I suppose working in a smaller town you have less of that?" Derek asked Rex.

He snickered. "I have to admit, it's been pretty busy since Sara came to town."

I picked up a throw pillow and lobbed it at him, then took a long pull on my beer. "None of this is my fault!" I said. That was all I had for a comeback.

"Yeah, you never ask for trouble," Rex offered, placing the pillow next to him.

"She wants the dock and pontoon in now," Derek told him.

"Oh, boy," Rex said.

"I just think it'd be a good day to get it done," I said. "Neither of us have anything going on, and Derek's staying here for the next two nights, so why not?"

Rex shook his head and finished his beer. "Well, you two let me know if you need another set of hands. I have the morning off tomorrow. Thanks for the beer and insider information. I'm going to go home and process it."

We all stood. Derek shook Rex's hand. I hugged him. "Please let me know if anything else happens . . . or if the cannon fires again," he said.

I laughed and closed the door behind him.

Derek and I settled on the couch for a movie. Afterwards, I put the bottles in the trash. We'd each drunk three more. I realized that when I stood up. Derek did too. He followed me to the kitchen.

"Room spinning for ya?" he asked as he pushed me up against the island counter.

"Lil' bit."

"Hmmm, hope it's not too bad," he said as he moved my hair to kiss my neck. "I hope you remember this in the morning." He bent over and scooped me up and carried me to the bedroom.

Yay! I hope this is memorable too! I thought as he turned off the light.

8

I woke to Pepper licking my hand in the middle of the night. I guess we'd kind of forgotten about letting him out before bed. I looked at the clock—1:35 a.m. I got up and followed Pepper halfway down the hall before I realized I was naked. Oh, well. That was the nice thing about living in the country. I flipped on the outside light and opened the door to let Pepper out. I watched him fade into the darkness of the backyard, looking for the perfect spot. When it seemed to be taking longer than normal, I opened the door and called quietly to him.

He didn't come. *He always comes.* I stepped out on the stoop and was pretty sure I saw his tail wagging behind Derek's Jeep. "Pepper, come!" I whisper-scolded. He wasn't coming. *Lord, please,* I thought, *do not let him have a skunk or a porcupine cornered.* It was freezing out, and I was losing patience. "Pepper, don't make me come get you!" Quickly, I jumped down the porch step and tippy toed to the back of the Jeep, to see what he was wagging at.

"AHHHHH!" I screamed.

"Aaaaaaarrrr!" They screamed. Three pirates huddled together behind the Jeep. All three of them stood up quickly. They looked scared. Or at least two of them did. There were in full outfits and two had binoculars hanging from their necks. All three were men. One looked young, probably in his early twenties. One of them yelled, "Retreat!" The two older ones took off down my driveway. The young one stood there stunned, staring at me. That's when I remembered I was still naked! Shit! I quickly covered myself.

"What are you doing here?" I demanded, more angry than scared.

"Shiver me timbers . . ." he slowly said in awe. "Fer an old wench, ye gots very nice . . ."

"Long John, get yer arse moving!" The young pirate snapped out of it, and ran down the driveway after the other two. I didn't see a vehicle, but I watched until they were out of sight.

Pepper sat down next to me and watched too. Some watchdog he was. His size was scary but other than that he was apparently pretty useless. I rushed back to the house still covering myself. Pepper walked solemnly behind me. He never ran. He'd had hip surgery a couple months ago, and I'd met him shortly before that. So I didn't even know if he *could* run. I stood at the door whispering to hurry up, shaking from the cold.

"What are you doing?"

I nearly jumped out of my skin! Derek's voice came from right behind me. Now *he'd* scared the shit out of *me*! I screamed a long, terror-ridden scream. I screamed harder at his voice than I did at the sight of the pirates.

"FUCK!" I said, "You scared me!" His eyes were bugging out of his head. I think my reaction scared him, too.

I grabbed him and hugged him. I was cold and frightened and angry. I buried my face in his neck and breathed heavily. He uncomfortably put his arms around me. "What are you doing? Were you outside naked?" he timidly asked.

"Yes," I told him and let go of him. "I need a robe!" I almost yelled. Running down the hall to the bathroom I grabbed my robe, and threw it on, then returned to the living room. Derek was still standing there in shock.

"I woke up," he said, "and you weren't there! And I thought I heard voices."

My heart was racing, and I was still shivering. I pointed sharply at the door and scowled, "There were three pirates in my yard!"

Derek pressed his eyebrows together. "So you chased them away, naked?"

"Yes!" I said. "Well, no, I mean, I didn't know they were there! Pepper had to pee, and he wouldn't come back in, so I went out to see what was keeping him and found him behind your Jeep looking at three men dressed as pirates. They were hiding behind it!"

"The ones from the ship?"

"No, I didn't recognize these guys. They looked like they were spying on the ship. They had binoculars!" Dang, I was amped up.

"Okay. Okay," Derek reached out and pulled me in for another hug. "Did you see a car?" he asked, holding me.

"No, but they took off down the driveway." I thought about it for a second, they didn't really seem dangerous, but it still upset me that they were on my property, *and* that they'd seen me naked!

"Do you want to call Rex?" Derek asked. "Or do you want me to go out and see if I can find them?"

"No, you don't have to go out. I'll call Rex in the morning. I don't think they'll be back. But it was scary."

"It was probably pretty exciting for them," he teased. "Come on, streaker, back to bed. And you, Pepper, could we get a bark or something?" he scolded.

I headed to the bedroom. Derek locked the door and left the porch light on. I pulled on shorts and an old t-shirt and climbed back in bed.

* * *

In the morning I woke to pots and pans clanging. Derek was making breakfast. I decided to wait on the shower until after the dock and pontoon were in the water.

We ate and then got dressed in warm clothes. I still had my dad's waders from when we took the dock out last fall, and I owned knee-high boots now. I guessed Derek would have to get in the deep part.

Outside we dragged all the pieces over to the lake. We stood and stared at the ship for a few minutes. There were three people aboard. One looked like Aunt Val. They seemed busy and didn't notice us.

I asked Derek, "Have you ever done this before?" He shook his head.

"But you took it out last fall. Can you remember how to put it back together?"

"Yeah . . . probably." I looked around at the four pieces of dock and all the poles and hoped I would. "Umm, maybe we should call Rex."

Derek looked annoyed. I wrinkled my nose and shrugged. Then I ran back to the house for my phone.

When I returned Derek was putting the dock together like a puzzle on land and asking if I had a pole pounder thing.

"Since I don't know what that is, I'm going with a no." I smiled again. He shook his head again. I could tell he really didn't want to be doing this today, but I was glad he was.

"Rex'll be here in fifteen minutes. Wanna go fishing later?" I asked, trying to lighten the mood.

He shook his head again. "No, opener isn't until May, and I'm not feeling the greatest. I've got a headache."

"Oh, sorry. I didn't know that."

"I took something, so hopefully it'll go away soon."

We waited with our waders on until Rex got there. He pulled in and parked behind Derek. After he grabbed his waist-high waders out of the back of his truck he waved and headed in our direction. When he walked past Derek's Jeep, he stopped and bent over to pick something up. It was long and looked like a stick.

"Lose something?" he asked as he approached. He was holding it up. I knew right away it probably belonged to the pirates. It looked like a mini telescope.

"Aye, me spyglass!" Derek said. I shot him a surprised look and he raised one eyebrow.

"What?" I asked.

I laughed as Rex handed it to me. He looked at me with squinty eyes and waited for an explanation.

"Ha, ha . . . funny story," I started.

"Ah, yes, yet another," Derek smirked.

"We had visitors last night. I was going to call you, but it was like 1:30 in the morning. And I scared them away," I told him.

"Yeah," Derek said grabbing a piece of the dock and sliding it up to the water. "She scared them, all right. I mean, if you were hiding behind a Jeep and a naked woman and her giant dog came up on you, you'd run too and never return, right?"

I shot Derek a shut-up look and turned my eyes back to Rex. His eyes were bulging out of his head. He seemed stuck between anger and laughter.

"I was trying to get Pepper back in the house. I didn't know someone was out there, and I wasn't expecting to leave the house, but Pepper wouldn't come, so I had to go and get him. They took me by surprise."

"What the hell? What were they doing?" Rex asked, seriously.

"I think they were spying on the ship. Two had binoculars, and obviously one must have dropped this," I told him. "They ran away when they saw me. They were dressed like pirates, too."

Rex shook his head. "What's wrong with people? This is a bigger deal than I thought." He looked at Derek.

"Man, I can't help you." Derek gave him a palms up. "I have no idea what I'd do if this were my jurisdiction. I mean, the ship and cannon are questionable, and now we've got trespassing."

"Yeah, I checked on the ship. It's licensed, so it's fine to be there as long as it's not breaking any laws that apply to any other water motor craft. As far as the cannon goes, black powder cannons do not need any licensing or permits to buy, own, or shoot. They're not regulated or subject to the provisions under the ATF, GCA or NFA. So shooting them is legal as long as it's blank loads and doesn't interfere with any city noise ordinances. And, technically, this lake is out of city limits so those ordinances may not hold up." Rex looked stressed.

"Well, that's great," I said with a laugh.

"Did you get a good look at the guys last night?" Rex asked me.

"There were three, two in their thirties or forties—they ran off quickly—and one in his early twenties. They called him Long John. I got a good look at him. He was nice looking. He seemed pretty harmless, but then again, he was a grown man dressed as a pirate."

"Long John? Ha! That'd be my pirate name too, if I were ever a pirate," Derek said and winked at me. I was pretty sure that comment was more for Rex than me. "Long John was a little stunned by her nudity and took a few seconds longer than the other two to run away," Derek said with a nod and grin.

Rex smiled a closed-lipped smile and shook his head.

All this head shaking, ugh. What must people think of me?

"I want to know if they come back. They have no right to be on your property," Rex told me.

"Yes, sir!" I said.

"All right, let's get this dock set up," Rex said and pulled on his waders.

Roughly an hour later the dock was secure. And then came the task of putting the pontoon in. "So, Sara, can you still remember how to back up a trailer?" Rex asked.

"Probably not."

"Ah, you'll do fine. We'll help you hook up the trailer, but you get to back it in."

Derek tossed the Jeep keys at me. I hadn't even realized he grabbed them. We walked up to the house, and I got in my little red Jeep and had a talk with her. *Now, listen here, Lil' Red, it's just us girls against Derek and his black Jeep and Rex and his big tough black truck. We got this, but please help me out. Let's not embarrass ourselves*, I pleaded as I rubbed the dash.

Backing up to the trailer went fine. Derek hooked up the pontoon, gave me a thumbs up and an approving smile and nod. Then he jumped up in the boat and sat in the driver's seat.

I drove across the yard and made a big circle next to the makeshift access by my dock. I remembered to look out the back window and not at the mirrors like Rex taught me last fall, and I did it! In one try I backed into the water. I was so proud! I looked out the window to my left and smiled at Rex. Yes! He gave me a nod and mouthed, "Good job."

I opened my door and jumped out not realizing that I'd backed up that far and landed in calf-deep water. I was moving away from the open door smiling at Rex. I slid in the mud and fell backwards, hitting my head hard on the floor of the Jeep. Everything went black.

It was bumpy, and I had a really bad headache. When I opened my eyes, I was looking up at Derek's face. It was full of concern.

"She's waking up!" he said quickly. "Stay still. Are you okay?" he asked. He was holding my head in his lap and it took me a second to remember that I had fallen. I reached up to touch my sore head. "No, don't touch. It's bad. I'm trying to stop the bleeding."

I looked around, still confused. We were in the back of Rex's truck. I was on my back with my head on Derek's lap by the passenger-side door. As Rex was driving, he looked through the rearview mirror at me with concerned eyes. "We're almost there!" Rex said. He was on his cell phone, describing me to what I assumed was the ER.

I closed my eyes again. My head hurt so bad. *Geez, I'm such a klutz! How embarrassing.* I must have looked like a fool, so excited one second and knocked out the next.

We got to the hospital, and Rex pulled into the emergency unloading area. Derek opened the truck door, and nurses were waiting for us.

"Are you able to sit up?" one asked.

"Hmm, I think so."

Rex opened the driver's-side rear door. When I sat up, I was face-to-face with him. "Go slow," he said gently. His caring eyes made my heart soften, and I wanted to cry. I reached up for my head and could feel Derek still holding the cloth against it. Slowly, with the help of Rex and Derek, I got out of the truck. Two nurses waited, and one had a wheelchair.

"Sit," she told me.

I did. I was really dizzy. Derek let me take over holding the cloth on my head and followed me in.

"I'll move my truck and then catch up with you," Rex said.

We went straight through the ER doors and into what looked like an operating room. I moved from the chair up to the table and lay on my side. An older male doctor entered and asked for the update. There were four nurses now, and I could feel people touching me. People were saying my name, age, how it happened, time, loss of consciousness and other stuff I didn't understand. The blood pressure cuff was tightening, my bed was tipping up, and someone was covering me with a warm blanket. The nurse said to let go and removed the cloth slowly from my head. All of the nurses, the doctor and Derek leaned in to look. I heard moans and gasps, so it must have been bad.

Derek wrinkled his nose and clenched his jaw. "Stitches for sure," he said with worried eyes.

I looked with concern at the doctor. He said, "Wow, you did a good job here! How did this happen?"

"I fell," I said strained.

"Looks like you'll need stitches and fluids. It's a deep cut and judging by the sweatshirt, it looks like you lost a lot of blood," he told me. "We'll get an IV started and get you something for the pain. I imagine you've got a nice headache."

"Yes, I do."

"All right, well you just lay there and rest and we'll get ready."

There was a voice from the doorway. "I have a visitor for you."

I nodded when I saw Rex, and made a quick mental note not to nod again in the near future. He came in and Derek gave him the update. Rex came over and rubbed my shoulder.

"How are you feeling?" he asked leaning over to look at the exposed wound.

"Not good."

"Ooh, geez. At least the bleeding's slowed. You bled a lot!" he told me.

The nurse walked past with a large blood-soaked sweatshirt, the one Derek had on earlier. I looked back at him and noticed he was in just a t-shirt now.

"Sorry about your sweatshirt," I said to him. He leaned down and kissed my forehead again.

Four hours, two glasses of orange juice and three cookies later I was feeling a little better. I had eleven stiches, and was missing a one-inch-by-four-inch section of my hair. The doctor had insisted we shave some of it. The stitches were under some of my hair, but I'm sure it was still noticeable. Derek and Rex tried to reassure me they could hardly tell.

We made it back home in one piece around 4:00 p.m. The boys got me onto the couch and then went out to finish putting the boat in the water. When I'd fallen they'd just pulled the Jeep forward so the trailer was out of the water and left it there.

After that was all taken care of, they came in. Rex said goodbye and headed off to work his shift, and Derek made us supper. I ate some, but it hurt my head to chew. I helped clean up a little then took some more pain meds and crawled back on the couch. We watched another movie, and just as it was ending the cannon fired again.

BOOM!

9

I woke up to blurred vision and a bad headache. I was on the couch, covered up. There was a note on the coffee table from Derek: *Ran to town for food. Be back soon.*

That poor guy. I was so bad about getting groceries. I've never liked getting groceries, and I didn't enjoy cooking, and I had money to go out to eat, so why bother? I didn't mind baking, but I wasn't very good at it. Most of the time the things I made were overcooked or undercooked. They were rarely perfect. Except cookies. I had mastered the chocolate chip cookie.

After rolling off of the couch and onto my knees, and then climbing to my feet, I took another round of pain killers and put a piece of toast in. I wasn't sure when Derek had left, and I'd puke if the meds hit my stomach empty. I was supposed to open Lost and Found this morning, and it was past eight already. I called Ginger and asked her if she would want to cover for me. She agreed and asked if I wanted her to cover my shift for tomorrow, too. I gave her my shifts for the rest of the week. She was saving for a trip and wanted the extra hours. That worked out great for me. I could rest my head and grow some hair back.

I went to the bathroom and grabbed a handheld mirror, turned around and looked at the back of my head. I had a bald spot. It was pretty visible, too. My hair was short in a tapered bob, and the bob was missing some tapering. AND SOME HAIR! I *totally* had a bald spot. Ugh!

I fought back the tears and brushed my teeth. I left the mirror and went to the kitchen for the toast. Maybe after I got some food in my stomach I would feel better.

I ate the toast. It didn't help, so I curled back up on the couch and put in *Dirty Dancing*. I was in the middle of my pity party when Derek came through the door.

"Hey, sweetness, did you sleep okay?" he asked, walking in with two full plastic bags.

"I slept fine, but my head hurts again. I called the shop and got all my shifts for the week covered so at least I can rest."

"Well, I'll be your personal chef for today. From there you're on your own. I work Thursday and Friday, but I can come back up on Friday night if you'd like. Or, if you come to the Cities, I can take care of you there." He wiggled his eyebrows at me. I smiled at the thought.

"Oh, and by the way," I told him, "you can totally tell they shaved around my cut."

"What were you doing looking in the mirror? You should be resting!"

"You two lied to me!"

"We just didn't want you to worry. And what do we know anyway?" He said, with a hand flip.

I glared at him, but he was too busy putting the food away to notice. I stomped back to the couch and plopped down.

"Pouting will get you nowhere with me, sweetness!" he called from the kitchen. My back was turned to him so I stuck my tongue out. "I saw that!" he said.

About thirty minutes later, he brought two plates into the living room and set them on the coffee table. Then he went back for orange juice. He'd poured the juice into a champagne glass for me and a regular glass for him.

"Oh, fancy!" I said.

"Nothing but the best for you, princess," he said, clinking my glass. BAM!

I jumped in surprise and spilled half the juice out of my glass. Faith, who was sitting on the window sill in the sun, squealed, jumped down, and ran off to the back of the house. Pepper got up and walked slowly to the window.

"Damn it!" Derek said and got up to get a towel. "How many times are they going to do that? What are they even shooting at?"

"Ugh, I don't know. How many cannonballs do you suppose they have?" I asked.

"Where do you even get cannonballs?"

"Ebay," I said. "You can find anything on ebay."

"Yeah, but the shipping would kill you. They're heavy!"

"These are the people that built a pirate ship in their back yard . . . for a LARP. I don't think they are really concerned about expenses."

"Idiots," Derek said. I nodded in agreement.

My phone rang, so I went to answer it. It was Aunt Val.

"Hi, Sara! I just called to apologize for the cannon."

"What's going on? Why are you shooting it? And at what?" I asked.

"Well," she whispered. "Captain is trying out the cannon. He's working his aim, or sighting it in or something. I don't really know. All I know is that it's loud and shakes the house. I hope nothing breaks. He just sent Willy over here to pick up the ones that landed in the yard and bring them back over to the ship. There are divots all over the yard! I'm afraid they're going to hit this house while I'm in here! Anyway, I just wanted to call and say sorry. I know yesterday the cops were out about the noise complaint and the captain told me I needed to take care of it. I'm now the one in charge of customer service and withholding the parley codes."

"Oh, wow, is that a promotion?" I asked.

"No, it's just more stuff that he doesn't want to deal with so I get to. We won't be firing them at night—that's against LARP rules. We, like campgrounds, respect the 'quiet hours' rule, but from 8:00 a.m. to 10:00 p.m. we may be firing . . . sorry."

"So how long is this going to go on?" I asked.

"You mean the LARP?"

"Yes, this isn't a lifestyle thing is it? He's not going to live this fantasy life forever, is he? I mean, at some point the ship has to go, right?"

"Uh . . . I don't know. Most LARPs are ongoing, but the ship can't stay in the water in the winter so it should be done by then. At least for the season," she said.

"Really? That's crazy!" I said.

"Yeah, but it's kind of fun, too!" Val said. I could hear the smile in her voice.

"By the way," I told her. "There were some pirates on my property late last night."

"What? Where? How many?" Her voice sounded very anxious.

"Yeah, about one this morning. There were three that I saw. They were ducking down behind Derek's Jeep spying on the ship with binoculars and a spy glass they left behind when they ran off."

"They're here."

"Who? Are you expecting more pirates?"

"Yes, well, no. Uh, I have to go. I'll call you in a little while. I have to ask you something, but I need to get this information to Captain Caesar Wayde and First Mate Willy right away!" she said and disconnected.

I hung up the phone and gave Derek the update. "Well, that's great. At least you have another place in the Cities you can run to if it gets too annoying."

I shrugged and sat to eat my breakfast. When I was done, I went to take a bath. I couldn't shower—the water would hurt my head. I guess I'd wait a day to wash my hair. Hopefully then it would be okay. The doctor said not to wash it or use hair spray near my stitches. That would be very challenging since I was not a natural beauty. Hopefully Derek would still find me attractive at the end of the week.

I relaxed in the hot water and thought about the ship. It was kind of exciting. I was trying not to show it around Derek and Rex, but I liked the mystery and adventure of it. I thought LARPing was stupid, but I secretly wanted to go play on and explore the ship. I closed my eyes, sank down deeper in the water and imagined myself on board, the wind blowing my hair, the water splashing on the boards, the smell of fresh paint. I pictured myself with perfectly tousled, long, blonde, beach-waved hair, dressed in a beautiful, yet slightly worn pirate dress, floor length with a drawstring bustier, my full, round, soft breasts squeezed tightly together by the strings and spilling over the top. My eyes were dark, and my lips full and red.

Derek was there. He was the captain. I had just been promoted from a deck swabber to his girl. I no longer mingled amongst the buccaneers but stayed in the captain's quarters. I ate off the china and drank the good rum. Suddenly the ship was buzzing with action. I came out of my quarters and investigated. I couldn't find Captain Derek anywhere. I went down to the lower deck, where I never went anymore, and peeked over the edge of the boat where the others were running around in panic.

Suddenly, I was grabbed from behind. My mouth was covered and I was pulled away. Everything went black. When I opened my eyes, I was in a strange room. It was a captain's quarter, but not Derek's. I picked up my head and looked around the room. There in the corner was a pirate. He wasn't wearing the hat, though. The hat was always worn when in the position of authority.

I knew who this was. I was pleasantly surprised. He turned slowly towards me, and I recognized him. My long lost lover, Captain Rex. The ship I was on with him went down, and everyone thought he was dead. Obviously he was not.

"Hello, beautiful," he said in the deep, suave, sexy tone I remembered. I smiled. He locked eyes with me and slowly removed his sword from his belt, and then his belt with the pistol hung in it, and set it on the table by the bed. He kicked off his boots and slowly climbed onto the bed. He was directly over the top of me. I could feel his breath on my lips. "Miss me?" he asked.

I opened my mouth to answer, not with words, but with a passionate kiss when—BAM! BAM! BAM! There was a knock on my bathroom door.

"You still alive in there?" Derek asked from the other side of the door.

And, I was awake. Dang it! "Yes. I'll be out in a minute." Man, I really wanted to finish that daydream.

I got dressed in jeans and long-sleeved t-shirt and quickly did a basic hair and make-up routine. Just as I was finishing, my phone rang again.

"Hello?" I answered to Tannya.

"Hey, girl! Is that ship still out there?" she asked.

"It sure is."

"So can Miss Kitty and I come over again and watch?"

"Watch what?" I asked.

"Ya know, in case anything happens! I don't want to miss it. I've been doing some research on LARPing on the internet."

"Tannya, you need to stay off the internet," I told her.

"No, no, this is all legit, just like Val said. I looked it up and found a pirate LARP on the internet, and you can join for free!"

I sighed, "Oh, Tannya, please don't tell me you—"

"Yes! I'm all signed up. And here's the best part—a few minutes after I signed up, I got a call from them!"

"A call from who?" I asked her.

"From the LARP people, the pirate guy who's in charge! He sounded just like a pirate on the phone. He asked me about my location, and asked where in Nisswa I lived. We talked for about thirty minutes. I think it was the guys from your ship."

"What did you talk about?"

"Well, I told him about the ship at your place and said I wanted to join the crew, part-time of course because I work at the diner. He said that was fine and then asked what your address was, and if I knew of any treasure I could add to their collection. He said it had to be "taken" treasure, like a pirate would just take it, ya know? It can't be paid for. Just like Val said. It was so cool to talk to a pirate," she said with a laugh.

"You mean stolen? The treasure is stolen. That's why she was in jail!" I warned. Derek shot me a look and turned back to the TV.

"Yeah, yeah. But anyways, I got a cousin that's out of town, and I don't know where she gets the junk but she has a garage full of stuff she tries to sell on ebay and at garage sales. She has a garage sale every week! It's like her job! And every time I go visit, she has more stuff instead of less. I bet she wouldn't notice if I took a few things. I guess all the new scallywags need to bring fifty pieces of gold treasure with them as their entry fee."

"You're not going to steal from her, are you?"

"Well, I figure I'll just take some of her stuff and leave some of my own stuff. That way we're square. I gotta bunch of old stuff around here I've been meaning to get rid anyway. It's only fifty pieces. She'll never notice."

"I don't think it's a good idea."

"You should sign up, too! We could get you some treasure, too. You got any old stuff you can replace it with?" she asked me.

"Yes," I shook my head. "I mean no. This is wrong!"

"My cousin's not going to care. If she finds out she'll probably want to sign up, too."

"Did you say you gave the pirate my address?" I asked.

There was a beat of silence. "Yes."

"Crap. Tannya, don't give out my address to people!"

"Why? It's just your neighbor anyways, not like he don't know where you live."

"I don't think it's the same group. I think there is more than one pirate group. I had pirates in my yard in the middle of the night last night."

"What? Way cool! Did you talk to them? Why didn't you call me?"

"They were hiding in my driveway behind Derek's Jeep and ran off when I saw them."

"You scared them with your nakedness!" Derek yelled from the couch.

"What did he say?" Tannya laughed. "Were you naked?"

"Ugh, never mind him," I told Tannya.

"I think they were spying on the ship. I think they're planning to attack, or steal treasure or who knows, but I don't think they're on the same team."

"Oh, really? So I signed up on the other team? So I'll be competing with Val and her crew? So which team are you going to sign up with then?"

I laughed out loud. "I'm not signing up at all!"

"So where were you yesterday? We tried to call."

"I had a minor slip and fall and ended up with stitches in my head. We were trying to get the pontoon and dock in, and I wiped out in the mud."

"Oh, bummer. Well, I hope you're feeling better. Miss Kitty and I are going to meet here at the diner this afternoon when I get off. She's going to bring her laptop, and I'm going to show her the LARP, and she might join too! You should come here and talk with us. I get off at 2:30. See you then, girl!" she said enthusiastically and hung up.

Huh. I stared at my phone and then set it on the counter.

"Making big plans with the girls?" Derek asked with a grin.

"No." I sat down on the couch next to him. "Well, they are. Tannya joined a LARP. I think it's the group that was out here. And now she's talking to Miss Kitty about it. Tannya's planning to rob her cousin's garage sale to get the treasure items required for entry into the LARP."

"Really? Wow," Derek responded.

We sat a few moments longer and then he turned from the TV and asked, "Are you joining?"

"Me? No, definitely not!" Probably not.

10

I finally got off my lazy butt and made Derek a homemade apple pie to take back with him. He had to work in the morning and wanted to get some laundry done before going to bed, so he was heading out a bit early. I walked him out to his car.

"Stay out of trouble," he said.

"I will."

"I see something in your eyes that tells me differently." Dang he was good! I *was* considering . . . not being good.

"Yeah, sure ya do," I leaned in and kissed him. I didn't want to make any promises I couldn't keep. So I used my mouth as a distraction. After a long while, the kiss ended with me in goosebumps, not wanting him to go.

"Good night. I'll call you tomorrow," I promised.

"Good night, sweetness," he said, then got in his Jeep and drove away.

It was about 2:00 p.m. and who was I kidding? I was going to meet Tannya and Miss Kitty. I don't know why. Usually I'm the good girl who tries to avoid trouble, even though it usually finds me anyway. But something made me want to be involved. I wanted to be bad. Maybe it was the new freedom of being single after so many years of marriage. Maybe it was too many years of being the good girl. Maybe it was the moon in alignment with my stars . . . maybe the bump on my head. I didn't know. I didn't care, either. All of a sudden I felt unstoppable, strong, brave, and angry that Long John trespassed on my property . . . and that he saw me naked! Ugh.

First thing I needed to do was figure out what the hell was going on. It sounded like Tannya might know a thing or two, so why not? I loaded myself into my big, strong, red Jeep and drove to Morning Glory.

When I got there, Tannya was just taking off her apron and talking through the pick-up window to Marv. I couldn't hear, but it looked like their normal, playful smack talk.

"I knew you'd come, girl!" Tannya said with a big smile.

I just smiled back. "Someone has to keep an eye on you!" Marv said.

"Exactly," I responded to him.

"Marv, you know you want in! You're just jealous I found something more fun than your boring video games before you did," Tannya yelled back.

The place was empty except for us three and another waitress, who was just putting on an apron. Although that didn't matter, as they yelled at each other all the time anyway.

"Pirates are nothing new to me, sista! I've seen all the *Pirates of the Caribbean* movies at least five times!"

"Yeah, Marv, we know you're a lonely loser with a lot of free time. Please don't remind us."

I looked at Marv, who was squinting his eyes at Tannya. "Lady, I gotta mind to join the other crew just so I can sink your fat ass to the bottom of the lake."

"Fat ass? Marv, please, I've been plump since I was born. Those comments have all been said before. Nothing you say is going to bother me. You live in your mom's basement, for the love of Pete! Don't even get me started on you!"

"Huh, well, that's because my parents sucked. It's not my fault, my dad left us, and my mom did a horrible job raising me."

"Your mom's a saint. She didn't kill you, and she still lets you in the door. I'd call her an angel," Tannya said.

He leaned even closer to the window and yelled back, "She's like a ninja mom. She just sneaks up, destroys your will to live, then disappears."

I laughed out loud. Marv shook his head. "It's true!" he said with wrinkled brows.

Just then Miss Kitty walked in the door. Tannya and I both turned our attention towards her. "Hi," I said.

"Hi, darling!" she sang and threw her arms around me. "What happened to your hair?" she asked. Tannya rushed over to see the damages too. I told them in detail what happened.

Miss Kitty was dressed to the tee, as usual—denim jeans with rhinestones all over the butt pockets and around the front pockets, a bright pink cashmere sweater with a black cami underneath, ears pulled to the max with diamond chandelier earrings, and matching necklace. Over her arm was a black leather jacket and an expensive purse with Smoochy Poo's head sticking out the top. She smelled amazing, too. Miss Kitty's hair was white blonde, and dry, but nice looking. And her make up always looked good, bright some days, but good.

"Hello, Smoochy," I said and reached out to pet her. She licked my hand.

Tannya walked over and gave her a hug too. Smoochy Poo growled and barked at Tannya.

Tannya instinctively pulled her hand back. Miss Kitty looked down at her. "No, no, Smoochy. Be nice!"

Having scolding the little dog, she turned to us. "Oooooh, girls, I'm so excited for this next adventure!" Then she gave me another hug.

We settled into a booth near the back and the waitress brought us all diet pops, on the house. Miss Kitty maneuvered around Smoochy and pulled an iPad out of her bag.

"Here," she said and handed it to Tannya. I bit my lip and watched as Tannya looked at it front and back, and then at all the ends.

"What the hell is this?" she finally asked.

"It's an iPad," I said.

"Oh, yeah!" she said as her face lit up. "I've heard about these. How's it work?" she asked.

Miss Kitty turned it on and asked for the website address. Tannya watched in amazement as Miss Kitty worked the touchscreen. "Wow, I was wondering how you were going to type on it. That's neato! I need to get me one of those!" I made a mental note—future gift idea.

We spent the next hour and a half looking it over and learning more. The crew Tannya had signed up for was on the ship named *Ocean's Lie*. The site didn't list all the crew, but it had the leads on there as "Captain Morgan," "The Flying Dutchman," and "Long John." The site listed the next LARP as on Thursday, May 1, and to inquire via email for more information. Information would only be given to members whose booty had been received.

We looked at other ones, too, and figured out that the ship on my lake was named *Poseidon's Zebra Mussel*. I let out a snort. I loved that name. They had the names of the lead crew: "Captain Caesar Wayde," "Willy," and "Gun-Powder Gertie."

"Ha! That has to be Aunt Val!" We all giggled.

"Oooh, *we* need pirate names too!" Tannya said with a grin and squirmed in her seat with excitement.

I raised my eyebrows and looked at Miss Kitty. She shrugged. "Sure, why not? Sign me up. Looks like fun," she said.

My jaw fell. *Oh, boy!*

"How about you, Sara? Are you in?" Tannya looked eager.

Miss Kitty giggled and elbowed me playfully in the ribs. "Aw, come on, Sara. You have to! You're our leader," she said.

"Leader? The hell I am! This was *not* my idea. I'm *not* the leader."

"Fine I'll be the leader," Tannya said. "Let's get you signed up!"

I wasn't sure I wanted to sign up, but signing up on a different ship than my neighbor and aunt seemed like a bad idea.

"I don't think I should. What would my aunt say if I had my name on crew list to the ship trying to take her loot?"

"You're right," Tannya said. "We can't do that. We have to start our own LARP crew." I looked over to Miss Kitty, who was playing on the iPad.

"That's not what I meant," I said.

Miss Kitty nodded and looked up. "Yup, I agree. And it's easy enough. You just have to register your ship's name and the names of at least three leads on your crew: a captain, first mate, and second mate. There's no charge. We just fill out this simple form. Then if we want to participate or plan any events we update those on this site."

"Seriously, you guys, this is dumb!" I tried to reason. Part of me was totally in, the other sane part was telling me not to get involved.

"It's not dumb! Sitting back and watching a pirate movie take place on your lake and not being involved is dumb," Tannya said.

"I think we should create our own crew and register, but I also think that Tannya should still sign up for the other one," Miss Kitty said. "She can be our spy."

"Yes! That's genius! I'll do it!" Tannya said with a fist pump. "You can count on me!"

Oh, geez. If this were a Lifetime movie, it wouldn't end well, and Tannya would die first. But the more I thought about it, which wasn't very much, the more I thought it might actually be a good idea. It'd be nice to have a spy on the inside, someone who knows when and where they're going to strike. It was all very silly. At the same time, Aunt Val worked very hard to steal treasure, and she cared very much about Wayde. I didn't want to see her get hurt. She didn't have a lot, and this was the longest she'd stuck around any location in a long time. She must really like him. I wanted to help, but I didn't want to join the *Ocean's Lie*, and *Poseidon's Zebra Mussel* had a crew that seemed a bit too crazy for me.

"I've already started registering our crew," Miss Kitty said. "We need names for the ship and names for us."

"We need a ship?" I asked.

"We have a ship, we just need a name," Tannya informed me.

"What ship?" I asked.

"Well, your pontoon, duh!" Tannya said.

"What? Whoa there! The pontoon? The pontoon is not a ship. It's a twenty-foot boat."

"Yeah, the pontoon! It'll work great! Besides, it's all we have." Miss Kitty said.

"It's too small. There's nowhere to hide on it!" I protested.

"We don't need to hide," Tannya said. She shot her fist in the air again and said, "We come to conquer!"

"All right," Miss Kitty said staring at her iPad and typing. "Names . . . what's your pirate name, Tannya?"

"Ohhhh! Gosh, let me think." We all got quiet and thought hard. After a few moments Tannya answered with a big grin. "You can call me Tannya Tytass."

We laughed. Miss Kitty said, "My name will be Candee Barre."

I couldn't come up with one so Miss Kitty decided for me that I would be "Sara Narra," as in "sayonara." They thought it was funny, and frankly I didn't care, so she typed them all in. Then Tannya proclaimed the name of the ship *Ella Vashow*. In my head I agreed that the three of us doing anything was in fact a hell of a show.

After a few more minutes, Miss Kitty put down her iPad and picked up her pop and raised it in a toast. "To our next adventure!" she said. We all clinked glasses and drank.

"Let's go to my house first and get some junk, and then we'll go over to my cousin's house and steal some treasure."

"We need gold spray paint and some gold Rit dye too," I told her. "The treasure has to be gold."

We all loaded into my Jeep. I had the cargo room. We headed to the hardware store. Miss Kitty ran in and bought six cans of spray paint and three small bottles of Rit dye. "It's all the gold they had," she said.

I made a right out of the lot and drove to Tannya's. I'd never been there before. I knew the area she lived in but had never seen it. She was a ways out of town and it took about twelve minutes to get there.

We pulled up into the driveway to see a modest rambler on the right side of the driveway with an attached garage. A bit further down the lot was a tin pole shed. The yard was nicely kept. The house looked good too. She was single, so I wouldn't have been surprised if it weren't.

"How many acres do you own?" I asked.

"Thirty."

"It's a nice place," Miss Kitty said. I guess she'd never seen it, either.

"Thanks! I do my best. I think we'll start in the shed. Scooter left a ton of stuff here and hasn't been back for it. I haven't seen or heard from him in quite a while, so I doubt he'll miss it. He's probably too high to remember he still has anything here, anyways."

"What kind of stuff?" Miss Kitty asked.

"Who knows what we'll find. That man was crazy for most of the year we were married. Shortly after our wedding, he lost his job and started entertaining himself with drugs and reality TV." She rubbed her eyes. "He was a bit obsessed with *Doomsday Preppers*." She let out a big sigh and looked at us nervously. "He was a really nice, responsible person when I met him. Drugs changed him." She seemed ashamed and apologetic.

I put the Jeep in park and we got out. "Tannya, we aren't here to judge you. Both our husbands were not who we thought they were when we married them. We're all in the same boat, love." I gave her a hug, and Miss Kitty wrapped her arms around both of us too.

"Men suck," Miss Kitty said. "I'm quitting men!"

We broke the hug. Tannya and I stared at her. "What? It was just a thought. But really, now who's judging? Think about it, you never hear talk about the divorce rate of homosexual couples, do you?"

"No, no you don't." Tannya nodded in agreement.

"Let's check out the shed, shall we?" I said.

"I'll be right back. I gotta get the key," Tannya said and walked to the house.

When she returned she unlocked the door and we stepped in. The shed had a large roll-up door on the front. Tannya hit the button and the door went up. As light entered the room we all three gasped at the sight.

11

The shed was full top to bottom! It was like something off the TV show *Hoarders*. Except that it was organized. Boxes of stuff were piled a foot or two above our heads. Along the left side of the shed, we saw a food hoard of cans and boxes to last a single person a year or more. To the right were all kinds of guy things—chain saws, vises, lawn mowers, a million hand tools, yard tools, boat motors, tackle boxes, fishing poles, and lots and lots of boxes of nails and screws.

Further down a bunch of scrap metal and large engine parts caught our attention. I didn't know what they were for, but there were a lot of them. Off to the left, way in the back corner behind the wall of food was a living area.

"What the fuck?" Tannya yelled in anger.

Against the back wall was a makeshift living room—a beat-up old couch, the cushions worn thin, and a couple old blankets tossed on it. An old console TV sat on the floor across from it. The screen had a crack in the corner, and the wood veneer was barely holding together on the front. Pizza boxes and empty cans of fruits, vegetables, and tons of empty two-liters overflowed a garbage can in the corner. A month's worth of newspapers were spread about, and an old desktop computer was set up on a few old palattes taking the role of a coffee table.

"Oh, my God!" Miss Kitty said.

I stepped forward and looked at the date on the newspaper on the top of the pile. It was last week's.

"Current," I told them.

Tannya had her hands on her hips. She was red with anger and started pacing. Then she noticed the wire from the computer and followed it. Miss Kitty and I followed her to the back of the shed. There was a little hole drilled in the tin near the bottom back corner. Three wires went through it.

After a few moments we figured out that someone had spliced and split her cable, her internet, and her phone lines. She went back in to the shed and used her cell phone to call her landline. A hand set under the blanket on the couch rang very quietly.

"What the hell?" Tannya said with a confused look as she picked it up and ended the call. "Why would he have this? I would know if someone called him."

"He could call out on it, though, and you wouldn't know," I said.

"And he could listen in on your calls, and you wouldn't know either," Miss Kitty added.

"He's stealing phone, internet, and cable!" she shouted.

"I'm assuming this is your ex we're talking about, right?" I asked.

"Has to be. That low-life son of a bitch! I'll kill him!"

"Easy, girl!" Miss Kitty said. "We 'Ella girls' don't get mad. We get even!"

"'Ella girls'?" I said.

"Yes, our ship is *Ella Vashow*. That's our new calling card," Tannya said with a nod at Miss Kitty. Miss Kitty smiled and fist bumped her.

Wowzers, I shouldn't be here. These two are going to get me wrapped up in a mess again, I thought as I looked around the shed.

"We need a plan!" Tannya said.

"Yes . . . yes we do," Miss Kitty said and rubbed her hands together.

"Maybe you should call Rex," I offered. "If it's Scooter, then he's trespassing . . . and stealing. Rex could put him in jail."

"If and when he returns," Tannya said. "I wanna kill him now." We stood there a moment while she thought. "No, I think for now we're going to pretend we didn't see anything. I want to think on this a bit. Scooter's gonna pay for this, but I'm not sure how yet."

"Well, what do you want us to grab for the treasure?" Miss Kitty asked.

"Nothing. Let's just go to my cousin's and get some stuff. We'll worry about replacing it later. She's gone for a while anyway, and I'm sure she won't care."

"When was the last time you talked to her? Are you sure she won't care?" I asked.

"Yeah, I'm sure. If she does, I'll just pay her for the stuff. We can just keep track of what we take. It'll be win-win either way."

We hauled ourselves back in the Jeep and drove away. While I was driving back towards town, Miss Kitty was pressing Tannya to discuss what she planned to do on the shed situation.

"Has he been there since you kicked him out?" she asked.

"I don't know," Tannya said shaking her head. "I never go out to that shed. Seriously, I've opened the door maybe twice since he left and that was to reach in and grab the rake that's right by the door. I never even looked in. For all I know he's been there all along."

"Judging by the shape the couch was in and garbage, I'd say it's been a while. It looked pretty settled."

"Man, that pisses me off!" She pulled her top lip into her mouth and tightened her eyes. She looked livid. I'd never seen her like this. She's always been the chipper or excited one. "I'll get him for this, but not just yet." She stared out the window hard at nothing while I drove.

"Take a right," she finally said a few miles later. "Milly lives down this road."

Miss Kitty leaned up from the back. "If she lives out here, why does she have garage sales? She can't get much traffic."

"She has nothing better to do. Like I said, she seems to add to her collection rather than get rid of anything. She's a hoarder."

"No! Really? Like the people on the show for real?" I said. I always thought it would be fun to climb through someone's house and then clean it. That show was motivating, too. Every time I watched it I got up and cleaned out a closet as soon as it was over.

"Well she's probably not that bad, but she has way too much stuff."

We pulled up to an old farmhouse. We saw no animals in the barn and the fields were grown over. Tannya informed us that her cousin had bought it from her grandparents when they moved to assisted living three years ago.

"Where's Milly?" I asked, getting nervous now that we were the trespassers.

"In Iowa for her sister's wedding. It was this past Saturday, but she planned to be gone this whole week, too. I'm supposed to stop over and feed the cat and scoop the litter and get the mail every few days."

"So, we don't actually have to go into the house with you, right?" Miss Kitty asked with a disgusted look.

"No, the stuff's in the attached garage. I'll run in and check the cat. You two start getting stuff from there. I'll meet ya when I'm done."

I parked right in front of the garage. Her cousin must have had the garage added onto the house after she bought it, because it looked brand new, and the house attached to it certainly wasn't.

We all got out and walked up to the service door of the garage and waited while Tannya opened the lock. She flipped on the light and we looked around.

"I'll be right back," Tannya said and disappeared through another door into the house.

The garage was full—tables set up everywhere and stuff set out and priced and nicely organized. I glanced around. She had very nice stuff. I was surprised.

Miss Kitty walked over by a smaller table near the automatic garage door and found a bunch of plastic bags. "Here," she said. "Let's load up."

I grabbed a bag and started walking around. I found myself by the far wall looking through the clothing rack. It was a dowel hanging from the rafters by chains and full of really nice looking clothes, most still with tags on them. Some were brand names, and the prices she had on them were great. "Wow, look at this!" I said and held out a beautiful rayon dress shirt.

"Very nice," Miss Kitty said with a smile. "Is that new?"

"Yeah, it still has tags! A lot of them do!"

"This is a beauty too!" she said and held up a crystal vase. "It's lead crystal! Two bucks!"

"What the heck?"

We continued showing each other great items, and then I found them . . . It was like sky opened up, and the sun gazed down on them as the choirs of heavenly angels sang . . . the one and only Louis Vuitton Vanity Pump in patent monogram canvas. MY DREAM SHOES! I had been in love with these shoes for months, ever since I saw them in a magazine. I actually picked that magazine up from time to time, just to look again.

I had looked them up on the internet a while back and found out that they retailed for $875. Which was a ton of money. I had money . . . I had lots of money, and I was pretty conservative considering I got a fresh ten Gs every month. These were going to be a treat to myself! And now here they were. I rushed across the room to an area under a table and dropped quickly to my knees and scooped them up and hugged them. "Oh, my God!" I screamed with excitement. I was literally bouncing with joy.

"What?" Miss Kitty asked and rushed over.

"Oh, please let them be my size!" I prayed.

Miss Kitty gasped and covered her mouth as I reached down and whipped my shoe off my foot. I didn't even look at the size of the Louis Vuittons. I just shoved my foot into them. "Are those—" Miss Kitty asked.

"Yes!" I interrupted and stood up.

Miss Kitty's face was lit up with excitement as she quickly turned her face under the table and looked for more. There were three more pairs! Dang, they were a bit tight, but I didn't care! We agreed that we each got two pairs. We stuck them into our bags and then tried to act normally. We decided we would not tell Tannya. We wanted to keep them and we weren't sure how she'd take that. She was pretty focused on getting some good treasure for her booty entry.

Tannya came and joined us, and we filled a bunch of plastic shopping bags with stuff, everything from household, to shoes, to clothes. I stuck a few shirts into my secret bag too. Before we walked away, Tannya looked around. "See, she won't even notice. There's still a ton of stuff here."

Miss Kitty winked at me. I smiled and felt an evil presence in my stomach. *Must be my bad girl coming out.* This was the first time I had stolen anything in my life.

I popped the hatch to the Jeep and Tannya dropped her bags in first and headed to the passenger-side door. Miss Kitty and I rearranged our bags, each putting our secret bag behind a blanket I had back there. "Get them to me later," Miss Kitty whispered. I nodded and winked at her, then skipped to my door.

Just as I got back into the Jeep, Derek called.

"Hello?"

"Hey, sweetness, you behaving?" he asked. I swear sometimes he was the psychic.

"Of course!"

"Good, I knew you would be."

Ugh, now my good mood was gone and guilt was taking over. "I hate when you think I'm a better person than I am," I told him.

"Oh? Now I'm worried."

Silence.

"Just kidding," I said to break the silence. "So what are you doing? How's work going?"

"Work's good."

"Well, that's good. Why ya calling?"

"Not sure, something just made me feel like I should check in on you."

"Ha, ha, what . . . are you my dad now? You're silly. You should get back to work and go catch those bad guys. Nothing interesting going on here," I told him.

Miss Kitty and Tannya laughed out loud. I shot them looks as I turned the Jeep onto the road.

"Where are you right now?"

"I'm just out and about with Tannya and Miss Kitty."

"Uh huh. Well, tell them hi for me and stay out of trouble. I'll talk to ya soon."

I disconnected and took a deep breath. He sounded annoyed. I would be too if he were as much work as I was.

I drove back to the diner and dropped the girls off so that they could get their cars. Then we went back to my place. Before they arrived, I took the secret bags in the house. I wondered where she got the designer stuff. She must not have known the value of them if she was selling them so cheap at a garage sale. Although Tannya said she did sell some online, too. I walked back to my bedroom and dumped the stuff on my bed. I had three gorgeous shirts, and two new pairs of LOUIS VUITTONS!

I did another happy dance then put the vanity pumps back on. Oh, gosh, they were so beautiful, and my feet never looked better. I could see why women loved them so much. I strutted down the hallway in them like I was on a cat walk. Back and forth up and down the hallway, adding dramatic turns and hair flips, and not smiling of course, just like the professionals.

I thought I better get back to the Jeep. Tannya and Miss Kitty would be right behind me. I was wrapping up my last turn and heading into my room when I stepped wrong and twisted my ankle. CRAP! I dropped to the ground and grabbed my ankle. Oh, my gosh, it hurt. The sting was incredible. I tried to wiggle it right away and get it loose so it wouldn't bruise and tighten up. I heard a car door and tried my best to get to my feet. I hobbled to my bedroom and threw the bags and the shoes into the closet just as I heard a knock at the door. I hobbled through the living room fighting back tears and opened the door to Tannya.

"Hey girl, oh . . . what's wrong?" she asked and noticed right away I was in pain.

"I just twisted my ankle. It hurts so badly!" I told her and hopped to the couch.

"Geez, how did you do that?" she asked and went to the kitchen.

"I was running into the house to go to the bathroom and just tripped. I must have just stepped wrong on it."

She returned with ice wrapped in a towel and handed it to me. "Here, ice it."

There was another door knock, and I yelled for Miss Kitty to come in. Tannya gave her the update, and she came over and looked at my foot. "Wow, you're kind of a mess lately."

"Thanks!"

"Take some Tylenol or something, 'cause we need you! You can't be out with an injury. Stitches and a sprained ankle won't stop Sara Narra, right?"

"I don't know. This hurts really bad," I whined.

"Here, take these," Miss Kitty said pulling two small pills from her purse and put them in my hand.

I looked at the unlabeled pills and asked her what they were. "Never mind that. They won't hurt you. They'll relax you and help with the pain and inflammation. Trust me. Think of them as little happy pills."

I was in desperate need of pain relief, and the lil' devil in me said to take them, so I did. While I waited for them to kick in, Tannya and Miss Kitty went out the Jeep and got the bags of soon-to-be-treasure. I sent Tannya out to the garage for old newspapers and Miss Kitty to the kitchen for beer. We clinked bottles. I made a toast, "To gold, and all the riches in the deep blue sea!" I was surprised by the words and enthusiasm. I didn't know that was coming out of my mouth until it was said. Weird.

We went out on the lawn and BAM! The cannon fired. "HOLY SHIT!" I yelled, and almost toppled over on my bad ankle. Tannya and Miss Kitty both screamed. It was much louder outside.

"Boy, I sure hope *Ocean's Lie* has a cannon!" Tannya said.

"We should get one!" Miss Kitty said. "We should get a cannon for *Ella Vashow!*"

"What? No, we don't know the first thing—" I started.

"We can learn! I bet there's a You Tube on it," Miss Kitty said.

Destroyed and Detained

"We don't have time! The pirates are coming tomorrow!" I protested, but, actually, I liked the idea.

"Where there's a will, there's a way," Miss Kitty said. "I have to go to the bathroom. I'll be right back," she said and excused herself.

Tannya brought me a chair from the patio and laid the newspapers on the lawn. Then she grabbed a few bags of stuff and spread out some of the items on the paper.

Miss Kitty finally joined us and grabbed the spray paint. They started shaking cans and spraying. We all felt a bit weird spray painting anything and everything gold. There were a few vases, some figurines, a couple small wood shelves, some old missmatched china, junk jewelry, old frying pans, a few picture frames, and then some soft items that needed to be material dyed. I started working on those. The girls brought me a five-gallon pail, the Rit dye, and the hose. I turned the water gold and threw in stuffed animals, some old throw pillows, a canvas bag, some old hats, and a couple blankets. When we were done, all of the items and half my yard was gold. Out of room on the newspaper, we'd just sprayed things in the grass. Fifty-six pieces, which was good because I didn't know if the blankets would dry in time.

Tannya's phone rang and she answered it. She looked very excited and pointed to the phone while trying to talk calm and normal. She stepped away while she spoke.

"Must be her pirate friends," I said to Miss Kitty.

"I bet they want her to join them tonight."

"Probably."

Miss Kitty went in and got us three more beers. It was getting cool and dark so we went inside and sat at the table, hoping the treasure would dry before the sun set all the way and the dew formed.

"That was Captain Morgan," Tannya eagerly told us. "He and First Mate Flying Dutchman and Long John want me to meet them tonight!"

"Really! Where?" I asked with a grin that again surprised me.

"At Morning Glory at 7:00 p.m. I have to bring the fifty pieces of booty in a discrete container," she told us. "And they said to come alone."

12

We all looked at each other kind of panicked. "That's in an hour!" I said and stood up. "The treasure won't be dry by then!" Why was I so excited? I was practically screaming.

Tannya and Miss Kitty both looked at me. "How's the ankle?" Miss Kitty asked.

"The pills kicked in, didn't they?" Tannya said with a smile and looked at Miss Kitty.

Miss Kitty smiled and winked back. I thought about it. It didn't hurt that bad anymore. The ankle was still swollen and getting black and blue, but the pain was barely noticeable. And I had a ton of energy.

"I feel great!" I told them, "but we have to dry the treasure." They went outside and hauled the treasure in. I had the clothes dryer running on high with the soft stuff inside. Tannya had my hair drier, and Miss Kitty had a box fan. They had the hard items on the dining room table and were moving the fan and hair drier back and forth trying to speed up the process. Everything was still very tacky because the sun had gone down and the temps were in the low sixties.

I ran through the house looking for boxes and finally found enough to fit all the treasure in. The blankets and the pillows stayed back because they were not dry yet, but Tannya had her fifty pieces. We packed the four boxes into her car and sent her on her way.

We had her wired, of course, and we had the listening device with us. We followed her to Morning Glory in Miss Kitty's Benz.

"We definitely got our money's worth out of this equipment," Miss Kitty said.

"Yes, we did!" I agreed. "We're professionals at this. We come to conquer!" I said and threw up my hand at her for a high five. She shot me a look and turned her eyes back on the road.

"Maybe next time one pill will be enough," Miss Kitty said.

We pulled onto Main Street and circled slowly as we watched Tannya park and walk in. A few cars were parked out front and one truck parked the long way on the street with a trailer on the back.

We parked down a few spaces and turned the car off. After a few minutes, we could hear Tannya introduce herself. We quietly leaned over the speaker box.

"Hi, I'm Tannya, you must be Captain Morgan."

"Yes, I am," a gruff voice said. "Sit yerself down." There was some rustling and then more voices.

"I'm Flying Dutchman."

"And I'm Long John."

"It's nice to meet you both. I'm so excited to be part of this. This will be so much fun! I read about this on the internet, and, boy, I wish I'd known about this years ago!" she told them.

"That's nice," Captain Morgan's voice said seriously with a pirate accent. "Did ye bring yar booty?"

"Ha! Ha! Ha!" Tannya let out a belt of laughter. "Oh, wow, you even talk like pirates! Love the outfits too, by the way."

"Yer captain asked ye a question. Ye be doing right by him by answer'n him," Flying Dutchman growled.

"Oh, yes. Sorry. Yes, sir . . . er, yes, Captain. My booty, fifty pieces of gold is in my car in boxes. I didn't know if you wanted it in here."

"No, we can get that later. Now here's what we are gonna be doing, first thing. I need to know everything ye know about the ship that's near yer friend's property. Sara was her name?"

There was a moment of silence.

"Arg! Answer ye captain!" Flying Dutchman snapped again.

"Ah . . . yes. But she doesn't know much. She just woke up and it was there. She was very surprised." Tannya sounded nervous now.

"Did she mention seeing us?" Captain Morgan asked.

"Yeah, did she ask about us?" Long John asked with energy in his voice. I could almost see his boyish grin.

"Yes, she mentioned she saw three pirates, and they ran away, but that was all she said."

"Was she angry? Did she call the police?" Long John asked her.

"No."

"Oh . . . good," Long John said. I heard a smack. "Hey!" he whined.

"Stay focused!" Flying Dutchman warned.

"Do ye know the location of their treasure?" Captain asked her.

"No, I don't know anything."

"How about the real name of the Captain."

"No," Tannya said again. "I'm new to all this. I just think it looks like fun to play pirates. I thought I'd join."

"Tell me about yar friend," Captain Morgan demanded.

"Like what?" Tannya asked him.

"Arg, like how long she's known about the ship, and who made it. Whose ship is it?"

"She doesn't know anything. She's owned the house for less than a year. She doesn't know the guy who built it. All she knows is he lives across the lake. She saw some trees cut down and that's it."

"Does she know what he looks like?"

There was a moment of silence. "No, she doesn't. Why? What does any of this have to do with my friend?" Tannya asked.

I looked at Miss Kitty. We both had confused looks.

"Argh! Nothing. It's just best to know all that we can to make a good attack."

Tannya sounded concerned. "This is all just role-playing, right? This is just a fun game for a day or so?"

Flying Dutchman laughed. "Bloody hell! I love these scallywags, they think this is all just a game, something to do on a weekend because they're bored. No, this ain't for a day or two, some of us been doing this for years. Some LARPS are generations deep and been organized for years and years. What say you? A day or two? Arrr! Maybe it be best ye find a different crew that doesn't care. We are here to—"

"That's enough!" Captain Morgan scolded. "She be learnin' as she goes. She'll be good to have around. We need more buccaneers anyways. I'll be given the information she'll need from now on. Ye settle in and shut yer trap."

Captain seemed angry at him. It didn't seem like he was enjoying the LARP as much as Dutchman, or maybe he was tired of playing it . . . or he was a good actor and staying in character. I didn't like either.

"All right," Captain continued. "Let me think for a moment."

There was an awkward silence and then he spoke again. "Tonight, in one hour, you'll lead us out to yer friend's house to show us where the ship was built. We'll wait here, eat, and leave when it's good and dark. I want to see the location of the ship owner's home. I want to know if anyone else is living there with him."

"Do we have a ship?" Tannya asked.

"Long John is going to launch it tomorrow at dawn," Flying Dutchman said.

"Is it big? How are you going to get it into the water?" Tannya asked.

"Arg, commanding the ship is my problem, not yours. It's big enough for now."

"Yeah, we only need it fer a short while, until we take over *Poseidon's Zebra Mussel* anyway," Long John said.

"Oh, we're taking the ship? I thought we were just stealing the treasure," Tannya said.

"They plan to sink the treasure, and none of us are certified scuba divers. We won't be able to get to it, if we don't get aboard," Flying Dutchman told her.

"If ye agree to be on our crew, then ye agree to do what you're told and not repeat any of what's made known to ye. This is a verbal, binding agreement," Captain told her sternly.

"Yeah we live by the pirate code!" Long John said.

"Parley?" Tannya asked.

"Aye, parley," Captain answered.

"Now let's eat!"

We listened in while they ate, but there wasn't much more said. When the meal was over, we watched as they walked out the door. They were all decked out in pirate outfits and looked really out of place.

"We be following ya to the lake. Ye need to be showing us where on the lake the ship was built. I want to know the location of the owner's residence," Captain Morgan said.

"Yes! Let's follow them!" I yelled with excitement. Miss Kitty jumped.

"Geez, you scared me!" she said with her hand on her chest.

"Sorry, I scared myself a little too. What were the pills you gave me? I keep getting these bursts of excitement out of nowhere."

"Never mind about the pills. I don't think we should follow. They'll see us. It's not like we can hide in traffic," Miss Kitty said. "I think I should drop you off at home, and we should call it a night when Tannya gets back. I doubt they're doing much more tonight."

We watched as Tannya went to her trunk and handed them each a box and then carried one herself over to the trailer parked on the street. They unlocked and opened the back and put the treasure in, then quickly closed and locked it again.

When Tannya got in her car and started down the road, the pirates followed in the truck. I really wanted to see what pirates put in their trailer.

I called Tannya's cell. She answered. I told her we'd heard everything and for her to come to my house when she was done with them and let me know what happened, and not to tell them that Val lived there or that she was my aunt, to just keep playing dumb. She agreed and I disconnected.

Miss Kitty dropped me off at home and turned down the invite to stay and wait for Tannya. "I need to get back to Smoochy Poo. I bet she's lonely. Call me and let me know if anything else happens."

"Okay. Otherwise I'll probably see you tomorrow," I told her.

"Oh, you will!" she said with a wink and left.

Something was up with her. Not sure what, but it felt like she was hiding something. This made me nervous because she could be very resourceful.

I hung my jacket and purse on the hook and then hobbled to my room to see my shoes again. I put one on and then tried the other but my ankle was still very swollen and it wouldn't fit. I was so bummed. After a minute I took them off and kissed them and set them in the closet and closed the doors so they didn't get dusty.

After I limped into the kitchen, I drank a big glass of water to push the pills through faster. They were awesome for the pain. My ankle didn't hurt at all anymore, but it was swollen and had limited range of motion. But the side effects made me feel bi-polar. One second I had energy and spirit, the next I could fall asleep, then a second later I was just so happy! I was trying to control it.

I heard my phone and did my best to hurry over to it. I missed the call. It was a "blocked" number. Hmmm. The time showed 9:25 p.m.

A moment later I got a text: *Guess who came to see me?*

I was staring at the words trying to figure out who they could be from, when my phone beeped again. *Message.* I opened it.

It was a picture, a close up of Derek's face. He wasn't looking at the camera, and it was close enough that I couldn't see the background to tell where it was taken. He was smiling and looking straight ahead, almost as if it were taken from the side of him, by someone close to him.

My first thought was Jodi. Rage filled me, and my heartbeat picked up. What should I do? Respond? Ignore. Call Derek. Let it go. Drive to the Cities, hunt her down and gut her like a fish? Hmm, so many choices. I think I'll go with the fish!

My phone beeped. I quickly opened the message.

It was from Derek. *Hey, done for the night, headed home early! I'll come up tomorrow after my shift. I get off at 9, is that okay?*

I responded: *Are you at home already?*

He replied: *Heading there shortly.*

Well, that didn't tell me anything. Now I was annoyed. My evil side texted the blocked caller back. *Who is this?*

She replied: *Jodi. Getting what I want. ;)*

I started marching around looking for my keys, and then I remembered that I probably shouldn't drive with the drugs in my system. It's times like this I hated that Derek lived and worked so far away. I was so frustrated. I was pissed off! I wanted to break something! I screamed at the top of my lungs, "AAAAAAHHHH!"

I took a deep breath to recover, and then was startled by a knock on my door. My heart was pumping, and I was so freaking angry. I'd already dealt with the bitch enough! I marched to the door and swung it open hard, expecting Tannya to be there. But it was Rex! God, he looked hot! My evil side reached out and grabbed his shirt in my fist and pulled him through the doorway. He stumbled up against me, and I kissed him!

13

I was breathing hard. I wanted to suck on his lip. Then I realized my mouth was actually on him, and that this wasn't a dream. As quick as our lips touched it was over. I pushed him off abruptly and stepped back.

"That DID NOT just happen!" I yelled at him with a pointed finger. He was frozen in shock. I wiped my mouth on the back of my hand and paced around the room, walking as quickly as I could and staring at the ground.

"Wha . . . wa . . . wao," Rex stammered with wide eyes.

"No. You be quiet! No talking. *I* get to talk," I told him with another finger point. I was shocked at my behavior and my own voice. It was like I was having an out-of-body experience. This must be what people mean when they say that. It was as if I was standing on the other side of the room, watching this unfold. It wasn't me doing that, and I was not talking like that. *That* wasn't *me*. Crap! Now what? I looked up at his face while I was still pacing, which was very hard on my ankle. I looked from him over to the door and noticed it was still open. I slammed it shut and stopped walking and sat on the couch. My heart was pounding so hard I could feel it in my foot.

I took a couple deep breaths and unwillingly made eye contact with Rex. He was still in shock. He hadn't moved a muscle since I shoved him back.

"I . . . ummm . . ." I squinted my eyes at him and wrinkled my nose. "I'm sorry!"

"What the hell? Are you drunk?"

"No. Well yes, well . . . not drunk. More like under the influence." I hoped that I knew Rex well enough that I could tell him a couple things and wouldn't get anyone into trouble.

"Are you high? What are you on?" he asked and sat down next to me on the couch.

"I'm on . . . I don't know," I started. "I'm not sure what I took. It helped my pain, though. I don't hurt at all."

"Pain from your stitches? Is it the pain killers?"

"No, gosh, I forgot about those!" I let out a bolt of laughter. And once again I couldn't stop. I had the giggles again.

I was thinking I was going to tell Rex about the pills, but then I needed to tell him about spraining my ankle, and where I had gotten the shoes. Well, from the garage sale that I just robbed, that's where! Why, you ask? Well, because I needed some treasure for my pirate captain, so that I could play pirates with the neighbors. Duh! And then I'd add that he'd caught me at a bad time. I was angry at my on-again boyfriend's ex, or maybe at my boyfriend, or maybe there was nothing to be mad about and she was just toying with me. And then I saw Rex and he was looking so good and I'd been attracted to him since the day I first saw him. And that my evil side temporarily took control and kissed him . . .

My mind was spinning all this up and it was funny! I mean, come on, if I told him the truth he'd have me committed and labeled 'crazy.' It was too absurd! I couldn't tell him. I wanted him to like me and think of me as normal . . . and smart, and sexy and capable, but lately that was not how I was coming off. Sheesh, what was I going to say?

This poor guy was going to wish he'd never met me. I finally got my laughing under control and took a deep breath. Dang, I was a case.

"Sara, what did you take?"

I just stared at his face and thought I totally ruined a first kiss with him, too! He would go home and think about it and how bad it was, and what a horrible experience it was to have Sara Martin's lips on his face. And then I shoved him away and yelled at him on top of it.

"I have a sprained ankle, and a friend, who shall remain nameless, gave me a pill to help with the pain. I guess I'm having some really crazy side effects. I'm so sorry. I didn't know that was going to happen, and I stopped it as soon as I could. I was angry about a text, and I guess the meds made me crazy, and you got the worst of it. Please forget that it happened, and let it stay between the two of us," I pleaded as I led the way into the living room. I flopped down on the couch.

Sitting down beside me, he showed me a half grin. "Forget about it? No, but it will stay between us," he said with a wink.

"Oh, gosh. Puuulease forget it! It was awful. I wasn't prepared. I was drugged and out of control of my body."

He let out a quiet laugh. "Actually it reminded me of a surprise kiss I once got on the playground in second grade. But don't worry, I won't declare that you have cooties and run away screaming."

"Aw, gee, thanks! I'm grateful. This town already thinks I'm weird. Cooties would make me another headliner."

He playfully elbowed me in the ribs. "Let me see your head."

I leaned forward towards him, and he carefully pushed my head down and moved some of my hair, just as the front door swung open.

"Whoa! So sorry!" Tannya said.

I quickly picked my head up. "Hey," I said, sitting up straight.

"I'll come back later," Tannya offered.

"Stop it! I was just showing Rex my stitches," I assured her.

"Oh, ha ha, of course, I knew that," she said and came in.

She smiled at Rex and he just stood there. We all kind of looked at each other awkwardly until I broke the silence. "Tannya was just coming over to help me decide on some window treatments. I just couldn't decide . . . . so she was going to help me," I told him.

Rex looked at me with quizzical eyes. I knew he wasn't falling for it. "Oh, of course. I just stopped by to see if you knew anything about the car on the road just down from your driveway."

"Uh, no," I told him. "I didn't see anything when I came home."

"I saw it, too." Tannya said. "It looks like . . . ." She stopped herself and thought for a second. "It looks like that one lady's car, that we met at the bar in the Cities, that one time. You remember, with Miss Kitty, *that* time. It looks like the car of that lady that we met there."

Jodi.

My heartrate was going up again. I knew Tannya was covering because Rex was in the room, but I didn't care if he knew about her, in fact I did want him to know. I looked at Rex. "Run the plates!" I demanded.

He looked at me and widened his eyes in fear. And then his face relaxed and he smiled, "Are you having side effects again?"

I reached out and punched him hard in the arm. "Just do it!" He went to the kitchen and called dispatch.

"What the hell would she be doing here?" Tannya asked.

"I don't know, but look what I got on my phone a minute ago," I said and showed her the messages and the picture. Rex was peeking in from the kitchen and listening. Dispatch put him on hold and he walked over and looked over my shoulder at the picture.

"That bitch probably took that from a zoom-lensed camera and then sent it. She probably followed him. There's no way he's with her. She's just messing with ya," Tannya said.

"What's the story here?" Rex asked with tight eyes.

"It's Derek's ex. We're having issues with her. I gave her a pretty good warning to stay away from him, but she's still bothering us," I told him.

"So has Derek told her to leave him alone too?"

"Yes."

"And she still bothers him? How long were they together?"

"For a while—"

"They lived together," Tannya interrupted. "They were ring shopping!"

"Really? Wow. But he's sure it's over," Rex asked with raised eyebrows.

"Yes! He's sure. She's behaving like a stalker and thinks she's the shit and can win him back," I said with my hand on my hip.

"How do you know she won't?"

"Because I know Derek loves me. He hasn't had feelings for her in a long time. She cheated on him!"

"Well, she kissed another guy," Tannya said.

"She kissed another guy, and he dumped her?" Rex said with a look I didn't like.

"Yes, but it was the guy across the hall, and she was half-dressed on top of him!"

"Oh, I see." Rex nodded his head.

"Tramp!" Tannya said.

"Just run the plates and find out why she's here, Officer!" I told him angrily.

"Sheesh! Okay," he said and stepped back to the kitchen.

"What's up with you?" Tannya asked me. "You're acting bitchy at him. You never talked to him like that before."

"I hate when people think I'm a better person than I am. Maybe I'm always an evil bitch and I've just been hiding it all this time, huh?"

"Ha, ha, haaaaaa . . . ahhhh. Oh, honey, you don't have a clue. You're so far from 'bitch' that a high school full of hormonal teenage girls would eat you breakfast."

"Whatever!"

"What did Rex mean about side effects, anyway?" she asked me.

"Well, I guess I just turned into a bitch, because I cheated on Derek. Yup, I kissed Rex two minutes ago, and now I'm a tramp, too!"

Rex came from around the corner.

Tannya raised her brows, "WHAT?"

"Ladies!" Rex said with authority. He squinted his eyes at me like a warning and continued. "No one is a tramp, and no one cheated. It was an accident that won't leave this room. Sara isn't herself and is feeling some side effects from some pain killers she took. It wasn't even a kiss. It was more of an attack . . . with a quick retreat. It was nothing, now both of you calm down."

"Nothing? It was nothing?" The rage building inside of me was uncontrollable.

"Uh oh! I ain't never seen that look in her eyes before!" Tannya said and stepped behind Rex.

"UGH!" I growled in frustration. *Could this get any worse?* I hobbled over to the couch and sat down.

"The plates are registered to a Jodi Vagerna."

"Oh! Oh! Ha ha ha!" Tannya was laughing again. She was doubled over holding her belly, trying to catch her breath. "Did you say Vagina? Ha ha ha! Serves the bitch right!"

"Vag-errrr-na," Rex corrected.

"That's her," I said with a grin. Then I giggled. When Tannya laughed it was contagious. I started laughing again and then realized how crazy I'd been acting and how strong my mood swings were. My head and foot were starting to hurt again. I looked up at Rex and the corner of his mouth curled but I guessed he didn't find it as funny as we did.

"I'm going to go have a look around the property and check on the car again," he said. "You two stay here, don't kill anyone, and stay out of the pain killers!"

"Uh, no promises, my ankle and head are starting to hurt again," I yelled after him as he went out the door.

I put my leg up on the coffee table and Tannya brought me some ice for it. I sat there and rested it for a bit while Tannya caught me up on what happened when she went to meet the pirates.

"We drove past Wayde's lot and then circled around, and came back. They got out of the truck and told me to wait in my car. They walked along the trees near the driveway and disappeared into the night. They were only gone for about fifteen minutes, and then they came back. Flying Dutchman came over to my car while the other two climbed into the truck. He said they wanted to see the place and if anyone else was with them, and now they were going back to basecamp to plan the attack. Dutchman said he had my number and would be in touch. I told him I wanted to come with, but he said no, that they wouldn't need my services until tomorrow. He said I could call him if I knew of any other information that might be important and that I should leave my cell phone on in case they had more questions for me. That was it. I drove over here after they turned off.

Something is strange about these guys, though. They take this shit way too seriously."

"Yeah, they do."

We sat there a bit longer and talked about what kind of plan they would come up with.

"They don't seem to have a ship. So what can they do without a ship?"

"Right? And what kind of *attack*? I don't get this. Wayde has a real cannon. Do you think he will use it? I thought that LARPs were for fun, like a play, with fake swords and knifes and stuff. But his cannon is real!" I added.

"I know. I don't get it either, but if your Aunt Val is over there we need to watch her back."

"Yes, no matter what, we need to make sure that she's happy and safe at all times. I wonder if she realizes this is going a bit far, or if this is in fact normal."

My phone beeped. I looked at it. It was another message from Jodi. All that was in the message was a colon and a capital 'P,' which looked like a face with a tongue sticking out.

I showed Tannya. "What the hell?" she said.

"I wish I could reply, but it was a blocked number." God, I hated her! She went through the trouble of getting on the internet to find my number, just to send a message to me through a blocked number? *And* she drove all the way to Nisswa to peep at me? She had serious issues.

There was a knock on the door, and we both looked up. Rex opened it and peeked in.

"Come on in," I said.

He stayed in the entryway and looked serious. "I walked around outside here and didn't see anything. And then I went out to the road and the car is gone now."

"Really? Well, at least she's gone. Good. I hope she crashes her car into a tree and dies," I said. I was a bit surprised at my own voice again. Tannya and Rex both shot me a look of uncertainty. "Oops! Did I say that out loud?" I asked with a wink. I'd said it, and my evil twin inside was nodding and rubbing her hands together. I supposed I should feel guilty about wishing pain or death on another person . . . but I didn't.

My phone buzzed and I looked at it again. Another message. This one was from Derek. My evil side wanted to yell at him. He'd caused all this this bullshit. I opened it and it was a picture. "It's a picture from Derek . . ." I told Rex and Tannya, who were both staring at me with anticipation. I clicked on it and waited for a moment while it opened.

When it finally appeared on my screen, my mouth hung slack. I couldn't believe what I was seeing!

14

"I'll kill her! I will fucking KILL HER!" I screamed. I threw the ice pack off my foot, limped to the living room window and looked out. That did me absolutely no good. I knew she was gone.

"What's going on?" Tannya asked.

I looked over at Rex, who had a very somber look on his face.

BEEP. Another message from Derek. I opened it: *Enjoying your evening, are ya?*

"FUUUUCK!" I screamed again. I looked at Tannya. "I should've killed her when I had the chance!"

"What? Tell me!" she demanded.

I showed the picture to Rex. He tucked his lips tightly inside his mouth, bit down, and nodded. Then he shook his head and made a call to dispatch on his shoulder CB. He asked dispatch to notify the county sheriff to keep an eye out for Jodi's car. He said she was wanted for questioning on a possible trespassing and harassment charge.

Tannya came over to us in the entryway. "Let me see!"

I showed her. She gasped and covered her mouth. "Oh, girl, you got some explaining to do! I bet he's pissed."

"Thank you, Captain Obvious!" I shouted at her.

The picture was of Rex sitting on the couch and me with my head in his lap. It didn't look good. It was innocent, but it still didn't look good in the photo. And I had a spring flower centerpiece on the coffee table, so from where the picture was taken, which was from outside my living room window, the centerpiece blocked the view from my head down. Which was not helping my case any.

"I'm gonna bounce!" Tannya said with a grin. "You two have a nice night. I'll be in touch in the morning, girl." She hugged me and left.

"I'm right behind you. I've got a trespasser to catch," Rex said and followed her out.

I shut the door behind them and went to the kitchen. My meds were totally worn off. The pain, on a scale of one to ten, was at an eight for my ankle and about a six for my stiches. I poured myself a glass of wine and went to the bedroom. I texted Derek back that I'd call him in a bit. He replied with another picture. This one was taken right after I kissed Rex. Our lips weren't touching, but we were very close, and I had my hands on his chest. I was just pushing him away. It didn't look good, either.

Ugh, how was I going to explain this? Should I? I mean, really, Rex was right, it was an attack and retreat. The details would be boring to anyone. I knew the right thing to do would be to fess up . . . but my evil side was running the show.

I got into my pajamas and brushed my teeth and then settled into bed with my foot propped up on a pillow. I dialed Derek's number and took a deep breath. My evil side was whispering bad ideas into the phone. I was trying to shush her when he answered.

"Well, hello, busy girl." They were playful words but there was irritation in his voice.

"Hi," I said slowly. "Well, to update you, your ex, Jodi, is harassing me AGAIN. She was trespassing on my property and has my phone number now, too."

"Yeah, looks like she's been busy, too."

"Ahh," I sighed and let out a long exhale. "Look, I know that the pictures look bad, but they are nothing. Rex was over wondering about the abandoned car and if I knew anything about it. Tannya was here, too. I sprained my ankle earlier today, between that and my stitches, I was in a lot of pain so I took some pain killers, and I was having some bad reactions to them, so Rex was helping me relax."

"Well, isn't that nice of him? He's a great guy!"

Silence.

The silence was bad because it gave my evil side a chance to return. "Look, Derek," my devilish twin said. "Think what you want. I don't care. I'm not going to sit here and defend myself. If you want to play into Jodi's games AGAIN then go right ahead. I don't need this. Do me a favor and figure out what you're going to do about her. It's getting on my last nerve, and I'm tired of it. I'm going to hang up and ENJOY my night! GOODBYE!" I said and slammed the phone down on the counter. UGH!

I drank the rest of my wine in one gulp. I just wanted to end this crazy day. I let Pepper out to go to the bathroom and then filled his and Faith's food and water dishes. I climbed back into bed. Faith curled up on the pillow next to me and purred. I turned off the light, closed my eyes and wished the day would go away.

I woke to a banging on the door. It was still dark. I looked at the clock . . . 6:00 a.m.

Shit! Who's waking me up this early? I stepped out of bed and yelped when I put pressure on my ankle. It was still swollen.

I padded down the hallway to the entry and opened the front door to Rex. "Morning, Sleeping Beauty," he said, looking all adorable in his uniform. I pinched my own arm to make sure it wasn't a dream.

I moaned at him with a wrinkly face. "What are you doing here? And why so early?"

"I work a lot this week," he said with a smile. "I thought that if I came out this way this early that you might still be in bed, so I brought you a treat." From behind his back he pulled out a large coffee from the coffee shop on Main Street in Nisswa and a waxy to-go bag that looked like Morning Glory's. I prayed that it contained a caramel roll.

Ahhh, now how could I be crabby? "It's a caramel mocha with espresso, and two caramel rolls. I know you like caramel. Oh, and Tannya says hi."

"Great, she's going to be gossiping about this. You were here late last night and now you're back in the early morning with treats. This looks bad," I told him.

"Not as bad as the picture your boyfriend got from his ex, who was stalking you last night," he joked.

I shook my head. "I don't want to think about that. Why are you here anyway?"

"I was wondering if you knew anything about the ship, er, boat, ah, floaty thing on the lake," he said with an eye roll.

"What?"

"Yup, it looks like there are more lunatics in the area than we thought."

He has no idea.

"Really?" I stepped aside and motioned him to come in. Then we went to the patio door and I pulled back the blinds. Holy crap! He was right! There was another . . . boat . . . out there. I set my coffee and rolls on the table behind me and grabbed my binoculars. This new one was an inflatable raft, large and octagon-shaped with three men in it dressed as pirates, and they looked to be Captain Morgan, Flying Dutchman, and Long John. They had rigged two flags on the raft. One was a skull and crossbones, the other said *"Ocean's Lie"* in big letters. *"Ocean's Lie"* was also painted on the side of the raft.

What are those morons doing? Do they think they are going to be a threat to the ship?

"Wow," I said out loud.

"Yup," Rex said. "So you don't know anything about this?"

I shook my head. "I'm sure it has to do with the LARP, just grown boys playing around."

"There's talk at the station about LARPing and some criminals out of Chicago being involved," Rex told me. He stared at me hard. "Know anything about that?"

"If I told you, I'd have to kill you," I said with a wink. Rex didn't smile back. "No, I don't know any criminals."

"I'll be around. If you hear anything, call me," he said seriously.

"Mmkay," I said and followed him to the door. "Thanks for the coffee and rolls. I love them!"

"You're welcome," he smiled slightly and winked. After he shut the door I called Tannya on her cell.

She answered quickly. "If you come here to Morning Glory, I'll tell you more of what I've learned. They've got me on the clock until 2:00 this afternoon, and then captain's supposed to call and let me know where to meet them. I think we're heading out on the ship."

I laughed out loud. Ship? She was in for a surprise! "I'll be there in an hour," I told her.

I sat in front of the TV and ate my breakfast. I washed some Tylenol down with what was left of my coffee. Now that my foot wasn't elevated it was throbbing again. It hurt, and so did my head. I was wishing Miss Kitty was here with some more magic pills. They sure did make me a bit crazy, but I had energy and no pain. I could use both right now.

After I showered, I dressed in jeans, a long-sleeved t-shirt, and a zippered sweatshirt. I put socks on, but it was a slow, painful process. I did minimal hair and make-up because I didn't want to stand in front of the mirror.

When I was finished with that I went to the entry and started the process of putting my size eight shoe on my size ten foot. I let Pepper out to do his thing and then left for Morning Glory.

When I got there it was 8:00 a.m. The regulars were there, and Tannya was running around to the tables with a coffee pot. "Hey, girl!" She said with a big grin and wave, which always made everyone look. I hobbled to the closest booth and sat down.

"Girl, we need to get you some crutches," she said with a laugh. "No doubt!"

She brought coffee over and a set of flavored creamers. "Miss Kitty called me this morning. She is very excited. She told me she has a surprise for us. She's going to meet us here at 9:00, if everything's on time."

"If what's on time?" I asked.

"I don't know. She was quick on the phone, maybe she's waiting on a dog sitter. Who knows with her?"

Bing! "Order up!" Marv yelled from the kitchen. "Hey, Sara! How are you today?" he asked me.

"I'm fine, Marv," I yelled back.

"Yes, you are!" he said through the window, then disappeared from sight.

I looked at Tannya, and she rolled her eyes. "I don't know what's up with him right now. He's been weird and . . . almost chipper all morning."

I read the paper in my booth until the crowd thinned out. Then I limped up to the bar area and sat on a stool. This way I was close to Tannya's work area.

Bing! Tannya looked at the window. "Marv, what are you doing? I don't have any orders out right now."

"Just wanted to tell you that you're doing a splendid job today, Tannya," he told her.

"Marv!" she snapped. "Are you trying to get in my head?"

"Just making a Pop-Tart in your head kitchen," he said with a smile. He looked at me and winked. He disappeared from sight again.

"Marv, you're up to something!" Tannya yelled at the window with her brows pressed together. "Did you get laid last night or what?"

I looked around the room to verify we were the only ones in there, and we were.

"Boy, you are sportin' four shades of ugly. *No one* is coming near that!" Tannya said.

"Tannya, Tannya, love, calm down," he said reappearing at the window. "I was out with the guys last night playing cards. There's no woman trying to take your place."

"My place! I ain't in no place. There ain't a place in my life that YOU'D fit into either, so you just enjoy your boys and your card games, it's the only excitement you're gonna see in this town."

"Ya know," Marv started, "bridge is a lot like sex. If you don't have a good partner, you'd better have a good hand."

Pfft! I almost shot my coffee across the room. Tannya shook her head and handed me some napkins. "Don't encourage him," she warned me. I swallowed back my laughter.

The bells on the door rang, and we turned. Miss Kitty. She was all dolled up again—shiny black leggings with a long, red, cashmere sweater belted at the waist. She wore a silver-colored scarf and silver earrings that would sink her straight to the bottom of the lake. On her feet were high-heeled, over-the-knee boots. Her hair and make-up were fully done up, and she smelled great. She was carrying a large bag on her shoulder, but it wasn't her usual dog bag.

"Hello, darlings!" she sang as she came in.

"No Smoochy Poo?" Tannya asked.

"No, she was up really early with me, and she was just too tired. I left her at home to nap."

"You look like you've been up for a while too," I told her.

"I was. I had to be ready for the surprise I have for us!" she said with a huge grin.

"What's the surprise?" I asked.

"You'll see soon enough," she declared. "But first, Tannya, tell us what you know," Miss Kitty said and sat down on the stool next to mine.

"First off, I know you're listening, MARV! Get back to work!" she said without looking at the window. A towel flew through the window and landed on the counter behind her.

"Last night after I left Sara's place, I was driving through town on my way home and looked in the lot of the little motel that the guys from *Ocean's Lie* said they were staying at. Their truck wasn't parked there, which I thought was strange since they said they were headed back to plan their attack. Anyways, I noticed that their truck *was* parked in front of Ye Old Pickle Factory, downtown, so I waited until they left at midnight and went in to talk to Bert."

"Oh, this is getting good!" Miss Kitty said.

Tannya looked at me. "Bert is an old high school friend. We dated for a while."

"Okay."

"I asked Bert if he'd heard them talking. He bought me a drink and said he didn't catch all of it, but it seemed like the big guy, who we know is Captain Morgan, was telling the other two about a plan to steal some gold back. He said the other two guys seemed shocked by the story, like whatever this guy was saying was really intense.

When Bert asked them if they needed another round, they'd quickly shoo him away and keep talking."

"Did you tell Bert about the LARP?" I asked.

"No, I told him it was my stepbrother's friends causing trouble and just thought I'd check it out. Total lie, I don't even have a stepbrother, but he didn't seem to mind sharing what he'd heard."

"What else?" Miss Kitty demanded.

"He said he was cleaning the glasses behind the bar and heard something about a jewelry store in Chicago. He wasn't really sure, and it was noisy by the glass sanitizer. He said it sounded like a guy had stolen some gold and this pirate was getting it back."

"Oh!" Miss Kitty gasped. "What a clever storyline for the LARP! Geez, these guys go all out. They really get into this."

"Yeah, they do." I agreed.

"I don't think it's a storyline," Tannya said. "I think this may be true."

15

"What do you mean you think it may be true?" Miss Kitty asked. I was thinking that too. This seemed too big for a role-playing game, but a clever way to go about it.

I remembered Derek talking about working a shift in Saint Paul for an event called the Zombie Pub Crawl. He said it was a bar crawl event where everyone dressed up like zombies. People were covered in fake blood and limping, stomping and moaning from bar to bar. Some carried fake weapons as part of their costume. The event was huge. There were over 20,000 people up and down both sides of the streets for miles, stopping off at every bar for drinks and for the live music at some of the bars.

He said the concern was that if someone was hurt or killed they would have no way of catching anyone. Every single person looked like a victim and every single person looked like a criminal. Trying to put out a description on a person at that event would do no good. That's if anyone ever noticed a victim. At the end of the night there were dozens of passed out, blood-covered people lying on the streets looking dead. It was *for real* dangerous and scary. If you were going to stab someone that would have been the place to do it.

Maybe the same was true of a LARP.

"What if the story is personal? What if Captain Morgan really is trying to steal from Wayde?" Tannya said and looked at us both.

"Steal what? The spray-painted-gold junk? That's stupid. It's fake!" Miss Kitty said. I wasn't so sure. Tannya shot me a look. I stayed out of the conversation for the moment.

"*Ocean's Lie* just wants to be on top! And I say we take them down from the inside! Tannya, do you know where their treasure is and when they'll have it unlocked so we can steal it?" Miss Kitty asked.

"No. They said they'd call me later when they needed extra hands on deck. I told them I had to work until 2:00 p.m. and they said it would be after that."

"Ah, FYI, there was a large raft on the lake this morning. Rex came by and asked if I knew anything about it," I informed them.

"What? A raft?" Tannya said and put her hands on her hips.

"Yup."

"Raft? What good is that going to do? How big is it?" Miss Kitty asked.

"It's a large octagon-shaped one, would hold maybe six people. It looked pretty crowded already with the three of them in it."

"They were in it?"

"Yup, they were all screwing around with the pole and the flags—two flags. One was the typical skull and crossbones, the other said '*Ocean's Lie*.' The side of the raft was painted '*Ocean's Lie*,' too."

"What a joke! I signed up for a *raft*? I got a peek inside the trailer and saw scuba gear, so I thought for sure there was at least a boat. What kind of lazy pirates are these guys? At least they could have a small boat! What kind of 'extra hands on deck' is needed for a raft? There is no deck! Sheesh! Now I'm really glad I signed up for two LARPs and I'm captain of the other one. At least we have a boat!"

"We do?" I asked.

"Yes, Sara Narra, the pontoon. Duh," Tannya said.

"My pontoon?"

"Let's refer to it as our mini ship. Her name is *Ella Vashow*. Remember?"

Oh, boy. Now who was taking this seriously?

My phone buzzed, a message from Derek. *Morning. Are you in a better mood?*

I replied, *Yes, the pills made me a bit cranky.*

Derek answered, *I'll be up after my shift, if there's room on your couch for me. It looked pretty crowded last night, but we can talk about that when I get there. I get off at 7:00.*

I replied, *K.*

"I think we should go get *Ella Vashow* ready for launch!" Miss Kitty said excitedly.

"I'm going to go check in at Lost and Found and make sure everything's good there. Then I'm going home to make cherry pies. My mom sent six gallon-sized bags of cherries home with me months ago. I stuck them in the freezer, and I haven't had time to make pies yet, but today, I plan to! We can meet at my house later," I said.

"I'll help you with the pies!" Miss Kitty said eagerly. This was not what I had in mind, but the look on her face made me feel bad for her. She had no one else at home to keep her company. Plus I could probably teach her a thing or two in the kitchen. She was such a diva I doubted she'd ever picked up a measuring cup in her life.

"Oh, okay. I have to make a stop at the grocery store too," I told her.

"No, problem. I'll just follow you," she said and stood up.

"You two have fun, and save me some. I'll let you know where I'm going and if I hear from the guys later," Tannya said and gave us a finger wave.

Miss Kitty followed me over to Lost and Found. I checked in with Ginger, checked the mail pile in the office, then did payroll quick.

Forty minutes later, Miss Kitty had done some shopping in my store and upped my sales marginally! I was done with work for the week. I loved my job. It was nice to just swing in and be done for the week in forty minutes, not forty hours.

We got into our vehicles and drove to the grocery store. I grabbed a cart and got all the ingredients I needed for the pies, starting with the ready-made pie crusts. I got two pastry shells and one graham cracker crust for the cherry cheesecake. I loaded up on snacks and other stuff too. Derek was coming, and I was always seemed to be out of food when he came.

We arrived back at my house and carried the groceries in. Miss Kitty was actually helpful. She had come down off her pedestal a bit since the divorce. Her demeanor had changed, and she was for the most part turning into a pleasant woman. When I'd first met her, she was very demanding and self-focused. Over the last few months she'd lost her valley-girl tone, some of it at least, and now asked people for things instead of expecting them. She still had a maid come three times a week to do the cleaning and the laundry, but I understood that because her house was huge. She made her own meals or ate out, but what she made was usually a salad or a sandwich. She spent a lot of her time in the gym and at the salon. And her dog was very spoiled. She appeared to be a full-time job for her, as well. I was very surprised that Smoochy Poo wasn't on her shoulder today.

We put the groceries away, except for the pie stuff, and then went to the patio door and opened the blinds. They had never been used as much as they had this week. Every time I was done looking or leaving the house, I closed them. I felt that if *I* had binoculars, then the ship and raft probably did too. And I didn't need anyone else invading my privacy. Between Long John and Jodi, I'd had enough!

The ship was still there, but the raft wasn't near it. I looked around and noticed it pulled up on land about 100 yards to the right of my dock. What the heck? That was my property. What the hell did they think they were doing? Now I was pissed.

"Let's go out there and take a look," Miss Kitty said with a big smile.

My evil twin nodded for me, and I followed her out the door. Everything in me told me to stay inside . . . so I went out. My evil twin smiled, which showed up on my face. It was kind of fun being the bad girl. I mean, who was I kidding in the grand scheme of things? I wasn't hurting anyone and it felt good. Well unless you counted the shoe stealing and ankle twisting. That was probably karma.

We threw on our spring jackets and made our way outside. I was focused on the raft beyond my dock as we walked, hoping pirates wouldn't come out of the woods and approach it. The tree line around the lake went right down to the water, so just a few feet from shore they could be hiding in the underbrush. We were just passing by my dock, when at the very last second, I noticed something on my pontoon. I stopped dead in my tracks. *What the fuck is that?*

"MISS KITTY! WHAT DID YOU DO?" I yelled.

16

There on the side of my pontoon, in huge letters that stretched the width of the panels, was the name '*Ella Vashow*,' in bright pink. I looked closer and noticed it was on the front, too.

"Surprise!" Miss Kitty said and threw her hands above her head. "Isn't it great? It's on all four sides. I ordered it last night, had it expedited and overnighted. I came out this morning and put it on quick. That's why I was late getting to the diner."

My mouth was hanging open. I wanted to kill her. She'd ruined my boat! I didn't want pink lettering all over my nice neutral-colored pontoon. And that name . . . "Uhuuhg!" was all I could manage. I was so mad. I looked at her, and she was standing there all smiley and proud, clapping and bouncing. My evil twin already had her in a mental head lock and down on the ground, rubbing her face in the dirt. I was debating the outcome of this one.

"You ruined my boat!" She was so going to pay for this!

Her eyes turned sad. She saw I was mad and shook her head and put her hands up in defense. "No, Sara, it's not permanent. They're magnetic! You can take them off!"

"Phew!" I blew a sigh of relief.

"Sorry, I should have mentioned that right away! I'd never ruin your boat. I know how much you love it!" she said with a caring smile.

"Oh, good! You had me scared for a second there!"

"No worries! If you want it off, I can take it off. I just thought it would be fun for the LARP today."

I thought about that. It *was* pretty cute. It would be fun! And, hey, it came right off, so why not. "Okay, well, thanks. We can leave it on for the LARP, but then it has to come off."

"Deal! I have one other surprise, but you'll have to wait a little bit for that one," she said, pulling her cell out of her pocket and checking the time. I was a little worried again.

"Just as long as it doesn't do permanent damage to my baby," I said.

"No, no, just another fun toy for the LARP," she assured me.

We continued on past the dock to the raft. It was bigger up close than it looked in the water from my window. It had a huge open space in the middle, no seats or anything. The flag pole wasn't very tall and looked to be made out of PVC pipe and duct tape. "Wow, Tannya is going to fit in here with three grown men? How's that going to work?" Miss Kitty asked.

I just shook my head. "I have no clue. I'm just glad we all didn't sign up for that one!" We giggled. There was nothing left inside of the raft except the flags lying in the bottom. The pole was still up, though. The flags looked homemade and were designed to slide over the pole.

We started back to the house. The weather was great, sunny, no wind and sixty degrees. The high was supposed to be sixty-three and it looked like there wouldn't be any problem reaching it. It was unseasonably warm, and I liked it. The trees were budding and the air was clean. I took a deep breath of the fresh air and relaxed as we walked. Just as we were stepping into the house, I heard a loud rumble. I turned around and noticed a truck backing down my driveway. This was an eighteen-wheeler backing down my long curvy driveway.

"What the hell is that?" I said out loud.

"Ahh!" Miss Kitty screeched. She was bouncing up and down again and clapping. "It's here! It's your other surprise!"

"In a giant truck? What is it?" Now I was really worried.

The truck continued backing up. It got up next to our cars, kept backing up and completely passed the driveway. "Ah! Where is it going?" I asked out loud.

"Stop!" I yelled and walked off the step and went towards it. It was backing up to the lake! "Stop!" I yelled again. I was chasing the front bumper of the truck as it kept going back towards the lake.

"It's okay!" Miss Kitty yelled. "I told them to!"

"What? Why? It's wrecking my yard!"

Finally the truck stopped and turned off. The driver climbed down and came over to us with a clip board in his hand. "Hello, ladies!" he said with a hand shake. "I'm Clive, from Nelson Trucking. I got a delivery here for Eleanore Kittsoff. Clive was in his late fifties—tall and stocky and had on jeans, and a flannel checkered shirt. He looked just like what you'd think a truck driver would look like, vented John Deer hat and all.

"That's me!" Miss Kitty said and shook his hand. "This is my friend, Sara."

We shook hands. My face was a combination of anger and confusion.

"Well, I have very specific delivery instructions. And let me tell you, there was a bit of a fight at the loading docks on who got to make this delivery. I won. Boy, this is a first. I have made a lot of strange deliveries but never one like this," he told us with a laugh. "What are you ladies up to?" he asked.

"Oh, nothing, just a bunch of girls and their toys!" Miss Kitty teased.

"Well, I see the pontoon and I'll do my best," he said with a hat tip. "In the meanwhile, you can sign and date this." He handed Miss Kitty the clip board and turned to the back of the truck. And for the first time he noticed the ship. "HOLY MOTHER . . ." he said, stunned. He was staring at the ship with his mouth hanging open. Seeing people's reactions to a pirate ship on a little lake never got old. "What the hell is that?"

"That's not ours," Miss Kitty said.

He looked at her and then to me. I just smiled and shrugged. Then he lifted his hat, adjusted it back on and went back to the truck.

When he was out of sight I turned my attention back to Miss Kitty. "What did you do? And what does my pontoon have to do with it?" I asked seriously.

"You'll see," Miss Kitty said. She followed me as I went to the back of the truck.

Clive had the door rolled up and two ramps laid out. He disappeared inside. We moved further around to see inside. He was hauling himself up onto a fork lift. He started it up, pulled it forward and lifted a large wooden crate.

"Where's he going with that?" I asked apprehensively.

"Wait for it . . ." Miss Kitty said with a smile, trying to contain her excitement.

Clive backed off the truck slowly, staying in line with the ramps, and then turned a bit at the bottom. Miss Kitty set the clipboard on the ground at my feet and ran to the dock and opened the door on the pontoon. He shifted into drive and moved forward. He drove up on my dock and I swear I thought the thing would break. I covered my mouth, waiting for the dock to snap, tip, or sink. Clive drove surprisingly fast. The dock was a nice wide, newer, strong dock, but still! The wheels barely fit on it. One false move and a wheel would go over the side and all of it into the lake. I held my breath and watched.

Clive drove to the end, where it widened. My pontoon was parked just perfectly. It was centered so the side door was lined up with the dock. If it wasn't, this never would have worked. He moved up to the pontoon and lowered the arms of the forklift. The beams barely fit through the door. Holy cow! I could not believe that worked. He set it down and had to tip it on the side a bit to get the legs out from under it. They were finally free and the crate slammed down flat. He then backed up perfectly and drove the forklift back up into the trailer.

I looked down at my feet and grabbed the clipboard. I scanned it as I listened for the fork lift to turn off. It didn't. It backed out again and hauled another, smaller, wooden crate out to the wide part of the dock and set it down. Once again it drove back into the trailer, but this time it shut off.

I scanned the clipboard. In bold at the top of the paper was a box labeled, "Special Delivery Instructions." Inside that box was typed and highlighted: *Deliver cannon lake side, and set onto pontoon. Uncrate. Deliver cannonballs to end of dock, leave in crate but open.*

My mouth hung slack. Miss Kitty was just approaching me as I looked up. "Surprise!" she yelled and again threw her arms in the air.

I was speechless. "A cannon! You bought a cannon?" I yelled. "That's so AWESOME!" I ran up and high-fived her, hugged her and then we did a quick little happy dance.

I was pretty sure my evil twin was running the show at this point, but I didn't care. I had a cannon! "Ahhh! I can't believe we have a cannon! This is so cool! Now we can play pirates!"

"And our boat is bigger than *Ocean's Lie*. They are no match for us girls!" Miss Kitty said.

"No doubt! This is so exciting!" I told her with a huge smile. "WE HAVE A CANNON! I can't wait to fire it!" According to what Rex had found the other night, it was apparently perfectly legal to fire one. The only law is noise restriction, which the Nisswa police didn't seem to care too much about. We had plenty of land and water to use it. This was fantastic! "Where did you find it?" I asked Miss Kitty.

"Online."

"Ebay?" I winked.

"No, I just did an internet search and a few places came up. I called the closest one and had it overnighted. The cannon wasn't very expensive at all, it was the delivery—that was super high."

"I bet!"

"I had asked for it to be placed on the boat and uncrated. I didn't think that the three of us could get it on there ourselves, and I didn't know what it would take to uncrate it."

"It takes one of these here!" Clive said as he strolled past us. In his hand was a crowbar. Miss Kitty and I followed him to the dock and watched.

"I also wasn't sure of how much weight your boat could hold. The guy on the phone said it should be fine, just to make sure the tops of the floats were completely above water." Miss Kitty, Clive and I all looked to the left at the front ones and then to the right at the back ones in unison.

"Looks good!" Clive said with a nod. He seemed as excited as we were to get it unwrapped.

"Eeeek! It's like Christmas Day!" Miss Kitty exclaimed and clapped.

"I know! This is so cool! And you got cannonballs too?"

"Yup I bought six of them. I hope that's enough."

"Well, it should be! What are we going to shoot six cannonballs at?" I said.

"That's what I . . . er, everyone at the shop was wondering, too," Clive said. "We all wanted to come and see this Eleanor who ordered a cannon, cannonballs and requested delivery to a pontoon deck. Would someone please fill me in?"

"We would, but the then we'd have to kill you," I told him with a serious face. He stared at me for a beat. Then I gave him a "forget about it" hand wave. "Just kidding!"

He raised his eyebrows and went to work on the crate. We watched eagerly. He finally got it open and removed all the packaging from it. It was smaller than I thought it would be. There was a lot of packing material and thick wood surrounding it.

It fit fine on the pontoon. It was on wheels, which was nice because it was blocking the front door right now. There was still room on the boat for people, too.

Clive took a phone out of his pocket. "Do you mind?" he asked holding it up for a picture.

"No, go ahead," Miss Kitty said.

"The guys are never going to believe this." Then he turned and took a picture of the ship, and one more of my pontoon with its new magnetic name. "What are you rednecks up to out here in the middle of nowhere?" he wondered out loud.

He looked again to us and we both did a "palms up." shrug "Some sort of secret society out here?" he mumbled and then hauled the wood and packaging to the trailer. It took four trips, but when he was done he could get to the cannonball crate. He pried that one open and then just set the cover back on top.

"So it's ready to go? We can just put a ball in and fire it?" Miss Kitty asked.

"Here's the instruction packet that came with it," he said and handed her the plastic bag with a white booklet inside."

"Beats me! I've never owned or fired a cannon," Clive admitted. He turned back to the crate and lifted the cover. He moved around the packaging and balls. "I don't see any fuses."

"Oh, shit! We need fuses?" Miss Kitty asked.

"Yes," Clive laughed. "You're gonna need fuses and charge bags. This here is a muzzle-loader cannon." He stepped past me into the pontoon and picked up what looked like a large Q-tip. "This is the ramrod. You need to put a bag of gun powder in, ram it down good with this, and then put in the cannonball." He adjusted his hat again. "Shoot, I wish you two good luck," he said and chortled quietly. He picked up his crowbar and clipboard and returned to his truck. We followed him and watched as he put the ramps back inside and pulled the overhead door down.

"Well, ladies, it's been a pleasure . . . for real. Glad I got to come and see it. You two be careful and try to stay out of trouble." He tipped his hat and climbed back into his truck. The engine roared, and off he went down the driveway, leaving behind long depressions in the grass.

"Shoot! I'll be back," Miss Kitty said as she marched towards the house.

"Where are you going?" I asked.

"Well, to get gun powder and fuses of course!" she snapped.

"Wait! Let me make a call," I told her as we neared the patio door.

"Why, do you know where to get powder and fuses around here?" she asked me.

"I might."

"Really?"

I dug through my purse looking for my phone. "Funny story . . . you see, a few months ago, I was helping my friend Joan clean out her garage. Her husband has a lot of stuff and no organizational skills, and I remember digging through a pile and coming across an unopened package of cannon fuses. I asked her, 'Joan, do you own a cannon?' She started talking about a camera and I said, 'Ah no, like a BOOOM cannon.' Then I threw her the package and she started laughing hysterically. She asked her husband later, and he had no idea where they'd come from. Maybe she still has them," I told Miss Kitty.

I had gone to high school with Joan and we had reconnected when she looked me up last year when I made the paper. She had been living up here for seven years, and we'd done coffee a couple times, and I helped her clean that one time. "She's great. If she's has them still, we're good to go!"

A few minutes later I was off the phone. "She's going to check and call me right back." I waited about ten minutes, and the phone rang again.

"Good news," I said as I put my phone down. "She still has them! She said they are cut-to-fit, and she has the one package with thirty feet of fuse in it. We can have them."

"Great! I'll run to Black Lion Tactical and get powder packets," Miss Kitty said. She grabbed her purse and headed out the door.

I put the pie stuff in the fridge and headed to Joan's house. She only lived a few minutes away. She and her husband lived on a fifty-acre lot that was half-wooded and half-field. He was a mechanic at a shop in town and she stayed at home with their seven kids, ages two months to fourteen years. Just visiting her was great birth control. I was not really sure how she did it. The most amazing part was her energy and the fact that every time I saw her she was all smiles and giggles.

After the short drive, I parked in the driveway, walked up to the house and knocked on the door. I could hear a ruckus inside. The door swung open and a boy about four years old came flying through it with a huge frog in his hands. He shoved it up at my face and made a growling noise. It made me scream. It all happened so fast that I was in shock. I wasn't afraid of frogs. I just wasn't prepared for that. He bolted past me and off the front steps into the yard. A small dog followed a few steps behind him, barking, and then came Joan, jogging after him with a newborn on her breast, nursing.

"You bring that in here again, and I'll make it into soup and feed it to you!" she yelled after him. Then she looked over at me. "Oh, hi, ha ha ha ha!" she laughed and winked at me, "I probably wouldn't make him eat it. Come on in!" she said and waved at me to follow her.

17

That was Joan, fun, loud and always full of energy. I followed her through the living room, dodging toys and small pets along the way, and into the kitchen. "Here they are," she said and handed me the package. "We never did figure out how those got in our garage, but now I'm trying to imagine what you would need them for." She squinted at me.

"Well, for the cannon, of course!" I said with a "duh" shrug.

"Ah, yes, the cannon." She just stared at me.

"MOMMY!" a tiny voice screamed. It was a shriek that gave me goosebumps. It sounded like some little girl was getting stabbed to death. I looked at Joan with fear in my eyes. "MOMMY!"

She moved slowly and rolled her eyes. "Here," she said and detached the infant girl from her breast and handed her to me. She yanked her shirt down and walked into the next room.

And there I was holding a baby. A little tiny beautiful creature that for a second made me want one. But then I heard a noise and looked up at the little dog in the living room. It had been busy chewing on something in the corner when we came in. It was a gray fluffball that stood maybe a foot and a half tall and was about ten pounds. He was bent over funny, coughing and gagging.

"Just as I thought. She needed her Dora movie started over again," Joan said calmly. I pointed to the dog.

HAK! AUF! HORK! The dog was really fighting to get something out. Joan leaned one arm on the counter and calmly watched. "Should we help him?" I asked, concerned.

"No, the little turd probably ate something he shouldn't have again. He does this. He'll get it out . . . and I'll have to clean it up," she said with another eye roll. "Serves you right! Maybe stick to the dog food for once!" she scolded. "This is the part where we make bets on what it is and who it belongs to."

I kept watching. The dog was still horking. His stomach was pumping hard! "We're getting close now. I'm going with Victoria's sock."

HAR HAR HAAAAACK! Out it came, a pile of . . . not sure. The little dog ran off, and Joan went in for a closer look. "Shoot! It's not a sock, it's a diaper. I lose!"

I had to turn away. I was starting to gag, too. "Honey," Joan warned. "If *you* throw up, you're cleaning up your own mess. I don't do messes after the age of thirteen."

I did my best to hold it in. I waited with my back turned until she got it done. I saw a bottle of air freshener on the counter, and I grabbed it and sprayed. The smell was worse than the sight.

After she washed her hands she peeked at the baby. "You may want to tip her up, if she hasn't burped yet."

"Oh, okay," I said and reached under her arms. She was two months old, so she was still very soft and wiggly. I tipped her head up and pulled her close to my face for a closer look. "She is so pretty!" I said. "Oh! She opened her eyes! Hiiii!" I squeaked at her. "Oh, are you going to smile for me?" I asked.

"Nope," Joan started, "that's not her smiley—"

At that very moment, that precious, tiny, beautiful baby, that couldn't have weighed more than ten pounds, spit up. Not just spit up, PROJECTILE vomited at least twelve ounces of breast milk onto my face. Most of which shot into my mouth!

I was frozen with fear! OH, MY GOD! I didn't know what to do, I had it in my eye, my mouth, down my shirt . . . I spit out what was in my mouth, and reached out to pass the baby to Joan. She quickly set her on a blanket on the living room floor and rushed back to me.

"Oh, my God! Let me help! I'm so sorry!" She pulled me to the sink and said, "Here, swish and spit!" She turned the water on and grabbed a cup from the closest cupboard. I leaned forward and started washing my mouth out. Meanwhile, she reached behind me, grabbed my shirt and in one swift move un-tucked it, and pulled it up and over my head. It took like a second!

"Drop your arms by your sides!" she demanded.

Still leaned over the sink, swishing a mouth full of water I dropped my arms. She yanked the shirt completely off, rolled it up and threw it in the other sink bowl.

"Here's a rag, and there's baby wash by the sink. I'll be right back with a shirt for you."

After about fifty swish-and-spits and a wipe-down, I was feeling a little better. I looked down at myself. I still had some milk puddled in the middle of my breasts, caught in the underwire. I turned away from the sink towards the light and reached the rag in there to wipe it out.

"BOOBIES! AHHH! I SEE BOOBIES!" I heard a little boy yell. There, in the corner of the kitchen, stood another little boy. This one was about six years old, and he was staring at me with a huge grin.

I quickly covered myself with the rag, which didn't cover much at all. "Shoo!" I said and waved my hand at him.

"Boobies, boobies, I see your boobies!" He sang in a teasing tone. And then he started dancing, smiling and pointing.

Joan came back into the room and shot him a stern look. "Charlie! Go outside and play!"

He turned to the door and sang the song all the way out. "Sorry," Joan said with a giggle. "That one's still working on manners. And he's obsessed with boobies, which is funny because out of all my kids, he's the only who wouldn't nurse." She shook her head and shrugged.

"Here," she said and tossed me a t-shirt. "You can keep that. It's my husband's, but he won't wear it. I looked through my closet, but they're all maternity clothes."

I held it up. It said "TEAMSTER" in big blue letters across the front. "Thanks," I said and quickly threw it over my head. "Sorry about exposing your son."

"Oh, please! Don't worry about it. It's a phase, and anyway, he's used to seeing me nurse all the time." She went to the sink and rinsed out my shirt. She offered to machine wash and dry it, but I told her I had to get back.

After she put it in a plastic grocery bag, I grabbed it and the fuses and started towards the door. I stopped by the baby, tickled her tummy and thanked her for the gift.

Just as I was slipping my shoes back on, the door burst open and in came both boys. "I wanna see her boobies too!" the four-year-old demanded. Joan lunged at them, but they took off out the door again.

She winced a smile at me. "Sorry," she said with a giggle.

I laughed. "We'll get together soon, and I'll tell you all about the cannon," I said with a wink.

"Okay," she said, holding the door open for me. "Or, you know, I get the newspaper, so I can just watch for you in there," she teased.

"Good grief, I hope not!" I said and waved goodbye. "Thanks for the fuses!" I walked to my car, opened the door and threw my stuff on the passenger's seat. To my left I could see the two boys hiding behind the swing set. They were smiling. I waved as I drove by and they ducked back more. *She sure has her hands full*, I thought as I drove slowly down the winding driveway. I felt something nudge my foot and looked down. HUGE FROG!

I pulled my feet up and swerved a little. Eww! I looked down at it. It was hopping all around trying to find a way out. I was going to have to put my foot down and hit the brake to stop the car. Ahhh! I really didn't want to but I was running out of driveway. Another fifty feet and I'd be at the county road.

Finally it hopped to the left. I swiftly put one foot down, slammed the Jeep to a stop, threw it in park, whipped open my door and jumped out, all in under two seconds!

Outside the Jeep, I did a little icky dance to shake off the cooties. There was laughing coming from the swing set area. "I see you, and I know what you did!" I yelled. The boys turned around, mooned me and then took off running to the trees. I was speechless. I reached down and grabbed the frog out and set it in the grass. Then I did one more icky dance and climbed back up in the Jeep and drove home.

Back home I quickly got the stuff out to make cherry pies. I started with washing all the cherries and pitting them. I really should have done that before I froze them because now they were all mushy and soft. It was much easier to do when they were fresh and firm.

After about thirty minutes of that, I got bored. My plan was to do two pies and a cheesecake all at once and get it done, but now it seemed like more work than I planned. I really just wanted to curl up on the couch a watch a movie. I got a can of diet Mountain Dew out of the fridge and cranked the radio up. I sauntered back to the kitchen.

I was making the sauce for the pies when my phone rang. It was Kat, a friend from the Cities. I hadn't talked to her in forever.

"Hi!" I answered.

"Hello, stranger. How are you?" Kat asked.

"I'm good," I said. "Busy, but good. Sorry I haven't been in touch lately."

"It's okay, all is good here. Same stuff, different day. I've been on a few dates with West, though!"

"Faith's vet? Really? How's that going?" I asked. I was excited for her. She hasn't had much luck in the dating field the last few years. A few months ago she came with to a vet appointment for Faith and met Doctor West Riggers.

"It's going good! Really good, actually that's the reason I'm calling. We're going to be passing through Nisswa on the way to his cabin about a half-hour from your place on Saturday afternoon. I was thinking we should get together."

"Yes, for sure! That's so cool that he has a cabin nearby. Why don't you guys come here for lunch on your way through?"

"Are you sure? We don't want to impose, but he'd love to see your place, and see Pepper and Faith again."

"Derek will be here too, it'll be fun. Let me know when you're on your way so I know what time to expect you. I'll plan for a meal," I told her. We talked a while longer. I didn't tell her about the strange stuff I was involved in, but I did fill her in on my head and ankle. I just told her I stepped wrong and twisted it. When she came on Saturday maybe I'd tell her. I didn't want her to think I was any more crazy than I already looked. By the time I disconnected with her I was ready to put the pies in the oven. I set the timer and decided to wait on the cheesecake. I was ready to be done.

After I cleaned up the kitchen, I went and took a quick shower. I swear I could still smell baby puke. Then I threw my jeans back on and went to my closet and got an old t-shirt and sweatshirt of my own. I picked a black one. *I must be planning for easy hiding later.* I was pretty sure I'd just heard my evil twin giggle.

On my way back to kitchen, I heard a car door. Pepper got up from his spot by the fireplace and proceeded slowly to the door. I opened it to Miss Kitty. Pepper sniffed her and went back to his bed by the fireplace. He was the laziest dog I'd ever known.

"Welcome back!" I said, stepping aside.

"I got 'em!" she said, holding up a bag. We opened up the package and looked at them. "I think we should go try it out right now," Miss Kitty said with a smile.

"Mmkay!" I said and slipped my shoes on. I went to the bathroom, just in case it got super exciting, and then waited for Miss Kitty to go. It was after two thirty already. The day was flying by. It was nice and sunny out still, slightly chilly but nice for May first.

I carried the fuses, and Miss Kitty grabbed the gun powder packets. "How do you know if we got the right ones?" I asked her.

"The guy at the store helped me. He was a little stunned when I told him I needed it for a cannon."

"I bet."

"He looked me up and down twice, stopping at my high heels and breasts for a few seconds. I didn't know what size cannon I bought, so I used my arms to show him, and he laughed at me. Then he had to talk with two other guys at the store. They thought these should be big enough. He wanted to know what I was shooting at and how far. I said it was really just for show and for fun, and that we'd be shooting into a yard."

"What did he say?"

"He asked how big the yard was. I told him we'd be starting from on a ship a ways out on water and the yard was huge and far from town. He said that cannons can fire at 1,000 feet per second."

"Really?"

"I guess. But ours is small, so I don't think we'll get more than a few feet."

"Yeah, you're probably right," I agreed. "I remember the one they used in the *Sweet Home Alabama* movie. That one was way bigger than ours and that didn't fire very far."

"Right! I remember that."

We went out to the pontoon and looked at the directions that came with the cannon. Miss Kitty opened the bag and handed them to me. I read them out loud.

1. Cover the air vent to choke the barrel and suffocate any sparks that may remain from previous firings. Failure to do this may result in the cannon firing when it is not safe for it to do so.
2. Insert a damp sponge rod into the barrel of the cannon to clear out any hot debris that may remain in the barrel from previous firings. This may seem like a waste of time, particularly in a real war situation, but it is another necessary safety measure.
3. Ready a charge by removing the charge from its bag and placing it down the barrel of the cannon.
4. Ram the charge down to the base of the cannon's barrel using a ramrod.
5. Insert a cannonball into the cannon.
6. Remove cover from the air vent and carefully insert a priming wire (fuse). Be certain to insert the fuse deep enough to make

contact with the charge, but not so deep that you cannot light it.
7. Aim the cannon, taking into account distance, trajectory, and wind speed.
8. Light the fuse, and run away.

"Well, that seems easy enough!" Miss Kitty said. I nodded in agreement.

"I forgot to grab a lighter and a scissors for the fuse. I'll be right back," I told her.

When I opened the door to the house, I heard my phone ringing. It was Tannya so I answered. "Hi!"

"Hey, girl. Well, I can't seem to find the guys anywhere. They said they'd call me by two thirty. It's way past that," she told me with a whiny voice.

"Well, their raft is still out here, and they're not, so they can't be too far."

"Still, they should've called by now."

"Well, why don't you come out here? Miss Kitty bought us a new toy. We're going to break it in right now. If you hurry we'll wait for you."

"Oh, boy! Really? Okay, I'll be right over. I have everything I could possibly need for the day in my car already. I'm on my way!" I could hear the smile in her voice now. Personally, I thought the guys were using her for information and treasure and didn't need her anymore, but I didn't want to tell her that and break her heart.

I stuck the phone in my pocket, found a lighter and scissors and limped back out to the pontoon. Miss Kitty was sitting in the driver's seat with the radio on, bobbing her head to the music. She looked like she was having fun.

"Ready?" she asked me and stood up.

"We have to wait for Tannya," I told her. "She's on her way. The guys never called her."

"Oh, was she mad?"

"It seemed like it, but I told her you'd bought us a new toy and we'd wait to break it in. I didn't tell her what it was, though."

"Oh, she'll be so excited!" Miss Kitty said. "I have one other surprise that should be coming soon, too," she said as she looked at her smart phone."

"What is it?" I asked. Miss Kitty had lots of money so I couldn't imagine what she had up her sleeve now.

"You'll see. It should be here in the next half-hour." She smiled at me and looked excited. I was excited too, with this little devil side that had made itself at home in me, I didn't really care what it was. I was in the mood to break some rules and be naughty.

I set the stuff down on the seat and asked her if she wanted to wait inside for Tannya since it would be about twenty minutes before she got here.

She said yes, amd that she was getting thirsty, so we headed in. Dang it, my ankle was really hurting again. I was limping more and more as the hours passed. I guess my Tylenol had worn off. It was throbbing by that time we got back to the house.

"You're limping bad. Is your ankle hurting again?"

"Yes, bad."

"How's the head?"

"That doesn't hurt too much unless I bump it, but my stiches are itchy."

We went inside and Miss Kitty grabbed a glass of water and a "happy pill" from her purse and told me to take it.

"Oh, I don't know. Last time I got pretty crabby when I took one," I told her, holding the pill in my hand.

"Nonsense, these are happy pills! If you were crabby, it was probably from the pain, or being tired. It wasn't from the pills. Just take one this time."

I remembered the pain going away completely last time, and I really liked that. "You're probably right." My evil twin agreed, and I swallowed it. Oh, well, if I was crabby, then too bad. It would wear off eventually.

Miss Kitty had me sit in the living room with my foot up and an ice pack on it while she made hot cider with cinnamon Schnapps. She brought me a mugful and joined me on the couch. We both took a sip and sank back in relaxation.

A few moments later I heard a rumble outside. Miss Kitty got up and walked to the window, along with Pepper. Faith was already on the window sill and looked out, too.

"Yay! It's the Fed Ex truck!" She skipped to the entryway and disappeared through the door.

I waited anxiously on the couch until she finally came back in with a medium-sized box. I could tell by the way she carried it that it wasn't too heavy.

She smiled and said, "We'll wait for Tannya." She set it down by the couch and reached for her cider.

18

"Oh man, I'm too excited to wait!" I said. Then my phone rang. I reached in my pocket and pulled it out.

"Hello?" It was my Aunt Val.

"Hey, chicky, just checking in. How are things over there?"

"Things are good. Why?"

"Oh, ya know, I'm in charge of customer service and such, and Captain's driving me crazy with all his demands. He's starting to annoy me."

"Really? Why, what's he demanding?" I asked her.

"Well, he asked me to call you and see what you were up too. He didn't say why. He just said to get a feel for your plans for the day."

"Why does he care what I'm up too?"

"I don't know." She let out a sigh. "He's been kind of a jerk the last couple days. He's constantly pacing and checking on things he's already checked on and looking all around with his spyglass. He hasn't been off the ship much in the last two days and hasn't slept much, either. And every time I try to talk to him he's rude and snappy."

"Did you try saying 'game off,'" I asked with a giggle.

"Yes," she answered seriously. "He won't go into 'game off' mode. I've been on the ship with him more and more these last two days and he's very adamant about getting the treasure sunk. That's what he's working on right now. Then all of a sudden he was looking at a truck in your yard and told me to call you."

"Oh. Well the truck was just delivering something for my boat. So tell him not to worry about it. Do you think he's scared to lose the LARP battle and that his treasure will be stolen before he sinks it?" I winked at Miss Kitty.

"Probably, and all of a sudden he's super protective of it. Up until yesterday I was helping to package it and tying the weights on, and now he snaps at me if I'm near it without him present. It's like he doesn't trust me all of a sudden. I mean really, I'm on his team! I love this dress up like a pirate and play games stuff! I haven't had this much fun in a while. But it doesn't seem fun for him anymore. He's taking it way too seriously."

"Well, if he bothers you too much, come over to my house. You're welcome here anytime," I told her.

"Thanks, hun. Before I let you go . . . you haven't seen any more of the other pirate guys have you? Apparently there's been some talk in town about ships and pirates. Captain's very unhappy about that. He wants total secrecy about this."

"Well, I doubt he's the only one who knows. Law enforcement has been out there, and Tannya works at the diner. She was with when we bailed you out. I think the secret's out!"

"I get that, but Captain's in a mood and not happy. He also wanted me to ask what was up with the raft you own. Why was it on the lake this morning, and why do you have it? He thinks you might be tied in with another pirate LARP group that's been stalking us."

"The raft belongs to *Ocean's Lie*. It's not mine and I don't know anything about them except that they seem to be trespassing over here a lot."

"So you're not on their team?"

"No, I'm not on their team." I half-lied. Even though Val was my aunt, all was fair in love and war, I told myself. I looked at Miss Kitty and she nodded and put her finger over her lips and smiled.

"All right. Well, keep me posted if anything changes or you notice anything strange."

"Okay, thanks. Have fun!" I told her and disconnected.

"It seems Captain Caesar's upset. He's getting nervous about his treasure," I told Miss Kitty.

"Wouldn't it be fun if we got the treasure from both of them and won?!"

"That'd be awesome!" I said with a smile. "We come from out of nowhere, knowing nothing about a LARP before three days ago, and suddenly we're the highest-valued group! Just a few small-town girls, kicking ass and takin' . . . gold!"

We giggled. Then I heard a car door in the driveway. Pepper and Miss Kitty got up and looked out the window. "She's here!" Miss Kitty said and opened the door.

"Hey, girls!" Tannya said. She looked at me and tipped her head. "Oh, no, your ankle still hurting?"

"Yeah it was, but it's getting better by the second. The throbbing is gone and swelling's down again," I told her peeking under the ice pack. I took the ice pack off and returned it to the freezer.

"So did I miss anything? What's the surprise?" Tannya asked eagerly.

"Well, one is right here," Miss Kitty said kneeling down by the box on the floor. "The other two we'll show you in a minute."

Tannya sat down on the floor by Miss Kitty and watched. I sat back down on the couch. Miss Kitty ripped the tape off the box and opened it up. She reached in and pulled out a black sweatshirt. It was a cute, fitted, front zip one. On the breast pocket area was a white skull and crossbones applique and the words "ELLA VASHOW" embroidered under it in bright pink thread. The bones were glittery.

"AHH!" I screamed. "That is super cute!"

"I love it! Do we all get one?" Tannya asked.

Miss Kitty flipped it around and showed us the other side. In big letters across the back it said CANDEE BARRE. She tossed it in her lap and grabbed another. That one said SARA NARRA. She tossed it to me. The last one was a few sizes bigger and said CAPTAIN TANNYA TYTASS on it. Tannya grabbed it, stood up and put it on over the long sleeve shirt she had on. I pulled off my sweatshirt and pulled mine on, too. It fit perfectly.

"Thank you so much! This is awesome!" Tannya said and gave Miss Kitty a hug.

"Yeah, thanks a lot!" I told her. "You work fast!"

"It wasn't easy to get next day stuff, but if you offer to pay more, they seem to be able to get it done!" she told us and pulled her sweatshirt on. "One more thing," she said, reaching inside the box again.

"Here," she said, passing us each a pink bandana. I looked it over. If I folded it correctly, it had a skull and crossbones on the front. We all went into the bathroom and folded them and tied them around our heads. Except mine was putting pressure on my stitches, so I had to take it right back off. I was super bummed about that, but Miss Kitty took it and tied it around my right bicep. It looked cool so I left it there.

"All right, let's get Tannya a spiked cider, and then we'll show her the other two surprises," Miss Kitty said and headed to the kitchen.

"Woohoo! Spiked cider? Okay!"

"Have you never had one?" Miss Kitty asked, shocked.

"Apple cider, right?" Tannya asked.

"Yes, but spiked with alcohol."

"No, ma'am. I told you before I ain't never had much more than a beer and that martini that one time."

"This will be much better than that!" I assured her.

Miss Kitty mixed her one up and handed it to her. Then she got our mugs from the living room and topped them off.

I was feeling pretty good. Pain was gone, and I wasn't crabby at all. We sat there and talked for a bit. Tannya was pretty pissed that she hadn't heard from *Ocean's Lie* yet.

"I bet you won't hear from them," I said.

"They have our treasure!" Tannya said.

"Oh, yeah! They do!" Miss Kitty remembered. "We'll have to get that back!"

"Oh, it's on!" Tannya said. "No one ignores Captain Tannya Tytass!" she said and threw her drink back. "Oh! Oh! Oh!" She had her head tipped back and cider still in her mouth. She covered her mouth with her hand and finally swallowed. "Bad idea, still hot!" she said panting.

We laughed at her as she ran to the freezer door and hit the ice button. She caught an ice cube and stuck it in her mouth. "Mmmm." She looked relieved. Until a second later when she looked scared. "HMMMM!" she mumbled pointing frantically at her closed lips.

"What?" Miss Kitty said with worry on her face.

"Her lips are frozen to the ice cube now!" I laughed. "Go to the sink and put your lips under the water."

She rushed over and did that and a few seconds later she was free and the ice cube was in the sink.

"Oh, my God!" she screamed. "Owww! I'm not sure what was more painful!" She went to the bathroom. Miss Kitty and I tried to hide our laughter. "I'm not going to be able to eat or drink for a week!" she said, looking upset.

"Well, let's go outside and show you the surprises. That'll make you feel better," I said.

"Oh, they're outside?"

Miss Kitty and I led her through the door and down the front steps. Then Miss Kitty covered her eyes and told her to walk forward. Slowly she did, and when they were in front of the pontoon Miss Kitty stopped her.

"Surprise!" she yelled and uncovered her eyes.

Tannya looked at the letters on the boat and started clapping and screeching. "Oh, wow, that looks great! I love it!" Miss Kitty and I watched her face as she spotted the cannon. "What is *that*?" she said, pointing. "Is it real? Do we get to shoot it?"

"Yes, it's real," I told her.

"Yes, we're going to shoot it right now! We waited for you to get here," Miss Kitty said.

"Oh, wow! This is so sweet," she said, looking at the cannon and the pontoon.

When we got to the end of the dock we each reached down and picked up a ball from the crate on the dock. They were heavy. We set them down on the floor of the boat next to the cannon. Miss Kitty sat down across from Tannya in the front, and I sat in the captain's chair.

"This is crazy," I said. I meant it, but I was also feeling *all in!*

"Crazy *good!*" Tannya said. "We need a plan!" she said and up went her fist again. I gave a huff of laughter.

"I think we should boat out a ways and shoot towards the left side of your driveway. There's plenty of room and even if it goes too far, there's trees to stop it back there.

We sat and looked at the property. "And if it goes too short it will just hit the water," Tannya added.

"Sounds good to me," I said with a nod. I reached in the dry storage compartment and got the key out. After I lowered the motor into the water, I turned the key. She started right up. It was just a four-stroke, forty-horse so it was fairly quiet and pretty slow. "Tannya, can you untie us from the dock?"

After Tannya pushed us off, I put it in gear and turned the boat to open water. We motored out towards the ship. The boat was lower in the water, and I could tell the weight was affecting the motor's strength, but the floats still looked okay. Low, but okay. We didn't want to get too close yet. As we motored around, we decided that as soon as we noticed the *Ocean's Lie* crew, we would do what we could to get their treasure and then take off to the other ship and take theirs too.

"What happens when we have everyone's treasure?" Miss Kitty asked. "Does someone sound a bell or bring you an award or something?"

We both looked to Tannya. "I'm not sure," she admitted. "I think that everyone just kind of heads home and then you go on the computer and change the rankings and list how big your treasure is and you're moved up. They list when the next battle is, and you can join in again if you want."

"Is today listed on the site?" I asked.

Tannya shrugged, so Miss Kitty pulled out her smart phone. "It's four o'clock already," she announced and then searched for the answers. I stopped the boat and put the anchor down. "It's not on the website," Miss Kitty told us.

"Huh, well good. Then we won't have much competition if it's just the three teams, and *Ocean's Lie* is short a player. It's four o'clock, they lost their chance with me." Tannya said and looked mad. "You say you're going to call, then you should call. At least have the decency to text!" She rolled her head around, angry.

"That's good, because for the record, this was *your* idea. *You're* the captain, and we need orders to follow," I told her.

She straightened up in her seat and looked proud. "That's right, I *am* the captain. My first order is that from now on we all are in 'game on' mode, and we have to use pirate voices."

"Aye, aye, Captain!" Miss Kitty said with a grin and a nod. She looked ready for fun. For a second I pictured her as a young child. I wondered if anyone ever played with her . . . if she ever got dirty, or maybe she was just the kid who stayed home and painted her nails. That was probably the case and why she was the way she was. I bet for the first time in her life she had friends, and just really wanted to play. It surprised me how different she seemed now compared to when I first met her. I liked her like this.

"Shiver me timbers! Methinks this here is our spot, mateys. You scallywags ready the cannon," she told us in her pirate voice.

I burst out laughing. She shot a glance in my direction and snapped at me. "Ye best be doing what yer told, or you'll be the first to walk the plank." She said it with a stern pirate voice and very serious eyes. I waited a second for the just-kidding head shake or smile, but it never came. She wasn't playing around. I looked at Miss Kitty, who was smiling and trying to hide it and look busy.

"Sara, did you bring the paper with the directions on it?" she asked me.

"Hey, it's Sara Narra, now!" Tannya snapped again.

"Sorry," Miss Kitty looked surprised.

"SORRY WHAT?"

Miss Kitty looked at me for support and I just shrugged my shoulders. "Ah, sorry . . . Captain! Sorry, CAPTAIN TYTASS!" she said, turning her voice to pirate and saluting her.

"Better!" Tannya said, then looked at me.

"Ah, yes . . . ahem . . . Aye, they're in me pocket," I said in my best accent and handed the paper to Miss Kitty. She read it out loud.

"'One, cover the air vent to choke the barrel and suffocate any sparks from any previous firings. Failure to do this may result in the cannon firing when it's not safe for it to do so.' We don't need to do that."

"Next it says, 'insert a damp sponge rod into the barrel of the cannon to clear out any hot debris that may remain in the barrel from previous firings. This may seem like a waste of time, particularly in a real war situation, but it is another necessary safety measure.'"

"Next!" Tannya said with authority.

"All right . . . next, 'ready a charge by removing the charge from its bag and placing it down the barrel of the cannon.'"

"What say you?" Tannya shot her a confused look. "What's a charge? And what's a bag?"

"That's the gun powder for the cannon, Captain." Miss Kitty opened the package and threw the contents into the cannon, then gave us a look and a shoulder shrug.

"Arrr, looks good to me," I said.

Miss Kitty looked back at the paper. "'Ram the charge down to the base of the cannon's barrel using a ramrod.'" Tannya picked up the ramrod and tapped it in. Then she set the rod back down.

Miss Kitty continued, "Insert a cannonball into the cannon.'"

Tannya reached down and grabbed one of the balls and heaved it up and into the opening. It rolled down and banged at the bottom. We all walked over and looked in to the dark opening.

"Okay?" Tannya said looking at Miss Kitty.

"Umm . . . 'remove cover from the air vent and carefully insert a priming wire (fuse). Be certain to insert the fuse deep enough to make contact with the charge, but not so deep that you can't light it.'"

I looked at the back end of the cannon, seeing a small circle with a cover. I popped the cover off and there was a small opening. I walked over to the seat near the rear of the pontoon and grabbed the scissors and fuse. I cut about a ten-inch section off. I slowly put it in the hole and fed it in until I felt resistance. At that point there was about three inches sticking out. I stepped back and looked up at them.

Tannya was wide-eyed. I couldn't tell if it was fear, or excitement. She looked over at Miss Kitty.

Miss Kitty quickly put her face back in the paper. "'Aim the cannon taking into account distance, trajectory, and wind speed.'" She paused and looked up. "There isn't any wind."

I opened the front door on the pontoon, which barely cleared the cannon's nose. I wasn't sure if we could push it forward, but I suggested we get it to the front. We all pushed and were able to move it forward. I tipped the nose of it up a little. The boat was facing the left side of my driveway. All of our cars were in the driveway, but we were pointed far to the left of them. It should land past the bank of the water but before the trees.

The front of the boat went down a little. So we all moved to the back to even the weight. I looked at Miss Kitty.

"'Light the fuse, and run away,'" she said, reading off the last point of the instructions with a half-smile. With that she folded the paper and sat down.

"Well, tighten your boot straps, wenches. We're going to light her up."

I handed Tannya the lighter. "Go fer it, Captain. Light 'er up!"

She lit the lighter and slowly moved it towards the cannon's fuse. Miss Kitty and I sat in the back on the sundeck. We plugged our ears and held our breaths . . .

"WAIT!" she yelled and pulled the lighter back.

19

"AYE! What is it?" Miss Kitty asked and let out a big breath. I, too, let my air out. My heart was pounding so hard it was shaking my vision.

"Remind me, what do pirates say? Was it 'fire in the hole,' or 'blast off,' or just 'fire'? Or do I count down? I can't remember," she said in her normal voice.

I was just about to answer, when Miss Kitty started pointing at her rapidly and said, "Oh! Oh! She didn't say 'game off'! You have to say game off if you're not going to talk like a pirate!" she tattled.

"UH!" Tannya shot her a dirty look and then turned to me. "FINE, GAME OFF!" she snuffed.

"ARRR!" I said in an effort to break up their quarrel. "I think it's the captain who's commanding the ship that chooses what to say before firing."

"Aye," she said back with raised eyebrows. "Game on!" She leaned over again and lit the lighter. We again held our breaths and plugged our ears.

"FIRE IN THE HOLE!" she yelled and lit the fuse. It sparkled quickly like a firework and made a crackling sound. Tannya bolted away from it and plopped down next to Miss Kitty and plugged her ears too. The fuse burned down and disappeared in the hole. We all shrank down and waited. A second later . . . BOOM!

I opened my eyes and looked. The cannonball had shot WAY farther than I thought. It went past my property, above the tree tops and disappeared. The cannon itself had moved all the way back in the pontoon until it hit the little table by the back row of seats with a hard bang. All of our feet were up on this seat. Thank goodness we sat up on the sundeck and not on the seats. The pole that the table sat on was bent and the table now leaned down.

"BLOODY HELL!" Tannya yelled in shock. "Did you see that?" She asked and started laughing nervously.

"Oh, fuck! That was scary!" I said.

"Shit, we almost lost our feet," Miss Kitty said stunned.

"Arrr, both of you use your pirate voices!" Tannya scolded.

"Wow, we should go see where that went," I said, staring off in the direction the cannonball had flown.

"I'm sure it's in the field across the county road," Miss Kitty said. I hoped she was right. I knew there were no houses over that way, and I didn't hear any tires squeal so hopefully we didn't hit any cars.

The smoke cloud slowly faded as we stood there looking at each other. "That was so cool! We should do it again, but this time let's tip it down a bit so it doesn't go so far," Miss Kitty said.

"Aye," Captain Tytass said and nodded to us.

She stood there and watched as Miss Kitty and I rolled the cannon back up to the door and repositioned it. Then we tipped it down a bit.

"I think we should wait a few minutes before we try again. It's still hot, and don't we have to clean it out, too?" I asked.

"Oh, barnacles, I forgot about that!" Tannya said. "Fine. Crew, sit and rest a bit. We'll fire again in ten minutes."

We sat there talking about how cool it was and how much crazy fun we were having. My phone rang. I pulled it out of my pocket. It was Aunt Val. Shit. I was busted.

"Hello?"

"Soooo, what's new?" she asked in a stretchy voice.

"Nothing . . . what's new with you?" I asked in the same way.

"Seriously, I'm on the ship, and Captain Caesar Wayde is next to me, and we can see one . . . *Ella Vashow* . . . on the water."

I laughed out loud. "Okay, fine! You caught us. We're on our pirate ship, and we're trying out our new cannon, too. We all thought it sounded fun and wanted to join in the game."

"So, you girls are your own group? You're not with *Ocean's Lie?*"

"Yup, we're our own group! I'm Sara Narra, and there's Candee Barre, and Captain Tannya Tytass," I said with a proud grin.

I heard her repeat that quietly to someone on her end. Then I heard a male's voice respond, "Tell 'em to go home! That's an order!" I put the phone on speaker and the girls came closer to listen in.

Val came back on the line. "Um, Captain would prefer if you guys would not be part of this. He has plenty of concern already with the others here and doesn't want you guys to get caught in the middle of it," she said gently.

"Screw him and his orders!" Tannya said in a loud pirate voice. "I'm captain of this ship, and *I* say when we're done. You can tell Captain Caesar Wayde of *Poseidon's Zebra Mussel* that we won't give up without a fight! We're coming for your treasure!"

"Did you catch that?" I asked Val.

"Yes. I have you on speaker. Captain heard it."

"Then this is war!" he yelled into the phone. The line went dead.

I stuck the phone back in my pocket, and we all busted out laughing. "He's so funny! He's way better at this than we are. He's been in costume all week and built his ship by hand. He's *really* in to this."

"That makes him crazy, and us fast and efficient. We pulled this together in a matter of two days!" Miss Kitty bragged.

"She's right," Tannya said and stood on the seat in front of the driver's console. She had her chest out and fist in the air. "We are the unstoppable trio of *Ella Vashow*!" she yelled at the top of her lungs. "No one can stop us now!" Just as she said the last word there was a loud BOOM!

It was *Poseidon's* cannon. BONG! The pontoon shook, and we all ducked down. Something had hit the boat! I looked up and saw that the pole the sun cover was attached to had completely broken lose. It was just dangling there. The sun cover was bent over from its own weight and now sitting on the sundeck.

"WHAT THE FUCK?" I shouted. "Is he firing at *us*? Like for *real*?"

"BLOODY HELL!" Tannya yelled. "Load the cannon, crew! We're firing back!"

"What's going on? I thought this was for fun?" Miss Kitty asked. "SEE, THAT GUY'S CRAZY!"

"Are you kidding me?" I asked. I was pissed. "Look what he did! He broke my fucking boat!" I paced in the two-foot area available to me, which was making me dizzy. Anger and rage were building. Now I was mad! "Reload the cannon!" I said and started the motor.

I yanked up the anchor and slowly turned the boat around. I felt my phone vibrate and quickly pulled it out. It was Val again. I put her on speaker and killed the motor.

"WHAT THE FUCK ARE YOU GUYS DOING?" I screamed into the phone.

"Oh, my God, Sara! Are you guys okay? I had no idea he would fire at you for real. He's lost it. He's crazy! I don't know what's going on. I thought this was for fun. Now I'm scared. I'm below deck and he's telling First Mate Willy to reload. This is not what I thought it was."

"Who's this Willy? Is he going along with him? Is he crazy too?" I asked.

"I don't know. Willy will do anything for Captain. He has no life and is at his beck and call all the time. He's a doofus, very nice looking younger guy, but a total doofus. He's from the area. He spends most of his time here and only goes home to sleep."

"What's his real name?"

"Scooter . . . something . . . it's really stupid-sounding . . . I can't remember."

I looked up. Tannya and Miss Kitty did too. We were all thinking it. "Scooter Potter?" Tannya said into the speaker.

"Yes! That's it!"

Tannya pressed her eyebrows together and lowered her voice. "RELOAD!"

"Oh, God!" Miss Kitty said and covered her mouth.

"Why?" Val asked.

"Oh, shit!" I said as I watched Tannya throw a powder packet in and ram it down, and then a ball. She cut a fuse and stuck that in too. She looked at the ship and tipped the nose of the cannon down so it was almost a straight shot.

"Tannya's gonna fire! TAKE COVER!" I yelled into the phone. Miss Kitty and I moved to the far end of the boat and ducked. Tannya lit the fuse and ran over by us.

"Shit, Tannya! My aunt is on that ship!"

"BOOM!" I watched as the cannonball flew at the ship.

"Hello?" I said into the phone. "HELLO? AUNT VAL?" The line was still open.

"I'm okay!" she said. I could hear voices and a commotion in the background. I waited and shot Tannya a look.

"Are you crazy?" I yelled at her.

"Scooter's on the ship, too! It's going down!" she said with a fist pump. "RELOAD!"

I looked at Miss Kitty. She was standing there in shock, but looked slightly amused.

"We are not reloading!" I said firmly.

"Sara! We've been hit!" Val said through the speaker. "The cannonball brushed the port side, there's a small hole. We're taking on water. It's a small hole and it's not much water but I can hear them talking about fixing right now. This will buy me time. Come and get me! I want off this ship. Quickly, while they're distracted."

"Are you sure? I thought you liked Wayde?"

"I did, until earlier this week when he went crazy! He's not the same guy. Hello, he just tried to kill you!" she reminded me.

We'd just tried to kill them, too, but I was not about to point that out. "Okay, I'm on my way."

I started the engine and drove full throttle towards the *Poseidon*. We were moving, but very slowly because of the weight in the boat, and the cannon placement didn't help. "Girls, go move the cannon back to the middle of the boat."

"That's Captain Tytass!" Tannya said.

"Yeah, and Candee Barre!" Miss Kitty reminded me.

I shot them a stern look. I was still pissed and not about to put up with their game or crap. We neared the ship, and Tannya gave me the finger over the lips signal. I slowed the motor and could see Aunt Val on deck. She waved at us and looked over her shoulder. Then she pointed down to a rope ladder that she'd thrown over the side. I motored quietly over to it. Tannya got up to grab the ladder and hold the boat steady, or so I thought. Actually, she grabbed onto the ladder and started climbing up the rope.

"What the hell are you doing? I whispered loudly.

"She was four rungs up already and hauling ass up the rope. She turned back and said, "I'm the captain, and we're boarding this ship. It's a mutiny! We're taking the aunt and the treasure!" She climbed higher. "This boat is taking on water. Get on here and get a look around before it sinks. When's the next time you get to see a pirate ship? Come on you scallywags, let's go!"

"She's right!" Miss Kitty said with a bunch of nods. "We're never going to get this chance again! I'm going!" She grabbed the rope and looked up at Tannya, who was on deck. Tannya gave her a hurried wave and looked behind her.

"Hurry!" she said quietly.

I killed the motor and went to grab the rope. "Fine! FINE! I guess I'll just stay with the ship then, CAPTAIN!" I yelled quietly up at her. Damn it! I wanted to go too, but someone had to hold the pontoon.

I looked up and saw Miss Kitty just getting to the top and then Aunt Val said, "We'll be right back." They disappeared from my sight. I sat there rocking on the pontoon for what seemed like hours, but was probably only five minutes or so. Finally I heard Miss Kitty.

"Hey!" she whispered loudly. "Catch!" She dropped down a medium-size package. I caught it. It was maybe five to ten pounds in weight and the size of a large backpack. It was wrapped in thick, black plastic and had a ton of tape around it. "Here!" she yelled again. And tossed another, and then another. Pretty soon the pontoon was full of plastic packages, each slightly different in shape and size and weight. All three were throwing them at me.

"Okay! That's enough! We're running out of room! Let's get out of here!"

Miss Kitty came down first. "That was so exhilarating!" she told me with a huge grin. I stuck my jealous tongue out at her.

"I bet it was. Hold the ladder!" I said and went to start the motor. Aunt Val came down next. "Thanks, Sara! I owe you another one!" she said and gave me a hug.

"You sure do!" I said with a smile. She sat in the back next to the broken table and looked around. "It's a fixer-upper," I said with a wink. "Is this all of the treasure?"

"No, there's more. This is the stuff he just loaded today that he's been so protective of. These packages are a bit smaller, and he hadn't weighted these yet. I figured they'd be the easiest to steal. Everything else is in crates and weighted."

Tannya was just starting down the ladder. We looked up when we heard voices and yelling. Tannya went up one rung and looked over the edge. "OH, SHIT! THEY'RE COMING!" she started moving faster down the ladder. I was scared for her. She was not the most graceful lady.

"Hurry!" I yelled up to her.

"Tannya?" A man's voice yelled. Two male pirates where leaning over and looking down at us. "Hey!"

"Do you know her?" asked the older one, who I assumed was Captain Caesar.

"Yes! She's my wife!"

"EX-WIFE, you jackass! You ruined our marriage two years ago!"

"What the hell are you doing?" Scooter, the first mate Willy, asked.

"It's a mutiny, dumb ass. I've got your wench and your treasure!" She laughed as she stepped onto the pontoon. "AND I shot your ship!"

"Thieves!" Wayde yelled. "Get 'em!" I was already motoring away. When I got turned around I opened it up, and we putted slowly back towards the house.

"Do they have any guns?" Miss Kitty asked.

"I don't think so," Val said. "But I guess I can't know for sure."

Tannya got up and started loading the cannon again. "This is our last one. We need to go back for more balls." I thought so too. Better safe than sorry.

The sun was moving behind the trees. It was a little after five. Tannya's newest orders were to go to the dock, get more cannonballs loaded up, and grab some drinks. As soon as I stopped at the dock, Miss Kitty ran in and got the cider, the Schnapps and our mugs, plus one more for Val. Val held the pontoon while Tannya and I loaded three more cannonballs on.

"That's all?" Val said looking in the empty box.

Miss Kitty was just climbing aboard, arms full. "I figured six was enough." She shrugged and then set the stuff on the seats. She got busy mixing drinks, and then we all toasted.

"If I may," Captain Tytass started. "I've always said, if your ship doesn't come in, you got to swim out to that bitch and steal your treasure, but this, my wenches, was beyond the fun that my civilian mind could have ever imagined." She shook her head and paused. "To us women! May the past pirates, that are no longer with us, look down on us with pride! I will forever remember this day with you, my closest friends!" She lifted her mug and we followed suit.

"Cheers!" We all said and clanked mugs. Then we decided to shift the treasure to the back of the ponton. Miss Kitty and Val moved it, while Tannya and I tried to tear down the rest of the awning. After we completely destroyed it we threw it up on the dock. That's when I noticed the three men in my yard just coming through the trees by the raft.

"*Ocean's Lie!*" I said quietly. Miss Kitty and Val stopped dead in their tracks, both holding packages. "Get down!" I whispered.

We all squatted on the floor of the pontoon and watched them. They were carrying boxes into their raft. They were all in full pirate uniform. "That's my treasure!" Tannya said. "Those assholes used me! They never even called!"

The three men all set their boxes in the raft and then disappeared in to the trees again.

"Quick, get the boxes!" Tannya said and took off running down the dock. We all stood there in shock. She turned around and whispered, "That's an order!"

"I'll stay with the boat," I said when the other two looked at me. They quickly followed Tannya, who stepped into the raft and handed them each a box and then took the last one. They ran back to us and put the boxes in the back of the pontoon. I pulled the bent pole and table out of their hole and set it quietly on dock next to the awning. We heard voices again.

"Start the motor, they're coming!" Aunt Val said nervously.

"Let's get out of here!" Miss Kitty said from the floor. She was ducking down to hide. I started the motor and bolted out of there. Except that with the now even heavier weight, we were going about twelve miles per hour.

We looked back at *Ocean's Lie*. The pirates were just coming through the trees, each carrying another box. They stopped short and were talking and looking around. They knew they were robbed! We were about 100 yards from them. I pulled the throttle back into neutral and idled there.

"That's right, boys!" Tannya yelled at them. "Captain Tannya Tytass got you! Can you say mutiny?" Then she turned to us with a grin and told us, "I love that word."

"We noticed," I said, not pointing out that it was the wrong word.

"THIEVES!" Captain Morgan yelled. "They've stolen our treasure."

"It's *my* treasure! You used me. Well, guess what, I used *you*! Now I'm captain of *this* boat! We *have* a boat, too. You don't even have a boat! We have *all* the treasure! We're the winners!" she yelled. She stood up on the seat. "YES! We win! We are the winners!" She was so loud and proud. I had never seen her so excited. I knew she got excited easily, but this was over the top, even for her. I was happy for her . . . well happy for us. But I was still pissed about the awning.

Tannya reached down and grabbed her mug and again toasted. "To us, winning! It's the all-girl power hour! We are the WINNERS!

We are one *Ella Vashow*! WOO HOO!" she screamed at the top of her lungs. It echoed around the lake. The rest of us laughed at her enthusiasm. We were watching her and didn't notice that meanwhile *Ocean's Lie* had pushed their raft out on to the water and had started paddling towards us.

"What are they going to do? Chase us down with paddles?" Miss Kitty laughed.

A phone rang. We all looked at each other. It was Aunt Val's. "It's Wayde," she said, looking at the screen.

"Answer it," Tannya said. She looked tough, like she wasn't afraid of anything. I slammed my drink and Miss Kitty and Tannya did the same.

"Hello," she answered and turned the speaker on.

"Val," he said in a nice, normal voice. "Look, I don't know what you're doing, but you need to bring that treasure back now! I *need* it. This isn't about the game, okay? It's very important to me, and I don't want you to get wrapped up in this mess." Val looked at us, confused.

"What mess?" Val started, but Tannya grabbed the phone away from her and yelled into it. "I'm the captain of this ship and Val is my prisoner. If you have a problem, you take it up with me!" Then she hit the off button and handed it back to Val with a firm nod.

We looked over at *Ocean's Lie*. They were about half a football field from shore and headed back towards land. "Wonder what they're up to," Miss Kitty said. "They gave up pretty easily for coming all this way and dressing up that much. Seems like a waste to just walk away now."

"Giving up, boys?" Tannya yelled. "That's right, back to the real world for you! Your game is over!"

"Arrr!" Flying Dutchman yelled. "Ye be mighty brave, but we got treasure left."

"What's that, a few more boxes of gold garage sale junk?" Tannya mumbled.

"Hey, some of that stuff wasn't junk!" Miss Kitty said. I stuck my leg out and kicked her.

When *Ocean's Lie* got back up on land, all three men disappeared into the woods again.

"Let's fire the cannon again!" I jumped. I'd scared myself with my own voice. Well, not my voice, but my dark side's voice. I loved the heart pounding excitement of the cannon. Miss Kitty got up and cut a fuse and stuck it in the hole.

"I get to light it this time!" I yelled. I turned the boat towards my land again. I figured that was the safest bet again since there was nothing but trees and highway over there. This time I aimed it down a little bit. Maybe it wouldn't sail over the tree tops if the projection was straight on. Hopefully it would just hit some trees and drop. "Can we reuse cannonballs?" I asked. Tannya, Miss Kitty and Aunt Val all shrugged.

"I don't see why not," Tannya said.

"All right. Is everyone ready?" I asked taking the lighter and moving towards the fuse. The three of them piled up onto the sundeck and pulled their feet up. Their fingers were in their ears, and they were shrunk up, ready for the blast. "Three . . . two . . . one!" I said and lit the fuse. When it started sparkling I leapt up onto the sundeck too.

BOOM!

We all opened our eyes and watched as the cannonball disappeared through the trees. You could hear twigs and branches snapping and falling. "That was so cool!" I said. I felt a sense of empowerment. Launching cannonballs was a great adrenaline rush. I was feeling tough, and unstoppable . . . and crazy. I also noticed my pain was completely gone. I was still pissed about my boat, but I did get Wayde back so I guessed I should get over that.

"This is really fun!" Miss Kitty said with a girlish grin.

"You guys are dangerous," Aunt Val said blatantly. "This game is getting out of hand."

"No, it's not! I love this! It's exciting and real," I protested.

"It's illegal!" Val said.

"What? No, it's not," I assured her. "I checked. The boats are licensed and the cannons are fine too, except the noise, which Rex doesn't seem to care about unless the neighbors do. It's perfectly legal to fire a cannon in Minnesota. You don't need a license or anything!"

"Only if it's a blank load," Val argued.

"It is!" Tannya told her. "These aren't the ones that blow up, they just land."

Miss Kitty and I nodded in agreement. Val put one hand on her forehead and the other on her hip.

"The cannonballs don't have to blow up. Just them hitting things is what does the damage. If you load a ball in to the cannon it's not a blank load. What we're doing is illegal."

Our humor turned to confused and worried looks. No one said anything for a few seconds as we all looked back and forth at each other. Finally Tannya broke the silence. "Check it!" she said with a bossy pirate voice at Miss Kitty.

Miss Kitty wrinkled her brows.

"On your smart phone!" Tannya snapped. "Check it, and see if it's legal or not, Candee Barre."

Miss Kitty reached in her pocket and took out her phone. While she did that we mixed more drinks. The cider was cooling down some but it was still good. We looked over at *Ocean's Lie*. We watched as the first two men pushed the raft half onto shore again.

I looked over my shoulder at the pirate ship. It was still floating so I guess they must have fixed it. When the girls saw me looking in that direction, they looked too.

"It's not sinking yet," Val said. She sounded bummed out.

"What do you suppose they're up to?" Tannya asked, looking over at the raft.

"Who knows. They're idiots," Miss Kitty said. "You're wasting your time in that dinky raft, boys!" she yelled over to them.

Long John looked up. He was headed back into the woods again. "Oh, yeah," he yelled back. "Just wait for a second. We've got something of yours that you're gonna to want back." He laughed and then disappeared from sight into the trees.

20

"What could they possibly have that we would want from them?" Miss Kitty asked.

"Probably just the rest of the treasure. I brought four boxes and we only stole three back," Tannya said.

"They can keep it. One box won't change the fact that we won," I added. "So, Aunt Val," I asked, still half watching the woods, waiting for Long John's return. "What happens now? Do we have some sort of awards party, or meet somewhere after and shake hands, or what? How is it declared over and that we won?"

"I don't know for sure. I think you just go onto the internet site and update that you are the winner."

"That's what we thought," I said.

We all sipped on our cider some more.

"She's right!" Miss Kitty said looking up from her phone. "It's a load, if it's loaded. Just putting the ball in makes it illegal."

"Oh, shit!" I said, surprised. "I didn't know that!"

"Oh, well. It's not like we're hurting anyone. And Wayde hasn't been arrested yet, so I don't think it matters too much to anyone." Tannya paused then looked at me. "Right?"

"Right," I said. I didn't care. I liked the evil, naughty feeling. I felt like going back to high school and slapping a few bitches that I'd been wanting to slap for many years. It felt good to be carefree. "We are criminals! We're breaking the law!"

"Yeah we are!" Miss Kitty said. "If we get into trouble, Sara Narra can get us out of it anyway."

"Yeah, she has a special way with Officer McHottie," Tannya said.

"Pffft! I do not."

"The photos on your phone would say otherwise," Tannya sassed.

"Please don't remind me. I will deal with that later!" I said.

"What? What pictures?" Miss Kitty elbowed Tannya. "Tell us."

"Yeah, we're a team. We all need to be in the loop," Val said.

I rolled my eyes at her. "You don't even have a sweatshirt, or a bandana."

"That's no problem! I can get one here for you by tomorrow," Miss Kitty said and looked at her phone again.

Tannya started telling them the story, while I kept an eye on the ship and the raft area. I finished my drink and set it down. Miss Kitty and Val were pretty pissed about Jodi too.

"Fucking bitch! She'd better stay off your property or we'll take her down," Miss Kitty said still looking at her phone.

Val nodded and added, "She better find her own life and stay out of yours or she'll have us to deal with!"

I smiled. This was why she was my favorite aunt.

"Done! I'm having it delivered tomorrow," Miss Kitty said proudly to Aunt Val.

"Really? That's great! Thank you so much!" Val slung an arm around her.

"No probs. I kept your name, 'Gun Powder Gertie,' for the back." Miss Kitty told her.

We all giggled. "That's fine!" Val told her.

I looked over to the ship and noticed the old wooden rowboat moving away from it. "Now what are they up to?" I said.

After they all looked. Val said, "That's Willy. I wonder where is he going?"

"You mean Scooter?" Tannya said. "Let's fire a ball at that boat."

"No! We'd sink it in a second, if we could actually hit it, which isn't very likely," Val said.

"It's worth a try," I said moving the cannon towards the door from where it had landed again after the last shot.

"True! We should at least try," Miss Kitty added.

"Really? You're all in agreement on this? You all think it's a good idea?" Val asked.

"That man ruined my life, and has stolen from me for months," Tannya said putting another gun powder bag in and ramming it down.

"Oh, what I wouldn't give to have one shot of *my* ex sitting in a boat, like a duck on the water," Miss Kitty said.

I looked at Val with raised eyebrows. "Oh, a boat full of scorned woman. I get it," she said.

While Tannya shoved the ball in, Miss Kitty cut a fuse and shoved it in to the hole. "Would you like to do the honors?" Miss Kitty asked holding the lighter up.

"My pleasure!" Tannya answered as I started the boat and turned it in the direction of the row boat. Tannya pointed the nose of the cannon down a little.

"You'd better hurry!" I said. "He's almost to the dock."

"Fire in the hole!" she yelled and we all jumped up on the sun deck and plugged our ears.

BOOM!

CRASH! The cannonball missed the boat by just a few feet and hit the dock. The dock exploded into a million pieces. Wood flew high into the air and in all directions. It was destroyed. All that was left were tiny pieces of wood the size of toothpicks.

"HOLY SHIT!" Miss Kitty laughed. "That was awesome!"

"Oh, fuck! I wasn't expecting that!" I said and shared in a bunch of high fives. We were hooting and yelling, and cheering. It was loud and exciting.

"Bloody hell!" Tannya said. She looked pissed. She wasn't high-fiving anyone. "We fucking missed! What are you people celebrating? RELOAD!" she demanded.

"What? We don't want to hurt him," I said. "Look at him, he's scared. That's all we really wanted to do. It worked."

"The fuck it did! I wanted to sink him! RELOAD!"

"We only have one ball left," Miss Kitty said.

Tannya thought about that for a moment. "I suppose we should save that."

"Probably best," I said. "Besides, look at him." Everyone looked in his direction.

He was out of the boat, just pulling it up on shore. He was yelling something and shaking his fist. We giggled as we watched him throw a temper tantrum. He was kicking the dirt and picking up pieces of the dock and throwing them in our direction all the while screaming at us. It was pretty amusing. He was way beyond pissed. We couldn't make out what he was saying but it didn't sound nice.

When he walked towards the house we turned our attention away from him. Val's cell phone rang. She looked up at us. "Wayde."

"Answer it," Tannya told her.

"Hello," she said reluctantly. She turned on the speaker and we all gather around.

"Game off!" Wayde said in a not so friendly voice.

"Okaaaaay."

"What the hell are you doing, Val?"

"Well, I was helping you win a game until you started acting like a jerk and not playing by the rules. You're firing at my niece's pontoon. It's personal now. What the hell is your problem?"

"He's just mad because we got some of his treasure," Tannya said into the phone from over her shoulder. "We got the most! We won!"

"You need to stop this and return the treasure. I'm not kidding around, Val. This is bigger than you know. I don't want to see you get involved in this."

"Involved in what? You think I'm not already involved? I've been with you for over two months. I helped build that ship. I dressed up like a goddamned pirate wench for days on end to make you happy. I'd say I'm pretty involved."

"Fine. I'll let you win, but will you trade some of the small treasure that you took for some of the larger crates? Then you'll for sure have more. You can have the win. I don't care."

"What? Why?"

"BULL SHIT! This treasure is ours. NO TRADE. If it wasn't better than what you have, you wouldn't want it back. No way!" Tannya told him. "You want your treasure back, you come and get it!"

"Game on, wench. Don't say I didn't warn you. If you get wrapped up in this and get hurt, it's not on me. I tried to reason with you. I've got bigger fish."

"Yeah, like who? Willy? He's a dick-head loser!" Tannya said.

"Take me off speaker," Wayde said.

"Anything you got to say you can say in front of my girls," Val said and winked at us.

"I got nothing more to say, except you're going to pay for that dock."

"Screw you! You're going to pay for my awning!" I yelled.

"Fuck you, lady! I got a hole in my ship!"

"GAME ON!" Miss Kitty yelled from beside me, and then Val ended the call.

After we all sat back down on the boat, we started discussing the conversation and wondering what was in the treasure. "Why don't we just unwrap it and look?" Miss Kitty said.

We all looked at one another and smiled. "Let's do it!" Tannya said.

As she went to the pile and grabbed a package, I looked past her to the woods. I could see people moving in the trees. "They're back," I said.

We watched as Captain Morgan appeared and threw what looked like a rope into the raft. Next through the woods came Long John. He looked in our direction, then turned back towards the woods. He was waiting for something. A few seconds later Flying Dutchman appeared. He was with someone else. When they were clear of the trees I could see what Long John and Captain Morgan were looking at.

Flying Dutchman was shoving a person towards the raft. The person had a t-shirt over his or her head, hands tied in back.

"Oh, my god!" I covered my mouth. "Who is that?"

"What are they doing?" Val asked nervously.

"I don't know," Tannya said slowly.

We were all chatting amongst ourselves, trying to figure out what was going on. The person was tall and thin, had on jeans and a sweatshirt. We had no idea what *Ocean's Lie* was doing or why.

"This is scaring me," Val admitted.

"Nah, I bet this is part of the game, they're playing hard ball, pulling out the big guns," Tannya said with a grin.

"Hey, ladies! We got something for ya!" Long John yelled.

"Don't yell back," Val said. "I don't like this. This doesn't feel right."

I was concerned too. The person they were pushing didn't seem to be participating, seemed to be struggling to walk while blindfolded, and Flying Dutchman was shoving hard.

They shoved the person into the boat and pushed it off shore. Then they started paddling over to us. We talked about it and decided to let them get close enough to talk.

When they were close enough I sat in the driver's seat and had my hand on the key. I wanted to be ready to make a getaway should they try anything funny.

"Let's just see what they want," Tannya said. It was a bit weird because they were lower than us in the raft, and they had to sit.

They got close enough for my liking. We could see their faces and hear them fine. I nodded to Tannya.

"Arrr! That's close enough, losers," Tannya said to them. "Ye jackasses didn't call me, so I did what any pirate would do. I got me own ship. Ye know what they say," she said in her tough pirate voice, "if you can't join 'em, beat 'em! Arr haaar harr har!" she laughed.

"What are you doing?" Miss Kitty asked the men, serious.

"We have a trade. It's my understanding that you've got some of the *Poseidon's* treasure. We want to trade your treasure for your friend," Captain Morgan said.

"What friend?" Val asked.

"This one!" Flying Dutchman said and pulled off the t-shirt.

All of us gasped, except Val.

Jodi.

"Fuuuck," Miss Kitty said in a quiet airy breath.

"What the hell?" I said in shock. What was she even doing here? My blood pressure picked up, and I was red hot. I could hear my heartbeat in my ears. Here came the anger. She was gagged with a bandana so she couldn't say anything.

Jodi looked around. Her face was priceless. It was total fear. I watched as she discovered she was in a raft, with three men dressed like pirates, and there, across the water, were her three worst nightmares. I couldn't imagine what was going through her mind. She had nowhere to run, and no one to help, and no one here cared about her. Her eyes showed total helplessness.

I was basking in it. I locked eyes with her. And slowly squinted my eyes. "Keep her! Do what you will with her. We don't want her!" I never broke eye contact with her.

"What?" Long John said surprised.

"Throw her ass overboard. She's no friend of ours," Tannya told him.

"No, no, we should make her walk the plank!" Miss Kitty said with a grin.

"Agreed! Make her walk the plank!" I said still glaring at her. "Make sure her phone is in her pocket and sinks with her, too."

Jodi raised her eyebrows, looking worried. It was awesome to see. Val leaned over my shoulder from behind and quietly asked, "Do we know her?"

"Yup, Jodi, Derek's ex, Jodi Vagina," I said with a tight-lipped smile.

"Oh, I see," Val said. "Sorry, boys, no deal." Val whispered to me, "Is that her real name?"

"Vagerna, but whatever," I whispered back.

"Mmmm," Jodi mumbled through the gag and shook her head. Then she tipped her head to the side. Her eyes said, "Help me."

I laughed a long, evil laugh. The pirates in the boat didn't look very excited to hear that response. "We can't sink her," Long John said.

"What are you doing here anyway, Jodi? Were you invited, or were you trespassing on my property again? Maybe peeping in my window, taking more pictures for your extortion? Did I miss anything?" I asked.

"That's a nice rap sheet, plus I'm sure there's a law against being a bitch, too," Tannya said. "You see, honey, in the Cities we just walk away and slap down some green for the clean-up, but out here, in *my* town, we handle things a little differently. Isn't that right, Sara?"

"Sure is. You're trespassing! I think it's legal for me to shoot you."

"I think you're right," Miss Kitty said and came and stood tall next to me and Tannya.

Captain Morgan and the boys were standing there with their mouths open. I guess it wasn't going as well as they'd planned.

We all stopped when we heard a phone ringing. It was mine. I looked at the screen. "Derek," I said and stared at Jodi. She tipped her head again.

"Hello?" I said in a sweet voice.

"Hey! Well, you sound chipper. Are you staying out of trouble?" he asked.

"Umm, well . . . funny story. I'll tell you all about it when you get here."

"Okay . . ."

"What time are you coming?" I asked.

"I got off early, not much happening here today. I guess the bad guys are taking it easy today."

"Ha, I bet!"

"I'm just leaving my apartment now. I'll be on the road in a few minutes."

"Okay, see ya in a bit."

I disconnected. "Jodi, that was your boyfriend on the phone. He's on his way! You must be so relieved," I said snidely.

She looked down and shook her head. She was defeated. I loved it.

"Well, now what, Captain?" Long John asked as he looked at Jodi sympathetically. *What's up with that? I think he feels sorry for her.*

"Hell, I don't know," Captain Morgan said. "You fools told me she was their friend."

"Well, she was just walking down the driveway, and is about their age, and is a girl, so I just assumed—" Long John said.

"You assumed wrong," I cut him off. "Keep her."

The pirates all looked at each other and discussed it. "We can't just let her go. She'll report us to the police."

Jodi shook her head and made some grunting noises.

"I can't be sure, because she's crazy and delusional, but I do know she's wanted in this county on trespassing charges already, so she probably won't report you," I said.

"Don't count on it. The bitch can't be trusted. We know that first-hand. She's blackmailing Sara as we speak," Tannya told them.

"So now what?" Flying Dutchman asked.

"So give us the treasure and we won't kill her!" Captain Morgan said.

I wrinkled my eyebrows at him. His own crew looked shocked by his words and Jodi looked at me with concern. I didn't like her and wished she drop off the face of the Earth but I didn't want to *see* her get hurt.

"No, go ahead and kill her. We don't like her." I heard myself say. "Now, is there anything else we can help you with?"

Everyone looked at me. "Okay then, we'll chat with you later," I said and started the motor and turned around and sat in my seat.

"Permission to come aboard," I heard Captain Morgan say. His tone was different. It made the hair on my neck stand up. I heard a gasp from Miss Kitty. I didn't turn around but I looked at Tannya's face and knew.

"Come about!" Flying Dutchman said sternly. That's when I turned around. Captain had a gun. It was an old fashioned, long barrel pistol.

"What the fuck, Morgan? This is a game. Guns are not allowed!" Val said.

"Neither are cannonballs!" he shot back. He was pointing the pistol in our direction.

He had us there. "This *was* a game. It's not anymore!" he growled. While he was talking, the other two were rowing closer. When they got up next to us, he stood up and opened the door on the pontoon and stepped aboard.

"Permission *not* granted." Damn my evil side! It's like I had no control over my voice. Part of me was *not* afraid of that gun. The other part was trying to reason. This was not the first time someone had pointed a gun at me, so I wasn't as upset as Miss Kitty, Tannya, and Val looked.

"Put the gun down," Tannya said, "Or I drop it."

We all shot our heads in her direction. She was standing back by the treasure and had two black plastic wrapped packages in her hands. She was holding them over the water. I grinned at her. "Well played, Captain Tytass," I said and nodded.

"DON'T!" I heard Morgan say. Then I felt him grab my hair. He pulled me back against him and pointed the gun at me. Shit. I was mentally kicking myself for never taking the self-defense classes that Community Ed always offered. I knew there was a really swift way to get out of this but I couldn't remember how it went.

Oddly though, I wasn't afraid of him, just pissed that he was in control. "Get on the boat, Dutchman," he ordered.

"Okay, now wait a minute. This boat can't hold the weight of all of us and the cannon and the treasure," I said calmly. "So just start tossing it, Tannya."

"NO! DON'T" He pulled my hair harder and took the safety off the gun. "Dutchman, we're taking the boat! Get them into the raft and our stuff on here! Long John, hold the boat."

Dutchman boarded and shoved Aunt Val towards the raft. She climbed in and sat down. Then he grabbed Miss Kitty by the arm.

"Get your paws off me," she said and shrugged free of his grip.

"Go!" He yelled at her meanly.

"I'm going!" she said. Then she gathered up the mugs, cider, and Schnapps and climbed into the raft. Tannya was still standing there with the packages. Morgan shoved me towards the raft. I got in. Dang it, I was pissed! But he *did* have a gun. I mentally told my evil twin that was trying to tell me to shove him overboard to calm down. Dutchman went over to Tannya and yanked her arm. She looked pissed, too. She dropped the one package that was still in her hand on the floor of the pontoon and stomped to the raft.

"I ain't getting in with Vagina in there. She's yours. You take her with *you!*" she said to Morgan, standing at the door.

"Get in!" Dutchman said and shoved her.

"No, get her out first!"

"We don't want her either!" Morgan said.

I looked over and stuck my tongue out at Jodi. She was sitting on the other side of Miss Kitty. Miss Kitty saw me and did it too. Jodi rolled her eyes. Val was on her other side.

"NOW!" Morgan yelled.

"You're pissing me off. You ain't going to get away with this," Tannya mumbled and moved towards the edge of the boat. She sat on the edge of the pontoon and then, when she should have moved to sit, she tried to stand and slipped. She plopped hard into the raft. She fell into the middle and landed on her belly with her head on Jodi's leg.

"Ugh," now I got Vagina cooties on my face!" she said and rubbed her cheek as she sat up. We all laughed, and Jodi rolled her eyes again. I stuck my tongue out at her again. Gosh that felt good. I hadn't stuck my tongue out in years, and there was some real satisfaction in it. I understood why kids did it now. It was the three-year-old's equivalent of flipping someone the bird.

And there we sat . . . five girls in a raft. Three had matching sweatshirts. One was dressed as a pirate and one tied up and gagged. I was sitting back with my feet stretched out in the middle. I noticed they'd left the oars. Miss Kitty was to my left, then Jodi, then Val, then Tannya.

The *Ocean's Lie* crew was now on *Ella Vashow*. We all looked in that direction as they started the motor and turned towards the ship.

"Sayonara!" Long John yelled and waved.

"That's my name," I mumbled. I noticed he locked eyes with Jodi and his face changed to kind of a sad look.

I looked at Tannya. She was all situated in her spot now. "What now, Captain Tytass?" I asked in a pirate voice.

"I need a drink!" Miss Kitty said and started filling up the mugs. There was only enough for half a glass for everyone, so she went a bit heavier on the Schnapps this time.

Tannya had her arms across her chest. "Humph. Assholes," she said and then she grinned. I looked in her eyes trying to figure out what she was thinking.

"At least I got this," she said and pulled out a black plastic wrapped package from her shirt.

"Whoa! Nice!" I said.

Jodi started mumbling and shaking her head. "Should I take the bandana off?" Val asked, reaching toward Jodi.

"NO!" The three of us shouted in unison.

"It stays on. She never has anything good to say anyway, do ya?" I asked her with a smirk. She growled back at me. I crawled over to her and put my head next to hers. "What's that? I'm sorry, I can't understand you! You got something in your mouth." I was in her face teasing her. She was getting pissed, which made me happy. "You just sit there and look pretty. Your boyfriend's coming soon. I'm sure he can't wait to see you again." She glared at me and then snapped her head forward and head-butted me right on the corner of my eye socket.

"OWW! You stupid bitch!" I tried to slap her face but I only got part of the side of her head because Miss Kitty and Val dove on me. I was fighting to get at her. I just wanted one good punch, but Miss

Kitty and Val both held me down until I agreed not to touch her. I finally relaxed and sat up.

"You gotta lotta nerve!" Tannya said to her, "We could throw your ass overboard. I bet it'd be weeks before anyone would even miss you!"

"Watch your back!" I told her with a finger point. Then I took what was left of my cold cider, which I thought I was going to slam, but I threw it in Jodi's face instead. I was as surprised as everyone else. They all looked at me. I shrugged.

"Not sure what happened there," I told them with a confused look.

"All right, we need to get out of this raft before someone gets killed," Val said. "Let's start paddling back to the dock."

"Oh, hell no!" Tannya said. "This ain't over."

"No, it's not," I agreed. "I want my boat back, and I'm returning Jodi. She's not getting back on my property." I touched my eye. I could already feel it swelling up.

"Let's go then!" Tannya said with a fist pump. "Val and Sara, grab the oars and start us on our way. TO THE SHIP!"

21

First thing Tannya did when we started paddling was open up the package. It was a small, plastic, Tupperware box, about the size of a child's shoe box. Inside was a gallon-sized Ziplock with a bunch of tissue paper. She set it out and carefully unwrapped it. It was a roll, and as she unrolled it she came across a gold necklace. "Wow," she said. "This looks real." She passed it around to us. We agreed, it did look real. There were more gold items in there too. She wrapped the necklace back up and put it back in the Ziplock and then in the container.

While we were rowing out to the ship, we discussed our plan. We were about two football fields' length behind the pontoon. The crew of *Ocean's Lie* looked like they were almost there and planning to board.

The wooden rowboat was still on land over by the house. We didn't see any movement over there, so we weren't sure what Scooter was up to. Miss Kitty took over rowing for a bit because Val's arms got tired. There was no wind and the raft was round so it was really hard to get it to move.

"Here's what we do," Tannya said. "We sneak up and take back the pontoon. We'll leave Vagina in the boat and then go back to the house and hide the treasure."

"Where?" Aunt Val asked.

"I know where!" I said. "But I can't tell you in front of this bitch." I looked at Jodi and again stuck my tongue out at her. Then I chuckled. Tongues were so offensive. This had amazing power. She turned her half-open eyes away from me. She made two short grunting noises that sounded a lot like "fuck you," but I ignored it. I loved this. She was like my prisoner, except I didn't do it.

We watched as the three men started up the rope ladder. "Geez, Captain should have pulled that up," Val pointed out.

"I suppose he was expecting Scooter to return shortly," Miss Kitty answered.

"Hey, we should all turn our phones on silent when we get close. We don't want to have them ring," Miss Kitty suggested.

We each reached in our pockets and turned them off. "Ya know, if they were good pirates, they'd have taken those too," Val said.

"Hey, Vagina!" Tannya said. "You got a phone too?"

"She sure does! She's been busy using it the last couple days a lot, haven't ya?" I said. I crawled over to her and pushed her down so she was laying back. I reached in her pocket and pulled one out. It was the most recent Apple iPhone. "Wow, nice phone! Did you just get this? It's a great upgrade," I told to her. "Gosh, I'm not even sure how to use these things," I said, fumbling around with it. "How do you silence it?" I asked, turning and flipping it obnoxiously. "OOPS!" I said sarcastically as it slipped out of my hand and into the lake.

I leaned over the raft and looked. "Gosh, so sorry, it went straight to the bottom." I tilted my head. "I hope you didn't need it for anything." I looked back at my crew. They were all smiling at me in disbelief. "At least we know it'll be silent now."

"Indeed," Miss Kitty said.

I looked at the time on my phone. It was five thirty. I silenced it and put it back in my pocket. We started rowing again. We were almost to the ship and pontoon. We couldn't see or hear anything which I guess was good.

"I wish we'd brought a bug or mini camera with," Miss Kitty said.

"Oh, yeah, shoot. That'd have been handy," I said.

Tannya nodded. "Get us close to the pontoon." We did our best to row up to it. Within a few minutes we had climbed aboard and untied the pontoon, then re-tied the raft to the ship's ladder.

Jodi was still sitting in the raft. She started making noise and wiggling around. "Oh, silly us," I said sarcastically. "Jodi's right, we *did* forget something." I maneuvered the raft to the door of the pontoon and stepped back onto to it. She looked relived. "Thanks for the reminder, not like *you're* going to use it," I said and picked up the half empty bottle of Schnapps. I patted her on the head. "It was good to see you again. You should stop by more often. This was fun!" I told her. Then I got back on the pontoon. I started the motor and Tannya pushed us off.

"Bubye, Jodi. Hope you enjoyed one *Ella Vashow!*" Miss Kitty said, using her arms like Vanna White to show her the name on the panels. Jodi was shaking her head and yelling something, but we couldn't make it out. We all blew kisses and waved. As we putted slowly home I suggested we turn our phones back on.

Tannya noticed that across the lake, Scooter was in the rowboat going back to the ship. He'd be in for a surprise. We didn't see anything large in the boat so we didn't know what he went back for.

We approached the dock and quickly tied up. "The spot that I wanted to hide it is in the cave that's out in the woods," I told them as we stood there on the dock contemplating our next move.

"The one the bodies were in?" Tannya asked.

Well, that made it sound bad. "Um, yeah, no one would find it there. The problem is it'd take us a long time."

"How about in the house," Val suggested. "They wouldn't just break in. If we leave it out here they'll find it for sure."

"Yeah, and it's not like your dog'll protect it for us. Ha ha," Miss Kitty laughed. I was slightly offended, but I was trying to control my mood swings, so I didn't tell her what a piece of worthless junk *her* dog was.

"How about the washer and dryer? You never see a robber look in there," Tannya said. We all looked at her. "Right? When was the last time you watched a movie and someone opened the door on a washer when they were ransacking the house?"

"She's right," I said. "Let's do that, at least for now. We need to hurry though, before they notice us. No one's been on the ship's deck yet, as far as I can tell." We looked over and noticed Scooter was in the raft. I was sure he was cutting Jodi loose.

We all grabbed packages and went into the house. The girls set them on the floor and went back out for more. It only took two trips with all of us helping. I took the gold blankets and stuffed animals from the dryer and put them in the trash and then put the packages in the washing machine and the dryer, completely filling them. We still had more left so I hid the rest in my closet behind my sweaters that were folded on the floor.

It was chilly in the house, so I made a fire. We locked all the doors and checked all the windows to make sure that they were all locked, too.

I took another of the packages, and we opened it. Inside that one was jewelry too, but it wasn't junk. It looked brand new. There was everything from gold, to silver, to white gold, and even diamond studded stuff in there.

"This just got real!" Val said. "That isn't the kind of stuff I was helping to package. This explains why he was so protective of it."

"Why would he hide it in the lake?" I asked. "Why not just bury it, or put it in a safe deposit box? I don't get it."

Tannya put her hand on her hip. "Like I said, he's trying to play this off as a game. But there's something real here, and I think that *Ocean's Lie* knows it."

"This is getting to be too much to process. I think we should stop drinking and get some food in our stomachs," I said.

After we all settled around the island countertop I pulled some snacks out, and we cut into one of the pies. The pie was amazing. We finished the whole thing, and then I made a pot of coffee. We'd all been a bit too excited on the pontoon and had polished off half a bottle of Schnapps, and it was only six o'clock. We laughed and talked loudly, in our buzzed state, about the day. And then we discussed what to do about Jodi. There was some talk about calling Rex, but I was pretty sure we might be in trouble too, so I didn't know if I wanted to do that.

"They have a gun. This is beyond a LARP now. I'm not sure, but I think there is something else going on here," Val said.

"I agree." Miss Kitty said.

"Me too, especially since that phone call from Wayde about not getting involved," I said.

My phone rang. I looked at the screen. Rex.

"Answer it!"

"No, don't!"

"If you do, he's going to have to investigate."

"We aren't exactly innocent here!"

They were all talking at once, and I wasn't sure what to do, so I panicked and set it down on the counter. We all stared at it in silence until it went quiet. No one said anything for a few seconds after it stopped. Then it beeped, indicating a message.

I picked it up and read it aloud: *"I'm on my way over."*

"Shiiiiit," I said quietly.

"We need a plan!" Tannya said.

"What is with you and the plans?" Miss Kitty snapped.

"I'm just sayin' we need to get our story straight," Tannya told her.

"I think in this case we all plead the fifth. I really have enough to deal with already. I don't want anything new on my record," Val said.

"It's probably best to answer as few questions as we can," Tannya said. "We'll let Sara do the talking." She jabbed her elbow at me.

I took the binoculars off the table and pulled the blinds slightly open. I couldn't see any action on the ship, and Jodi was still in the raft, but her hands were in front of her and her bandana was off. She was just sitting there. I giggled to myself quietly. It was starting to get dark, and I bet she was getting chilly, too. This sure would teach her to mess with me again.

I told the girls what I saw and no one seemed to care about her wellbeing. "We'll send Derek out there to save her when he gets here," I said snidely.

We munched on some more snacks I had and drank the pot of coffee. After a bit we calmed down.

"Maybe we should go to Wayde's house and get my stuff. I have a bunch of clothes, my makeup, my purse and car there," Val said.

"We could do that now. Then we wouldn't be here when Rex arrives. We could avoid all the questions," I suggested.

"Sounds good to me, I'd like to get my stuff before he gets off the ship. He won't stay on it at night."

"Should we all go? What if *Ocean's Lie* comes back?" Miss Kitty asked.

"Oh, shit. I should probably get the key off the pontoon. I'm so used to just leaving it on there that I forgot. I'll run out there now." I bolted out the door and ran to the dock. It was quiet. No pirates in the trees, and no cannonballs flying. I looked at the ship and didn't see any activity, but I did notice that Jodi was no longer in the raft.

The raft was still tied there, but no Jodi. Huh. I grabbed the keys from the ignition and ran back to the house.

"Jodi's gone."

They all looked at me and followed me when I went to the window with the binoculars. I couldn't see anyone on deck. They were either at the far side of the ship or below deck.

"I don't see anything!" I said.

The girls all took turns with the two sets of binoculars but no one could see anything.

"Hopefully she jumped overboard," Miss Kitty said.

"Yeah, she's probably fish bait!" Tannya said.

"I hope not, we left her there. We might be in trouble for that," Val said.

Val was usually the wild one. I guess being recently arrested calmed her down at bit.

"We should get going if we're going to beat Rex out of here," I said.

We all used the bathroom and then hauled ourselves into the Jeep. Just as I started it Miss Kitty yelled, "Wait, I have an idea." She jumped out of the Jeep and ran to the house. I followed because I had locked it.

"The door's locked. What do you need?" I asked chasing her up the steps.

"My bag, the one I brought over. It has all the surveillance equipment in it."

"Oh!" I said. I turned the key and she ran in and grabbed the bag. I locked the door behind her.

On the short drive over, we decided to bug Wayde's house and see if we could get any information on what was really going on. Miss Kitty dug through the bag and handed stuff to the others and told them to check the batteries and make sure that everything was working. We went around the lake and parked at the end of the driveway so that if they looked at the house from the ship we would be hidden well from view.

We were pretty sure everyone was on the ship. We still wanted to make sure no one saw us go in the house. "My car is up by the house. I'll make sure it's unlocked. Then we can go into the house and get my stuff, and I'll put it in my car and follow you guys back," she said and ran to the car.

Miss Kitty threw the things back in the bag and we all exited the vehicle, closing our doors quietly. We quickly ran along the tree line towards the house. When we got close to the open, cut area around the house, we stopped and looked through the binoculars at the ship. I couldn't see anything on deck. The ship was closer to this side of the lake. It made it easier to see it, but harder for us to hide.

I gave them the wave to go on and they all passed me and ran to the side of the house. I followed. We pressed up against the house and waited for Val. When she joined us she tried the side door that faced the driveway. "Shit, locked!" she whispered. "Wait here." She went around to the front. She was visible to the ship now. I peeked around at the ship. There were people on the deck now. I could see Jodi. Her hands looked tied behind her back again. *Ocean's* crew was standing there next to Jodi, and Wayde and Scooter were across from them.

"Hurry, Val, they're on the ship deck," I whispered from around the corner.

A moment later she came back around the corner. "It's locked and the hide-a-key is gone."

We all looked at each other, except Tannya. She was already on her way back over the side door. She quickly took her sweatshirt off wrapped it around her right hand in a big ball and punched the window on the door. The glass broke. She removed the big pieces and reached through the door and unlocked it. Then she opened the door, stepped back and waved us in. "After you, ladies," she said with a proud smile.

"Oooh, girl, you's in trouble!" I sang.

"Thank you kindly!" Val said.

"Nice!" Miss Kitty said and fist bumped her.

"Candee Barre and Sara Narra, you set up the equipment. Me and Gun Powder Gertie will get her things together. Be quick, we don't know when they'll be back," Tannya ordered, shaking out her sweatshirt in case any glass had become lodged in the fabric.

Miss Kitty dumped the bag on the living room floor. We looked around the house. It was a very simple rambler with an open floorplan. Where we entered brought us in the middle of the house. The entire house was decorated in pirate stuff—posters, framed prints, and small trinkets everywhere had something to do with pirates. To the right was a simple kitchen. Cabinets, sink, fridge and stove were all in an L shape. At the end of the L was the other door. A small island counter and a small dinette set stood to the right as well. Straight ahead was a living room area—a couch, chair with a large coffee table. The TV was an older model sitting on an old end table.

Further to the left was a hallway. After a quick peek, we figured out there were two bedrooms and one bathroom. Aunt Val and Tannya were in the first one, gathering stuff into a big garbage bag. The other was a bit messy and had pirate clothing and posters of *Pirates of the Caribbean* movies on every wall. There were a lot of ships in bottles everywhere too. The house was overdecorated, but it was fairly clean and not overly cluttered. It was better than I'd thought it would be.

Miss Kitty and I decided to put the small pen camera behind the TV. There were a few trinkets sitting next to the TV so we taped the pen on to one of them. Then we hid a bug, that sent sound instantly to a hand-held radio thingy, under the kitchen cabinet.

"Where does he hang out the most?" I asked Val.

"Well, it used to be in the shed, working on the ship, but since that's been launched it's been on the ship or in the living room area." We moved it to the cabinet closest to the living room.

Val and Tannya went into the bathroom and got her toiletries and then the hall closet for her shoes and jackets. I looked out the window facing the lake and could see *Ocean's Lie* loading back into the raft with Jodi. Scooter and Wayde were watching them from on the deck. I quickly went to the hall and flipped off the light we had turned on and told them what I saw.

After we all got out of the side door we stayed there until Val peeked and gave us the all clear. She and Tannya ran to her car and Miss Kitty and I ran to the Jeep. We jumped in and drove to my house.

I pulled into my driveway and saw a Nisswa police car and noticed Rex standing on my dock.

22

After Val and I parked, we all got out. Val was still in her pirate outfit and the rest of us had on our matching sweatshirts and bandanas. The girls went into the house, and I walked to over to meet Rex. He'd seen us come up the driveway and was walking towards me.

"Hi!" I said like any other day.

"Hey," he said back with raised eyebrows.

"So what brings you out this way?" I asked.

"Nothing in particular." He was looking around the property as he talked. He was not here on a social call. That was evident.

"What's going on with the pontoon?" He asked. "*Ella Vashow?*"

"Oh, that's just Miss Kitty being funny. She thought she'd jazz it up a bit," I told him.

It was getting darker by the minute. I was sure he'd noticed the raft over by the ship. I could see people but no details about them so I wasn't sure what he'd figured out.

"So did she also jazz it up with a cannon, too?"

"Oh, ah, that? Yes. She thought it would be fun."

"And did you fire it?" he asked.

I looked at him, studied his eyes. I couldn't tell if he'd blow it off, give me a warning or cuff me. "Ah . . . yeah, we wanted to try it out."

"Where did she get it?"

"The internet." I studied his eyes again. He looked disappointed. "You're not putting cannonballs into it, are you?"

"Meeee?" I asked pointing at my chest. I thought about it for a minute. "No, I don't think I did."

"Did *anyone* put cannonballs into it?" he asked with a little more pressure in his voice.

"Um," I started. Then the front door swung open and Tannya yelled from across the yard.

"Hey, Sara, where do you keep the crackers?"

"I'll be right in!" I yelled back. I looked at Rex. "I better get back before they tear the place apart."

"We can head in. I may have some questions for them, too," he said and motioned for me to lead the way.

Shit, shit, shit. "Sure come on in," I said turning on my heels.

When we got inside, the girls were bellied up to the island countertop. I glanced over to the dining room table and saw two pairs of binoculars on it. I wished I'd put those away.

When we stepped in, everyone looked over to us. I slipped my shoes off and walked to the kitchen. "Come on in, Rex. Can I get you something to drink?"

"No, thank you," he told me and then walked up to the counter and greeted my friends. "Hello, ladies."

They all said hi back. After that there was some uncomfortable silence.

"So, what's the occasion? Everyone's over here. Are we celebrating something?" he asked.

"Oh no, just a few girls having a nice afternoon together," Miss Kitty said.

Rex turned his eyes to her. "Yes, I see that. I noticed that the pontoon got a few upgrades? Or shall I say downgrades. I noticed the sun cover was broken. Did you have the boat out today?"

We all looked at each other. Tannya was finally the first to answer. "We went for a little cruise around the lake and the dang thing caught some wind and got all twisted, so we took it off."

"Wind? Today?" Rex said, knowing perfectly well that there was no wind at all today. "Interesting," he said, holding her stare. "Looks like the boat got some new decorations, too. And it seems to match your outfits," he said, moving his eyes across each of us. "Are you a LARP team now?

"What? Nah," Tannya said. He squinted his eyes at her.

"Ladies, be straight with me. Don't make me be all official and take you down to the station to have this conversation." His voice changed tone a bit. It was still friendly, but he was letting us know he was done with the games. "There's a cannon on your pontoon," he said looking at me.

"Yeah, that's new!" I said.

"And have you used it?"

"Why do you ask?" Val interrupted just as I was about to answer.

"Well, for one thing there's a car sitting on the road again. The car that belongs to Jodi Vagerna."

"What? Where? I didn't see it when we came home a second ago," I told him.

"It's on County Road 12, about a quarter-mile down."

That road was to the left of the field across from my driveway approach, so I guess I wouldn't have noticed. "What the heck is she doing back here?" Miss Kitty asked.

He looked around at all of us again. We all shrugged. "So then I guess you have no idea how the hole got in her roof or the cannonball got in her passenger-side seat . . ." he said.

Tannya gave out a huff of laughter, and then put her drink to her mouth. Miss Kitty's eyes got really round, and Val covered her mouth.

"Nope," I said, "didn't even know she was in the area."

"Captain Wayde's been firing all morning. Maybe one went too far," Val suggested.

"Is that what you saw?" Rex asked.

She looked unsure. "Are we on the record right now or just friends having a conversation?" He just stared at her. I saw the hint of a smile.

"Please tell me you didn't intentionally fire a cannon at Jodi's car," he said looking at me.

I put my hands up in defense. "I did not intentionally fire a cannon at Jodi's car. I had no idea she was even *trespassing* again. Although, I thought I saw someone who looked like her hanging out with *Ocean's Lie*, the other LARP group that's been hanging around here. They, too, have been trespassing a lot lately," I said and folded my arms across my chest.

"Are those the guys who were out here late the other night?"

"Yes."

His eyes studied me. "You have a strange life, Sara," he said.

I just looked at him and shrugged. It was pretty strange lately but also a lot of fun.

"So why do you have a cannon and a crate that says it contains six cannonballs that's empty on your dock?"

"Oh, pffft! That's just for fun," I told him with a hand flick.

"Did you fire it?"

My phone buzzed in my pocket. I looked at the caller ID, and gave Rex the "one second" finger. "Hello," I answered to Derek.

"Hey, I'm just coming into town. Do you need anything? I'm at the gas station."

"Nope, I'm good. See you in a few," I said and disconnected. I looked at Rex again.

"Sara, can I talk to you for a moment?" he asked and stepped towards the entryway.

"Sure."

We got to the door, and Rex gave me a good stare down. "Look," he said. "I don't want to see anyone get in to trouble. But if you are firing actual balls from the cannon, it turns out it *is* illegal. So don't. If you already have, I don't want to know about it. This game you're very obviously participating in is dangerous. I don't want to see any of you get hurt. You've had enough going on in your life. You don't need to get wrapped up in this."

"I am concerned," he continued. "We have a cop in the office who's been in contact with the Chicago PD. They think there's a link to criminal activity that went on in the past. I told them about the LARP, and they're checking into it. We all agreed a LARP would be a great cover. I don't think this is a game being played. I'm not sure what it is, but we're going to find out soon. Just keep your distance and stay out of it. It's dangerous, Sara. If these are the same men, they are professionals and can't be trusted." He looked at me and I smiled.

"Thank you for your concern. I'll be careful. I'd say I'd keep my distance, but it's all happening in kind of close proximity." I shrugged.

"You haven't seen Jodi around, have you?"

I waited a moment. "Maybe check with Wayde on that. He might have seen her."

"Okay," he said with a smirk. "I'm headed over there now. Behave."

He rubbed my arm and went out the door.

I returned to the kitchen and wiped my forehead. "Phew!"

"Do you think he bought it?" Val asked.

"No, but I think he's too nice a guy to get angry at us," I said. "He's going over to Wayde's right now."

We all got up and looked out the window. "I wonder what we missed," Val said. "When we left it looked like *Ocean's Lie* was getting ready to leave." We glanced around. There was no one on the ship that we could see. The raft was gone and it didn't look like it was anywhere near Wayde's house or what was left of his dock. We all turned our heads towards my dock. I gasped. There was *Ocean's Lie*! The raft was back in its hidden spot near the tree line. Jodi was still sitting in it, gagged and tied again. I didn't like her but that made me nervous. Morgan and Long John were walking quickly towards my pontoon.

"What the hell do they think they're doing?" I asked.

"They're going to take your boat again!" Tannya said. "Let's stop them!"

"No," Val said quietly. "This doesn't feel right."

We watched as Morgan and Long John dug through the boat. They were flipping up seats and opening doors and coming up empty handed.

"They're looking for the treasure," Miss Kitty said.

"Well, they ain't going to find it!" Tannya said proudly.

"Maybe we should give it to them," I said quietly. "Rex said that they might be criminals from Chicago. Rex thinks they may be involved in a LARP as a cover story.

"Really?" Miss Kitty said.

I nodded. "I don't think we want to get wrapped up in this."

Val spoke up. "I agree. I have a bad feeling with all the little things that have changed in Wayde lately. I don't doubt he loves pirates and always has, but I think there's more to the story. We never stole anything of real value. I mean, once in a while we might find some small amounts of cash or a watch or something, but never anything of *real* value. People don't just forget or not care about their bags. If you value anything in your bag you'll go straight there and get it. You don't leave it lying around. And the only ones we ever stole were the ones left unattended. I don't know what's in *all* those packages we got, but I don't think I'm supposed to know. He got that stuff from somewhere. Illegally I'm sure."

"Where's Flying Dutchman at?" Miss Kitty asked.

We all jumped as the front door swung open. Flying Dutchman was suddenly standing in my entryway "Hello, ladies!" he said in a gruff voice.

"Get out!" I yelled, half brave and half scared to death.

"I'll depart your company just as soon as you hand over the treasure."

"Bullshit! That's my treasure! You lied to me, and took my treasure, and now I took it back!" Tannya yelled.

"Ladies, I have orders." He was still using his pirate voice. "I need the treasure or I take you into our custody."

"Really?" Miss Kitty said. "How are you going to do that?"

"Well, Captain gave me this, just in case," he said and pulled out a gun.

"That's seems really unfair. I'm pretty sure that you *can't* use guns in a LARP," I said.

"This isn't a LARP! Now tell me where you hid the treasure or I take all of you instead!" he yelled.

"No, you can take us," Tannya said and walked towards him. She leaned over, picked up her shoes and started putting them on.

She looked over and gave us a good stare. I had no idea what she was planning, but we listened to her eyes. The rest of us got our shoes on, too.

"Okay we're ready," Val announced when we all had our shoes tied.

He looked annoyed, and surprised. "Let's go then, out to the boat."

"Wait!" I said. "Are we going to be out there for long, because I have to pee."

"What? I don't know!"

"Well, can I go to the bathroom first?" I asked. He thought about it for a second and then told me to show him where it was. I led him around the corner of the hall and he peeked inside. Once he saw there were no windows he said it was fine. I stepped in and shut the door behind me. I reached into my pocket and dialed Rex.

From inside the bathroom I heard Dutchman yell, "FUCK!" and then a car start. Rex didn't pick up, so I hung up after the second or third ring. He'd see my missed call and hopefully return to my house. I set my phone to silent and stuck it in my bra. Hopefully they wouldn't notice it there. I peeked out the door. Flying Dutchman was nowhere in sight. After I put my keys in my pocket I went to the front door and shut and locked it. I noticed that Miss Kitty's car was gone.

Out the living room window I could see Long John and Morgan talking with Flying Dutchman. They didn't look happy. Morgan said something to Flying Dutchman and he turned towards the house and started marching towards it. As soon as he passed the patio's view I snuck out the patio door and called for Pepper to come with. He'd been napping by the fire and for the last half of the day didn't even bothered to get up and sniff us.

"Pepper! Come!" I whispered and patted my leg. He tipped his head at me but didn't look like he was going to move. Faith came bounding over, so I grabbed her and shut the door. I wondered if Dutchman had even noticed Pepper when he was in there before. I went around the back side of the house. My Jeep was parked near the front door, but I needed to make it to the Jeep without being spotted. I didn't think that was possible. While I waited there my phone was buzzing in my bra. I pulled it out. It was Rex calling.

"Hello?" I whispered.

"Are you okay? Where are you? Miss Kitty, Tannya and Val came here to Wayde's house and told me what happened. I'm on my way. I've called for back-up. Tell me where you are!"

"I'm behind the house. I was going to try to make a run for my Jeep—"

"Don't! Stay hidden. Where are . . . the pirates?"

"One just went up to my house and kicked the front door in. The other two are on my pontoon," I whispered.

"How many guns?"

"One for sure. Oh, and I think they might have kidnapped Jodi," I told him.

Just then I felt a hard hit on the back of my head and everything went black.

23

I woke up with a headache. It took a few seconds for everything to come into focus. I was in the raft. Jodi was kicking her foot at me. Oww! My head hurt! Jodi's face was not what I wanted to see when I came to.

I was lying on my side. I had a gag in my mouth and my hands were tied behind my back. I wiggled away from Jodi's foot and got myself to a sitting position. I glared at her and tried to get my hands free. I could hear voices and distant yelling but I couldn't make out what they were saying. I looked around. We were up on the shore. Jodi was shivering. It was pretty cold out now that the sun was down, and it was almost dark. We could barely see the ship. Jodi kicked me and made a noise. When I looked at her, she jerked her head twice towards the tree line behind her.

We could hear rustling in the trees. I wasn't sure who it would be. My heartrate was up. I happened to glance down and notice a puddle of blood next to me. I looked at it and then scanned my body. It had to be from my head. Jodi looked at me and shook her head hard. I knew she was trying to tell me that it was my head. My stitches must have split.

The rustling grew louder and closer. I could hear voices whispering. I recognized them. "Here she is!" whispered Tannya. She and Miss Kitty ran over to me. We all glanced towards the dock. There wasn't anyone over there that we could see. Tannya took my gag off, and Miss Kitty tried to untie my hands.

Just then we heard more noise. Flying Dutchman was walking out of the woods. He had a gun pointed at us.

"You guys just don't know when to quit, do you? Stand up."

I stood with Miss Kitty and Tannya's help. He walked over and yanked Jodi to her feet. "Walk."

We walked through the woods while he followed close behind us.

"Where's Rex?" I whispered to Tannya. She shrugged. "Where's Val?"

"She was in the car with Rex."

"Shut up!" Flying Dutchman warned.

He continued to direct us through the woods. About halfway through the woods he told us to head left. There was a somewhat beaten path they'd been using.

This was a power fight. I didn't think he should win. It was all of us against him. We clearly had him outnumbered. My mind was racing with ideas. I figured we'd be getting to the truck and trailer soon and he'd take us somewhere or lock us in.

"Where's your captain?" I asked.

"Let's just say he went down with his ship."

"So you mean he got arrested?"

"I think he's getting questioned, but I don't think he's been arrested. I wasn't going to wait around to find out. You don't need to worry about it. Just walk."

His tone seemed a bit more relaxed. And I thought since he was willing to talk he was probably not overly focused on his intent.

I whispered to Tannya, who was on my right, "Run when you can, bring help."

"Where are we walking to?" I asked. I turned my head to look at him for the answer and while I did that, I slowed my pace for a couple steps so I was now next to Miss Kitty.

"Just walk! Geez, do I need to put your gag back in?"

I turned to Miss Kitty and whispered, "Run with Tannya."

"Walk to *where*?" I asked Flying Dutchman again. I stopped, shot Tannya a look, and then turned around and walked towards him and Jodi. "I mean, this path doesn't lead anywhere. This isn't the way to my house," I said and walked in the other direction. "If we go this way, we can end all this foolishness right now. Come on!" I quickly tromped off in the direction of my house.

"Stop!" he yelled, turning in my direction.

"No, it's this way!" I said and head nodded that way. "Ouch! My ankle," I yelled.

He looked at me on the ground. I was lying half on my side, because my hands were still tied.

Miss Kitty and Tannya took off on foot. The trees were thick, and so was the underbrush. So although we could hear them, we couldn't see them anymore.

"Stop!" he yelled again in their direction. Jodi noticed and started running that way too. It was harder for her to keep up with her hands tied around her back. Dutchman ran after her and grabbed her, then went down on the ground. I quickly scampered to my knees and then feet and started running in the opposite direction.

"Damn it!" Dutchman said with frustration in his voice. "Stop or I'll shoot!" he yelled, but the devil inside my head that had been controlling me lately was pissed off and still wanted to run. So I ran. Ran like never before. I got into the thick underbrush, took a sharp left, went a few yards and dropped to my knees. Then I went quiet.

My heart was pounding hard in my chest, making my vision blurry. It was getting darker. I could see the flashing lights from Rex's car. I sat still trying to control my breathing. And now my ankle really did hurt. I felt weak. I wondered how much blood I'd lost. The back of my shirt felt sticky and cold, so I knew it was at least that much. It probably didn't help that I had alcohol and happy pills in my system.

I listened hard. I could hear someone running near me, but I couldn't see anyone. I waited and listened longer. In the distance I could hear yelling. "Hey! Hey! Stop!" It was Miss Kitty and Tannya's voices. They were probably out on the road flagging someone down.

Suddenly I heard heavy steps. It was Dutchman. Shit! He was coming right at me, gun drawn. "Get up, bitch. If you run again I'll kill you."

I believed him. He looked pretty serious. My evil twin stuck up my middle finger at him, but my hands were tied behind my back so fortunately he didn't see it. I rolled my eyes and stood up. I started to wobble and everything went blurry, so I dropped back to my knees.

"Get up!" he demanded.

"Geezus! Give me a minute. I got hit in the head and my stitches from two days ago split. I've lost a lot of blood. I'm a little dizzy here," I shouted. He looked surprised by my voice.

"Just get moving!" he said and grabbed my arm. He shoved me forward and marched me along for a while. We stayed on the path and passed Jodi along the way. She was tied to a tree with the belt that used to be around his waist.

When we got to the road, I recognized the pickup truck and trailer from Morning Glory. I was half relieved. I was getting cold. At this point I would rather be in the truck than the woods, except he turned and shoved me towards the trailer. I couldn't see the adjacent road, but I knew where I was. The main road to my drive should be straight ahead. He opened the back and shoved me in. Then shut the door.

It was pitch black. Oh no, this was not happening. I was pretty sure I could feel horns growing on my head at this point. I was so pissed my face felt like it was a thousand degrees. *He must be going back for Jodi*, I thought. I played with the rope on my wrists. Miss Kitty had started to untie them before. Maybe she'd helped it a bit. I pulled and pushed and tugged on the pieces. A few moments later I felt the ropes loosen. I got my hands free and stood up. I took the gag off. It was a bandana. I tied it tight around my head in case I was still bleeding. I still had my cell phone in my bra! I quickly pulled it out and turned it on.

Rex or Derek? Rex or Derek? I contemplated. Ugh. I chose Rex since I knew for sure that he was nearby. I assumed that Derek was here or close by now too.

The line opened. "Hello!"

"I'm locked in a trailer off the county road south of my woods. I was in the woods between here and my house. He has Jodi, too. I assume he went back for her. When he opens the door I'm going to make a run for it, through the trees, to you."

I could hear footsteps. "They're coming! Shhh!" I said into the phone then locked the screen and put it back into my bra. I felt around for the door and stood ready.

As soon as the trailer latch was loose, I gave it a hard kick and jumped out. I turned left and ran back into the woods. I just kept running as fast as I could. When I'd jumped down, Dutchman was holding Jodi's arm and was bent over at the waist with his face in his hands. I guess the door hit him in the face. I just kept running and running. I never stopped to look back and never stopped to breathe. I was on pure adrenaline. I was fast. There was no way he could keep up. I wasn't even tired. It was close to a quarter mile to my house.

When I finally got to the tree opening on the edge of my property I felt an overwhelming sense of relief. The security light on my property dimly lit the area. I could see Derek's Jeep, Miss Kitty, Val, and Tannya straight ahead about fifty yards. Over by the Nisswa police car, I could see Derek and Rex. They were huddled together over something. There were two heads in the back of the squad car, so at least I knew they had Captain Morgan and Long John in custody.

Upon seeing all that, the reality of what was happening and the danger behind it set in. Well, that, and my loss of blood, lack of athletic ability, fear, and exhaustion, hit me out of left field. I started breathing heavy and crying, which made me almost hyperventilate. I did my best to control it for a few breaths.

"Hey! Over here!" I bellowed and then dropped to the ground. I lay there listening to them yelling and talking and running towards me.

I closed my eyes and waited for them to get to me, concentrating on my breaths so I didn't hyperventilate. Feeling my heart knocking on my ribs, I knew I needed to lie there until I could muster the strength to stand up.

When I opened my eyes I was staring at Tannya. She was leaning right over the top of me. "Guuurl, you are one brave bitch! I can't believe you got away! And you saved us, too." She was hugging me and squeezing too tight. I couldn't believe that out of all the people standing way over there, she'd gotten to me first. "We were so worried. We were on our way to come search for you. Rex called for back-up *again*, but there was a barn fire on the other side of Nisswa, so the other cop is on his way but it's going to take a bit. Rex caught the two of them and got them into his car."

"I just got here, and I'm still getting bits and pieces of the story," Derek said. "Are you okay?"

"My head," I whimpered, leaning to my side so he could look. "They hit me with something hard and knocked me out. I think I lost a lot of blood. I'm not feeling great."

"Let's get you to the hospital," he said. He leaned over and scooped me up. "You left the cell phone line open. We were listening to you running."

"Oh, yeah, I did. I did that on purpose. I'd just forgotten that I did it." I reached in my shirt and pulled out my phone and turned it off. Derek took it and put it in his jacket pocket.

We got about half way to the Jeep and I could tell I was getting heavy for him. "I can walk. I'm okay," I told him. Derek set me down and reached into his pocket for the keys.

After he tossed the CB back in his car, Rex came towards us. "Thank God you're okay!"

"Flying Dutchman was throwing Jodi into a trailer on the East side of County Road 12 when I ran away."

"Okay, we'll get him. You just go get checked out. We saw the blood in the raft. We were worried," Rex said.

"I'll call your mom!" Val announced.

"NO!" I said. "She'll come down here and be freaked out and cause me more stress. I'll get ahold of her later."

"You're probably right. Okay, but I'm coming with you!" Val said.

Tannya looked at me. "Miss Kitty and I will stay here and protect the house and the dog."

"Oh, my God! I forgot about Pepper and Faith. Are they okay?"

"Yes," Miss Kitty answered. "Pepper is, as always, still by the fireplace, and Faith *was* exploring the yard but is back in the house now."

"Oh, good, will you guys feed them and make sure Pepper goes out before bed if I'm not back in time."

"Sure thing! You don't worry about us, just get better and keep us posted," Tannya said.

"I will. I probably just need some more cookies and juice," I said with a sniffle.

Derek opened the door to his Jeep and helped me up into the seat. He took a gauze wrap from Rex and stuck it under my head. "Don't mess up my seat," he said with a wink.

"I'm going to go look for the truck. Back-up should be here shortly. Keep in touch," Rex said to me. Then he ran to his car and took off down the driveway.

Val jumped in the back and off we went down the road. We got to the hospital. They remembered me from earlier in the week. Before the doctor came in, I told Derek and Val to let me do the talking and not to mention the pirates.

They both grinned and agreed. The doctor didn't ask a lot of questions, which was nice. I just told him I'd slipped on my porch steps and fell back and hit my head. He did a thorough exam because I had lost consciousness. After I passed all of that, he washed me up and put a few more stitches in. They put me on an IV and gave me juice and cookies. Finally, after two bags of fluid, they let me leave.

I called Rex. He said they'd looked for the truck, but it was gone. He dropped the other two pirates off at city hall for booking and then went back out. But he hadn't seen Flying Dutchman and Jodi yet. Dispatch was spreading the word to surrounding counties, so they'd hoped to hear something soon.

I gave Derek and Val the update as we walked out of the hospital. On the drive home, Derek ask me for details about the day. I wasn't really sure I wanted him to know everything. So I left a lot of pieces out, like the cannon.

"Sara, you can either be straight with me or you can keep your secrets, but I can't help you if I'm not in the loop."

"I don't need your help," my evil twin snapped. Actually, I wasn't sure now who said that. With all the time that had passed, the adrenaline, and IV fluids I'd had, I was pretty sure the drugs and alcohol were flushed out of my system by now. Maybe it was just my bitchy side.

Derek rolled his eyes at me and kept driving. When we got to my place, I settled on the couch. Tannya brought me water and sat down.

Miss Kitty told me, "The animals are fine. Pepper just went out to pee."

"Well, I'm fine too, just tired. It's been a busy day," I said. "Thanks for helping me."

"So how did you escape?" Tannya asked.

I told them what happened after they had taken off running. It turned out they ended up running back to the house, too. They made it to the road but no one would stop and help. Derek pulled in right behind them. Just as they were telling Derek about it, Rex's phone had rang with my call.

"They still have Jodi . . ." Val said with apprehension.

We all nodded somberly. I hated that bitch. "Well, I'd like to feel sorry for her but she brought this on herself," I said bluntly.

"I don't understand, why was she here in the first place?" Derek asked.

"Because she's been stalking Sara! She's trying to win you back. She's been trespassing and peeping in windows and now, well, the karma got her! This here is from karma. You don't mess with karma!" Tannya said and shook her head. Her lips were pierced tight, and she had a finger up, too.

"Well, what would make her come all the way here and make her feel she needed to peek into windows and take pictures?" Derek asked in an accusing tone.

I put my hand up and opened my mouth and I was just about to rip him a new one, when Aunt Val caught my eye and interrupted. "Well, jealousy, that's what! If a woman has her heart broken she'll do anything to get a man back." Aunt Val was a smart woman.

"I don't know. But I'm getting real tired of it. And I'll leave it at that," I said in snappy fragments.

"Well, I'm going to hit the hay. You ladies can hang out and discuss the day's events. Sara, I'll meet you in the room later?"

"Yup, good night."

He went to the entryway and grabbed his bag, then proceeded down the hall. When the door was shut, I took a deep breath and shot my angry eyes over to Miss Kitty.

I put my hand out. "I'm going to need another happy pill!"

24

Miss Kitty looked at me like she was scared. Then she looked at Tannya and Val. I looked at them too. Harder. They were like deer in the headlights, afraid to answer anything.

"COME ON!" I jerked my hand at her again.

"Ummm, I'm not sure you should have any more," Miss Kitty said cautiously.

"ELEANORE, I have been through hell and back to day. All of it was because of you three! Tannya, you and your LARP group, which you just HAD to sign up for. Aunt Val and your crazy pirate boyfriend. And YOU, you put a cannon on my pontoon, decorated it in glitter, called it a ship, AND named it *ELLA VASHOW*! Then . . . THEN there's Jodi! I got knocked out, bound and gagged and dropped in a raft with *her*. I was chased through the woods and stuffed in a trailer by a man in a pirate costume, who will only answer to Flying Dutchman. I've re-ripped my head open, lost a quart of blood, and then had the joy of getting it re-stitched. I'm pretty sure that qualifies me for a HAPPY PILL!" I shouted and extended my hand again.

Miss Kitty quickly rummaged through her purse and handed me one. I put it in my mouth and picked up the glass of water that Tannya brought me. I looked at Tannya, raised the glass in salute and tossed it back.

"There, now would anyone like more pie?" I asked calmly.

"Please, let me help," Val said. "I'll find something to fill our stomachs." I glanced at the clock, and it showed ten o'clock.

"Has there been any action on the ship?"

"No," Miss Kitty said. But we should get out the listening devices and see if anything is going on at the house.

We all moved to the dining room. Val brought over chips, dips, veggies, some pie, and a pitcher of water. We munched while we set up.

Pepper looked up at us. He got up, sauntered over to the table and sniffed in the pitcher. He could reach with all four paws on the floor. Then he walked back to the fireplace and lay down.

"Guess he's a margarita dog," Miss Kitty said.

"What if Derek comes out?" Tannya said.

"Screw him. It's not his jurisdiction," I told her.

We set up the video screen for the mini camera pen and the listening device for the bug. We could hear voices, but no one was on the screen. I had the video screen, I turned up the audio as far as it went, and Tannya did the same on the bug listening device. The screen was small, only three inches, and quite grainy. The camera was in the living room and there was no one in there. We quietly munched on snacks and kept watch over the video screen.

Finally on the screen we saw Wayde and Scooter come into the living room and sit down on the couch. They had a bunch of paper out in front of them on the coffee table.

We all leaned forward to hear. "All right, Scooter, sit," Wayde said.

"He sounds funny," Val said seriously. "He's talking in a normal tone. No more pirate." She looked kind of saddened by that.

"Honest, I didn't do it and I don't know who did. The last time I was in the house, the window was fine," Scooter whined.

"Fine, I'm past that. Let's move on."

"Sir, you're not using your pirate voice. Are we in game off mode?" Scooter asked him.

"Yes, game off. Geez, you can't be that dumb. Have you not noticed that this has moved past a LARP? There are few things you need to know. You're already involved, you know that, right? You're an accessory already, so you can leave if you want, but you're involved. You're going to get in trouble if we stay here and wait to get caught.

Your other choice is to help me, make a cut on the money, and get the hell out of Dodge ASAP. So what do you say? Are you in?"

"I . . . ahh . . ." Scooter stumbled.

"He'll do it," Tannya said.

"Ah . . . ahhh . . ." Wayde mocked. "WHAT? This isn't difficult. Make a choice. In or out, and if you're out, get the fuck out. I got shit to do."

"Well, shit, I'd like to know what the hell I'm involved in first."

"Burglary! Okay?" Wayde spat.

"Burglary? Like the treasure Val stole?"

We all looked at Val and she shook her head. "Bastard."

"No." Wayde paused and took a deep breath then continued. "Look, we don't have a lot of time. The stupid cop just left here and he had a lot of questions. Having the broken window helped make us look like victims, and it bought us some time, but he'll be back with more questions. They're getting too close, and if those jackasses open their mouths during questioning later, we're going down fast. So the way I see it we got a matter of hours, maybe less."

"So if this isn't a LARP, what the hell is it?" Scooter asked.

"It's a gang I was in four years ago when I lived in Chicago."

"A gang?" Scooter asked, confused. "But you're white."

Tannya covered her mouth and gave a huff of laughter.

"Shut up, fool! Anyone can be in a gang." Wayde shook his head and continued. "We were a group of friends sitting around one night, a few of us down on our luck and all of us under the influence of a variety of drugs. We came up with a plan to steal stuff for a living and came up with a name. Pirates steal for a living so we went with that theme. We came up with Low-life American Rebel Pirates. Which it turns out is also the acronym for Live Action Role-Playing."

"We started out small, teaming up together. Each of us had our own roles: stalkers, look-outs, route planners and drivers and robbers. We would do our parts, sit down and hatch a plan then break into houses, and garages and small sheds."

"Then we got better and more confident and moved on to storage sheds. We started with four of us but brought on a fifth, a brother to one of the guys. He was to keep track of the money and split it up evenly amongst the five of us. He would sell the stuff on the internet and to other buyers and then divvy up the money. Things were going really good. We carried guns but never ran into anyone while on the jobs and never got caught. We were professionals.

"One of the guys thought we should move to bigger and better things like jewelry stores, banks, and casinos. I was on board with that but the other three weren't. So our group split up. Me and Mike decided to keep going without them and ended up moving to the Twin Cities. Clint, Brad and Rick, from what we knew, went back to their old lives. They were happy and had some money in the bank, so they gave it up. They didn't want to take any bigger risks.

"So one night a few months after the split, Mike and I took a jewelry store. It was a Jared store just opening in the Maple Grove area. We did our research and found out their grand opening date. We knew it would be a busy day with a bunch of new, under-trained employees. We emptied the place out just before they opened. The shelves were well stocked for the event and we made off good.

"Mike and I went back to the apartment we shared and split it. We were up late celebrating and when I went to my room to go to bed, Mike stayed up. He was really high and was on the phone with someone. I heard my name mentioned so I crept in the next room and listened. He told the person on the phone that he was going to steal my share, all except a few items, and then rat me out to the police while he made a getaway. I was fucking pissed. Instead I put a gun to his head and took his share."

"Dude," Scooter said slowly.

"Yeah. I'm not proud of myself. It's something I live with every day, but he *was* planning on stealing my life too. I cleaned the apartment of anything that might link me and left. I moved back in with my mother after that. I've been here for three years. I can't stop thinking about the Low-life American Rebel Pirates. It's stuck in my head. I guess I was born to be a pirate, born to steal . . . and born to protect my treasure in any way I had to.

"I never told my mother what I'd done but she knew something was wrong. I used to put ships in bottles to pass the time. She said it was a waste of time, that I should do something bigger with my life."

"So why didn't you?"

"Well, dipshit, for one thing I'd need to pass a background check for most jobs and give an address on the application and show a license. I'm not sure how much the police know, but I don't want my name rolling around. My mother was remarried three times, so her last name has changed a bunch, and the last time not legally. Her ex paid cash for this place so her name isn't linked to this house or to me. So they'd have a hard time tracking me down."

"Where's her ex?"

"Don't know, he ran off with some young broad from the bar one night. They left the state, and she never heard from him again. So since I can't really go and get a job, instead I built a big ship. I sold a few pieces of the jewelry and bought a 'ship kit' off the internet.

"When Mom died that's all I did, just built the ship all day long. Then about six months ago I was trying to decide on a name for my ship and I came across a LARP website. It was the same letters as our gang and I sort of got sucked into it."

"I'd say! So you thought that dressing like a pirate and talking like one would heal your loss and your hurt?" Scooter said, sounding like a therapist. We all glanced at Tannya who also looked surprised at his question and loving tone.

"What the shit?" Tannya said with a wrinkled face.

"I guess. It was pretty therapeutic though. When I was in 'game on' mode I didn't have to think about the real world and my real world problems. It was a fun game that I could keep playing. Real people and the real world didn't know anything about Captain Wayde. It was nice to escape."

"So do you think the police are still looking for you?"

"I know they are. When *Ocean's Lie* came aboard, and I told you to go below deck and check on the leak, that's when I knew it was happening. Clint, Rick and Brad had figured out what I did and, well, they weren't happy. They've been trying to find me since that night. I spoke to Rick, a.k.a., Captain Morgan, a few months back when I registered my ship and LARP crew. I was out there."

"Out where?"

"Out on the internet. Rick said he found the name Wayde on the internet, listed under a LARP group. He looked at it, figured out it was about pirates and knew I'd loved pirates since I was a kid, and took a long shot that it might be me. Flying Dutchman is his brother, the one that came on later as our book keeper. His real name is Butch. Long John, whose real name is John something, was just another jerk that came along. They needed him for his computer knowledge and he'll do anything for his next hit."

"So Rick wants the real treasure?"

"Yes."

"Well, he didn't kill you when he came aboard, so what's his deal?"

"He didn't kill me because he needed the treasure. I don't know where it is. But I agreed to help him find it. I told him if he didn't kill me I'd give him and his men a seventy/thirty split. I informed him the value of the entire treasure is over four million dollars. I'd give them seventy percent of it to walk away and move on with their lives, or he could kill me and leave with nothing. We decided to go to the house where *Ella Vashow* is parked and find out what those women did with it.

"Rick and I are in agreement that those women are in on it together. Val was over here stalking me and learning my plans months ago. She played me to a 'T.' I don't know how she found me, but she's good," he paused and looked down at the coffee table. "She was very good."

We all looked at Val. She had hurt in her eyes.

"Are you in love with her?" Scooter asked him.

"What? No . . . no, I'm not."

"He's lying," Miss Kitty announced.

Val looked at her somberly and tightened her lips.

"And now she's teamed up with her niece and your ex? They're out to get us. We have to watch our backs, Scooter. I don't know what their backgrounds are and what their motive is, but those women can't be trusted."

Scooter shrugged. "I don't think it was a plan. I think it just happened."

"No, think about it. Val worked her way in long ago, played along with everything, and it was just last year that they moved into that house. There's no way she wasn't in on this for a long while. They've had a plan from the get-go. They got a cannon on the pontoon, and decals, and they even had matching uniforms. You don't just pull that shit together overnight!"

"Yes, I did!" Miss Kitty said proudly. We all fist bumped her.

"They're afraid of us! This is great!" Tannya said. "*Yeah*, we had a plan. We *always* have a plan!"

We turned our attention back to the screen.

"Maybe, but what does Tannya and the blonde, skinny bitch have to do with it? No way Tannya figured any of this out on her own."

"Heeey!" they both said.

"Well, I don't know. But what I *do* know is that they were supposed to go to the pontoon and get the treasure and meet here at the house. But now it seems the cops have detained Long John and Rick. And apparently Flying Dutchman is on the loose with a kidnapped woman named Jodi. And I've got a broken window!"

"Who is this Jodi anyway?" Wayde continued. "She said she wasn't with *Ocean's Lie* or *Ella Vashow*. And I believe her because neither of them seemed to care about her safety. They keep leaving her behind, yet they tie her up like she's a threat. I don't get it."

"I don't know. Maybe she's a hostage, a bargaining chip," Scooter said. "Maybe we could exchange some gold for her."

Wayde reached out and slapped him upside the head.

"She isn't worth her weight in gold," I said. Tannya and Miss Kitty fist bumped me.

"Well, what's my cut in all this? Seventy/thirty doesn't leave a whole lot for me," Scooter said.

Tannya chuckled.

"You're sharing my part."

"So we each are only getting fifteen percent? That's a bunch of bullshit! No, if I'm going to risk jail time then I want more than that! Fuck this!"

"Well, then what do you propose? I already made an agreement with them."

"They're in jail or hiding from the law. There *is* no them. Let's go get the girls and find the treasure right now. We don't need to wait for them. We'll get the gold and get out of Dodge before they rat us out in jail."

My heartrate increased. "Come on! Let's go now! Throw what you need in the truck and let's head over there. Then we'll leave town. By the time it's reported we'll be miles away."

Wayde stood. "Okay, but what about the ship?"

"Just leave it. The police'll probably take it anyway," Scooter said.

"But that ship is my life," Wayde said sadly.

"It *was* his life," Val agreed.

"Change out of your pirate get-up and let's go!" Scooter ordered.

"All right! All right! But you'd better remember who's in charge here."

"Yeah, yeah, I'll meet you in the truck."

I turned around and grabbed the binoculars. "I see Scooter! He's getting in the truck!" I said anxiously.

"Oh, shit! What do we do?" Miss Kitty said.

"They won't never find it!" Tannya said.

"Still, I don't want them in here! And remember, Wayde killed a man once already over this!"

"He's about to lose it all! He's threatened and he has nothing to lose. That makes him extra dangerous!" Val said.

"We need a plan!" Tannya said. She was about to pump her fist in the air. I put my hand out, shoved her fist down, and gave her a warning look.

"I think we should call Rex!" Miss Kitty said.

"Rex is busy trying to find Jodi," Val said. "He's probably miles away."

Suddenly the door to my bedroom opened up. It startled us and we all jumped. "What is all the excitement about? You guys are loud," Derek said. He walked towards us to the dining room. He was sleepy eyed, and in a t-shirt and lounge pants.

"Honey, you're awake," I said and walked up to him.

"Thank God he's here," Val said to me.

Derek looked at me with confusion. "What's going on *now*? Haven't we all had enough excitement for one day? What is that on the table?" he asked with a finger point.

BAM! The front door flew open. We all jumped, and Miss Kitty let out a high-pitched scream that lasted until she ran out of breath.

Standing in the doorway were Scooter and Wayde, both with pistols pointed at us.

25

"Scooter Potter, what the hell?" Tannya scolded. She got up out of her chair. "Don't you knock? You think you can just invite yourself in without someone's permission?" she yelled. We all stood there in shock as Tannya marched towards him. "You son of a bitch!" she said with a finger point. "How dare you! I know what you've been up to. I know about your secrets. I've seen the bat cave you live in, in *my* shed!" She was right up in his face pointing her finger in his chest.

He looked scared. Wayde looked scared too. Pepper got up and sauntered towards them. I feared they'd shoot him so I acted like I fully controlled him. "Pepper! Down! No attack. NO ATTACK! Sit!" Thankfully he stopped dead in his tracks and sat.

Tannya kept right on going. By this time we were all on our feet. Derek had stepped in front of me but I could still see. I felt something poking in my back. It was hard. Miss Kitty had stepped up behind me. "Here," she whispered. "Give it to Derek."

I reached one hand behind my back and grabbed what felt like a small gun. I never turned my head to look at it, because I didn't want Wayde and Scooter to notice. I had no idea how Miss Kitty had gotten it out of her purse so quickly. I was shaking so much I almost dropped it. I wasn't used to handling guns. I was so scared. They were done playing games and were serious now, yet Tannya didn't seem to care at all. All that pent-up anger at Scooter was coming out right now. Not the best timing, but it seemed to be working to calm them down a little.

"You're stealing phone and internet and cable TV from me," Tannya kept yelling. "Do you know what they do to you if you steal cable TV? Do you? Are you crazy? You trespassing jackass. I hate you! I'm going to have you arrested for all of that! I hope they throw the book at you!" she screamed.

"Tannya, I'm sorry! I did it because you threw me out. I missed you and wanted to be close to you. And, well, who's going to watch the house for you and make sure you're safe way out there by yourself?"

"No one! You left me. You chose drugs over me! I threw you out because you were dangerous! I asked you to get help and you wouldn't. You don't *get* to be by me anymore."

"I know. But, baby, I've changed. I don't do drugs anymore. I've been clean for almost a year. I've been watching over you and the house and trying to be there for you . . . even though you didn't know it," he said sincerely.

Tannya looked at him, stunned. She shook her head and dropped her finger.

"Here," I whispered to Derek and poked him with the gun. He reached his hand back and took it. I could feel him fumbling with it, but I kept my eyes on Wayde and Scooter. He was probably trying to figure out what kind it was and where the safety was.

"OKAY! I think we've gotten a bit off track!" Wayde said. "Ladies and . . . whoever the fuck you are," he said referring to Derek. "We need the packages you stole. They're ours, and we want them back *now*!"

No one said anything.

"NOW!" he screamed out of frustration.

"Whoa! Gentleman . . . I think you've got the wrong house. These ladies are just having a girl's night in, and telling stories. We have no idea what you're talking about. We're more than willing to help you find what you're missing, but we don't need guns for that. So put the guns away and tell us what you lost."

I was very impressed with Derek's demeanor. He was holding it together really well.

"Who the hell are you?" Wayde asked.

"I'm staying here. The owner is my friend. Who are *you*? *You're* the one who kicked in the door. Why don't you tell us who you are and what you need," Derek said calmly.

"What, now you're in charge?" Wayde teased.

Tannya stepped back by us. Derek continued talking. "We're more than willing to work with you. Just tell me who you are and what you're here for."

"I'm Wayde, and I'm here for the stolen packages."

Derek studied him. I was surprised as hell that Derek just got him to do exactly what he'd asked.

"Okay, Wayde, I'm Derek, Sara's boyfriend. I don't think we know which packages you're talking about. What's this about stolen treasure that Tannya keeps referring to?"

"She thinks it's her treasure but it's not. The packages stolen were mine."

"So where are hers then?"

"I don't know! I didn't have anything to do with her treasure. But these women stole packages from my ship, and I want them back."

"Okay," Derek said calmly. "Ladies, is this true? Did you take this man's stuff from his ship?" He carefully eyed each of us. He tucked the gun in the back of his pants and turned away from Wayde and Scooter.

"What happened was, they fired a cannon at Sara's pontoon and broke the awning. We knew in this LARP, if you break anything that belongs to anyone else you need to replace it or compensate for it. Well, they didn't want to compensate for it so we took a few packages to cover the cost of the damage," Val said. "But now they're gone. The other LARP group must have taken them."

Wayde huffed. "You fired at us first! And you blew up my dock!"

"Whaaat?" We all said in unison with confused expressions.

"Look, you're more than welcome to look around. We didn't steal your treasure. I don't know who did, but it wasn't us. We're willing to help you out though. Feel free . . ." I said gesturing my arms open.

"Take a look around if you want. Derek can escort you around, just stay out of my private laundry areas."

Everyone looked at me. "Go ahead, we have nothing to hide," I said and sat back down at the table. Tannya sat down too, and then Val and Miss Kitty.

Derek looked a bit freaked out. "Well, gentleman, would you like the tour?" he asked unsurely. "I'd appreciate if you'd put the guns away though."

Scooter put his gun away and slipped off his shoes. He was ready for the tour. He looked happy at the opportunity. He stood there proud, with his hands on his hips and set the gun down by his shoes. This guy had to be the world's worst criminal. We were all in shock at how soft he suddenly was. Wayde stood there dumbfounded. He smacked Scooter on the back of his head and told him to bring his gun with. Wayde left his shoes on for the tour.

"Feel free to look in rooms, behind doors and cupboards. Just don't make a mess, okay?" I said.

"Okay," Scooter answered. Wayde shot him a look. Derek led them into the kitchen first, where they looked in all the cupboards and drawers, and then moved down the hall to the bathroom. The washer and dryer were in the closet at the end of the hall. The doors on it were closed.

When they stepped into the bathroom Tannya fist bumped me. "Good plan, they'll never find it, and they'll stop bothering us," she said.

"Yeah, good thinking. Then tomorrow we can take it to a buyer and get cash instead," Miss Kitty said. "That's much easier to hide."

I looked at Val. She didn't seem on board with it. I think seeing Wayde again was pulling at her heart strings.

I heard them come out of the spare bedroom and stop at the laundry closet. The doors opened and then the cupboards above the washer and dryer opened and shut. Then, like the polite gentleman he was, Scooter closed the closet doors.

We all grinned. "Now we just have to get through my closet. There are a few packages under my winter sweaters folded up on the floor." I crossed my fingers. I could hear a few drawers slide in and out, then my closet opened and a few seconds later closed.

"Well, guys, that's the house. There's no basement, just a crawlspace," Derek told them.

"We like to see that too!" Wayde demanded.

Derek showed them the way. A few moments later they were back. The crawl space was completely empty so it only took a second to realize there was no treasure in there.

"Well, boys, I guess this was all just a misunderstanding. Sorry you wasted your time," I said as I stood to meet them.

Scooter was already putting his shoes back on as Wayne angrily said, "This isn't over. I don't know where you girls hid it, but I know that you have it. I'll be in contact tomorrow. Get the treasure ready. We *will* be getting it back. You have twelve hours." Then the two stepped out and slammed the door.

Derek turned the lock then faced me and gave me a look that I'd never seen before. I was a bit nervous. "Sara, I told you to stay out of trouble and keep out of this mess."

Uh-oh, the horns were growing. "Excuse me? I didn't ask for your advice or your help. We can handle this ourselves," I snapped and put my hands on my hips.

"Really?"

"Yeah, really. We're strong independent women!"

"Oh, yes, I can see that," he said with a sarcastic tone. "Then *you* will need this, not me," he said and reached behind him. He pulled the gun out of his pants and looked at it. It was a tiny, bright pink pistol. He looked at it with disgust and handed it to Miss Kitty.

She took it and put it back in her purse. "I'm sure you have a permit for that," Derek said to her.

"Pffft, somewhere at home in a file, I'm sure," she said with a nonsense hand wave.

Derek rolled his eyes and rubbed his head. "You need to call Rex."

"Why? They already left."

"Just do it. He's trying to solve a case, and in case you forgot, there is woman being held against her will out there somewhere."

"Who? Jodi? I doubt it's against her will. She probably likes the action and the attention. If they untied her, she'd probably jump on them first chance she got!" I slapped my hand over my mouth. Whoops, might have gone too far there. I was surprised by my venomous words towards her. Guess the happy pill was working. "Okay, I'll call him," I said and went for my phone.

They all watched me while I put the phone to my ear. I felt like they were judging me. Maybe I was too harsh. I didn't care. I was tired of being the smart, quiet, nice, morally right one. I just wanted to scream and break something.

"Hello."

"Hey, Rex, its Sara."

"What's up? You okay?"

"Yes, I'm fine. I've been home for a while. Just a wash and a few replacement stitches. Then I had two IV bags and some cookies and juice and now I'm great. Well, except that Wayde and Scooter Potter were just over here."

"Really? What happened? Is Derek there? What did they want?"

"Woah! Slow down there, robo-cop. Yeah, yeah, Derek's still here. They just wanted a tour of the place to look for some packages they think we stole," I said and winked at the girls.

Derek was looking at me with wrinkled brows. He went to the table and picked up my water glass and smelled it, and then took a sip. When he looked back at me, I stuck my tongue out at him. He puffed air out his nose, and squeezed his brows together.

"Are they gone now?"

"Yes, they didn't find anything so they left. They said that we had twelve hours to get the treasure together and that they'd be in touch in the morning."

"All right, I'm going to swing by Wayde's house again. Let me know if you hear from them again."

"All righty!" I sang and hung up. "He's going to drive over to Wayde's and see if he can find them. He said to keep him posted."

"Fine, I've got a killer migraine. I'm going back to bed," Derek said. "Happy to be of assistance," he said and gave us a fake hat tip.

"Thank you!"

"Thanks, Derek."

"We appreciate it, Derek" they all said to his back as he walked down the hall. He waved one arm over his head and shut the door.

I gave them all a look. "Whatever! We didn't need him. We can totally do this by ourselves."

"I really think we should go to bed," Val said. "By the sounds of it, we're going to have another long day tomorrow."

"Do you think they're going home?" Miss Kitty asked.

"No," I said. "They're not that dumb."

"All right. Well, let's all meet at Morning Glory tomorrow for breakfast and see what happens," Tannya said. "I have to work starting at six, but I bet I can get someone to cover for me later if I need to." Miss Kitty offered Val a wing of her house. She'd have her own bathroom and bedroom, and she told her she'd love the company. Aunt Val said she'd love that. I offered for her to stay with me, too, but she wanted to stay in the mansion. She still had all her stuff in the car so it was just as easy.

I walked to them to the door and shut and locked it behind them. I fed Faith, scooped her litter box and took the kitchen garbage out. Then I swept and washed my bathroom and kitchen floors.

After that I scoured the shower and tub . . . and the sink . . . and the toilet. By that time, I was finally starting to feel tired. Stupid happy pills!

After I brushed my teeth, I changed into my pajamas and climbed into bed. I laid there and tossed and turned. I couldn't sleep. I still had way too much energy. I watched the clock until 2:30 a.m., when finally Derek rolled over.

"Seriously? What's the matter with you? Aren't you tired? You had a really long day. You should be sleeping like a baby."

"Sorry, I can't sleep," I said and sat up. I flipped the light on next to the bed. "Are you tired?"

"I don't know. For the last half-hour I've been laying here awake waiting for you to finally lie still. At least the headache's gone."

"Good. So are you up for an adventure?"

"What?"

"Come on, you only live once. Come with me on an adventure."

He studied my face. "Now?"

"Yes."

"Wha wha . . . what kind of adventure?" he asked and rubbed his eyes. He sat up a little straighter.

"Just trust me. There's something that I want to do. Come with me, please."

"Umm, okay. Do I need to get dressed?"

"Yes, brush your teeth and throw on some warm clothes. We're going outside, but no one else will see us. We'll leave in five minutes," I told him. Then I whipped the covers off and ran to the bathroom. I brushed my teeth too and then went back to my room and got dressed. I passed Derek in the hall. He looked at me like he was amused.

"Do I get to know?"

"Nope, but you'll figure it out soon enough."

After he was ready, I went to the entryway and told him to put on his shoes on. He did and then we grabbed our jackets. I grabbed a bottle of wine from the fridge and the keys.

Outside it was quiet. There was no wind, and the city noise was far away. The moon was big and bright and high in the sky. It reflected beautifully off the lake. When Derek veered off towards the Jeeps I whistled. "Hey, sexy, it's this way." I made my way towards the pontoon.

"A boat ride?"

"Not exactly," I said with a wink. "We're getting on the pontoon and going on a short trip."

He shot me a look. "Sara . . ."

"Shh!" I said and placed my finger over his lips. "You don't get to be in charge. I'm the captain now, and what I say goes."

He stopped talking and a sly smile formed on his lips.

"Now, untie us and have a seat," I said. "Sorry about the mess."

He looked around and shook his head.

I drove us slowly over to the ship. I was hoping it was still above water. It was, but I swear one side looked lower than the other. I didn't say anything to Derek, though. I didn't want it to ruin my plans.

"So what exactly are we doing?" he asked.

"Well, when was the last time you were on pirate ship?" I asked with a grin.

"I guess, never."

"Well, that's about to change, baby!" I was so excited. This was going to be fun.

"Sara, I think this is a bad idea," he said. "How do you know there aren't any people on it?" he asked as we approached.

"There's no way they'd risk coming back here. I don't see any lights, and the rowboat is still over there, too," I told him. "I want a tour. I've never been on a pirate ship before either," I said slowly, almost begging.

I stopped the pontoon, and Derek grabbed the rope ladder and held us steady until I tied us off. I slipped the keys into my pocket. Then I went back by my seat and grabbed both the wine and an electric lantern from under one of the seats.

"All right, climb aboard, matey!" I told Derek and started up the ladder. When I got to the top I took a quick peek around. There was no sign of anyone. "Come on up. Nobody's home."

I looked over the edge while he climbed. "This is trespassing, you know."

"Really? Nah, I don't think so. I think this ship was built for a LARP, and I am part of a LARP. I *am* new, so maybe I was confused about the rules," I told him with a wink. "Who's going to tell anyway? I know I won't."

He got to the top of the rope and climbed aboard. "Sara, you're very . . . adventurous lately," he said with a look of concern. I knew he meant moody. "What's going on with you?"

"Nothing. Everything! I don't know. Just look at this!" I stepped back on the deck of the ship and spun in a circle with my arms out, still holding a flashlight and bottle of wine. "Gosh, Derek, doesn't it feel good to just be free? Doesn't it feel good not having to worry about getting caught or behaving or doing the right thing? It's amazing!" I said with a huge smile. "I've never felt this free. I've always had to answer to someone for every action I ever made—to my parents, my husband, my teachers, my boss, my friends. But lately," I said, stopping and relaxing with a deep exhale. "Lately, it's just been *me*. I'm living for *me*. And I'm enjoying it."

"I hope I have some part in that," Derek said putting his hands on my hips and pulling me close.

"You do. A small part for now, but a part nonetheless," I said quietly. "I want you in my life. I just don't want to rush anything. I like where we're at."

"I like this, too. You never cease to surprise me, that's for sure." I tipped my head and smiled. "Like tonight, for instance. It's the middle of the night, and I'm on pirate ship with you, trespassing!" I leaned forward and kissed him.

I lifted up the wine bottle. "I didn't bring glasses. I hope you don't mind sharing the bottle."

"Not at all."

I twisted the top of the bottle.

"Oh, the expensive kind, eh?"

"Hey, it's not in a box. And just for the record, some pretty good wines come in boxes, and twist tops as well," I told him with a tip of my chin.

"I'll take your word on that."

I smiled and took a swig, then passed it to him. He took a drink too.

"Mmm, not too bad."

I grabbed his hand. "Come on, let's go check this out!" I led him across the boat. There wasn't much to see up on the deck except the cannon, which was much bigger than mine. We went down the ladder to the lower deck. Down there we found a bathroom smaller than those on an airplane and a tiny kitchen. It had a sink, a hot plate and a pizza oven. "So there must be electricity?" I questioned.

Derek found a socket and plugged in the hot plate but nothing happened. I swung the light around and noticed a switch on the wall. I flipped it up and nothing happened with that either. "I've never noticed lights on it at night before," I stated.

"This might explain why," Derek said and picked up a book off the card table to our left. *Electrical Work for Dummies*. There were four folding chairs around the table and some empty take-out food containers. We both giggled. I heard a trickling of water.

"Let's go see how big the leak is," I told Derek and walked out the doorway.

"The leak?"

"Yeah, this ship has a bit of damage."

"Damage from what?"

"Um, I'm not sure how bad the damage is."

"That's not what I asked, Sara," he said, in a fatherly tone.

Outside of the kitchen and the tiny little bathroom the rest of the area was open. We saw a bed on metal legs that looked like it would fold up like a lawn chair. It had a blow-up mattress on it and foam on top of that. "That's a nice bed, better than I thought we'd find," I told him.

Along the outside walls of the boat was a built-in bench. I raised the light to see farther. The sound of trickling was getting closer. "There we go."

We found the place that had been hit. It was a small area. It looked like they had used spray foam to fill the cracks in the wood.

On the ground were six cans of spray foam, some plastic on a roll, duct tape and some scraps of wood. The wood looked untouched. It was still neatly piled. There were a few pieces of duct tape on the ship wall, too. That's where the water was trickling in. There was a large puddle on the floor in front of us so we couldn't get any closer. "This ship is sinking." Derek said, pointing out the obvious.

"How long do you think that'll take?" I asked.

"I have no idea. A while I suppose, a day, maybe more."

"Well, that gives us plenty of time," I said. I leaned forward and kissed him again. He kissed me back and then grabbed the wine from my hand and took another drink. He passed it back to me, and I took a sip. We stared into each other eyes for a moment then he took the lantern from my hand and walked halfway across the ship and set it on the bench. I took another sip while I waited for him to come back. The placement of the lantern gave us a dim glow.

He took the bottle from my hand and set in on the bench close to us. Then he came back to me, took my face in his hands, and kissed me passionately. It lasted a couple minutes. He pulled back and slowly unzipped my winter coat and laid it on the floor. He removed his too and laid it below mine. Then he knelt and pulled me down gently to my knees and kissed me again. Our bodies' activities kept us warm inside the ship, even though it was cold outside. I was certain that, if the ship had had glass windows, we would have fogged them up.

26

Thirty minutes later we were chilled to the bone and on the pontoon heading back to my place. At the dock Derek tied up, and I put the light back under the seat. He grabbed my hand and walked with me to the house. "That's was . . . a fun adventure," he said.

"Sure was. That's one to check off the bucket list," I said with a wink.

Pepper met us at the door and needed to go out. Derek waited for him while I crawled back into my pajamas and under the covers. I was freezing. A few minutes later Derek joined me. He cuddled nice and close and whispered, "So did the invasion tonight make you nervous? Is that why you couldn't sleep?"

"No, I wasn't scared. I think I was just amped up on caffeine." *Or happy pills.*

I closed my eyes and fell right to sleep.

* * *

I woke to Pepper licking my hand. Derek was gone, and the room smelled like bacon. Dang, I wished I had his morning energy. I glanced at the clock—8:00. I needed to be a Morning Glory at nine to meet the girls. I rolled out of bed, took a fast shower, threw on some clothes and padded into the kitchen. Derek was just setting plates out. "Morning, sweetness," he said.

"Morning," I mumbled and went straight for the coffee.

"What are you plans for the day?"

"I'm meeting the girls at nine. We have to . . . do some stuff." *Like figure out what to do with the treasure in my washer and dryer.*

"So tell me, Sara, do you have their treasure?" he asked me as he set the pancakes and eggs on the table.

"Umm, are we on the record?" I said slyly.

"This isn't my jurisdiction," he said with a shoulder shrug.

"I know, but I'm not sure I want to share the . . . the details of my LARP's activities with . . . an outsider." He set the bacon down and sat at the table across from me. And gave me a look. "Ya see, there are certain rules we're expected to follow. I'd hate to get in trouble with the group for divulging too much information to someone not in the group."

He looked at me with a serious look.

"I take the fifth." I reached for the bacon. "Breakfast looks great. Thanks for making it," I said, trying to change the subject.

"You know how I feel about this. I'll leave it at that. You're going to get in over your head. The guys who broke in here had guns. The people they're involved with took Jodi. They aren't messing around. This isn't a game, and you know that."

"Does it bother you that they took Jodi?"

Derek frowned at me. "Yes, Sara, it does. Of course, it does. I hope it bothers you, too."

I continued chewing, but my appetite was ruined. I supposed I should feel bad, but part of me didn't. "Here's how I see it," I said and set down my fork. "She came here for a reason. That reason was to cause problems between us. She drove for hours to stalk me, take pictures like a peeping tom and send them to you, to get us to break up so she can have you back. She was warned not once, but twice, to stay away and she came back again! So, ya know what, Derek, it kind of doesn't bother me. She got *herself* into this mess." I excused myself and went to get ready.

I was in the middle of blow-drying my hair when Derek knocked on the door. I opened it, and he stepped in. "Hey, sorry. I didn't mean to ruin breakfast. Your plate is still there if you're hungry. I'm going to run a few errands. I catch up with you later," he said and gave me a kiss on the cheek. "Last night was a fun adventure. Thank you," he whispered in my ear. Then he closed the door behind himself and left.

After I was ready, I went the kitchen, microwaved my plate and finished. Derek had cleaned up the kitchen already. He was so nice and so efficient that he kind of hurt my self-esteem. I grabbed a to-go mug and filled it up with coffee for the road.

I took a little detour over to Jodi's car still parked on the side of County Road 12, not far from my driveway. I pulled up behind it and got out to take a look. Yup, there was a perfect hole in the roof the size of a cannonball, which was sitting on the passenger seat.

The doors were all locked, so I grabbed a large rock from the ground with my sleeve-covered hand and broke the passenger-side window. I reached in, unlocked the door with my sleeved fingers and grabbed my cannonball. After I put it in my trunk, I got back in my Jeep and drove away. *She doesn't get to keep my ball.*

I arrived at Morning Glory at five minutes to nine. Tannya was taking an order from someone in a booth across the room. Another booth had four older men in it in the far corner. Other than that the place was empty. I bellied up to the bar and set my purse on the floor.

"Hey, girl!" Tannya said as she walked by me. "You're the first one here."

"Morning."

"Boy, you look tired. Did you have trouble sleeping last night?"

"Yeah, I only got a few hours of good sleep," I told her.

"Heeey, Sara!" Marv yelled from the window. He was sporting a big grin.

"Hi, Marv."

"Marv, get to work! I just put an order up for you," Tannya scolded.

"I just put something up too," he said with a wink.

I put my head down in my hands.

"Marv!" Tannya yelled. He disappeared from view. Tannya shook her head. "I think he's got a bit of a crush."

"Great."

The door opened and everyone in the room looked at who was arriving—my aunt Val and Miss Kitty.

"Morning," I said as they walked in. Miss Kitty had her large dog purse with her.

Aunt Val wrapped an arm around me. "How are you doing? You look tired." she said.

"Thanks, I keep hearing that. I am tired. I only got a few hours last night."

"It's the pills. They keep you up. You can't take them that late at night. I tried to tell you that," Miss Kitty said with an "I told you so" tone.

"It's fine. I'll just take a nap later," I said with a half-grin.

"Did you two sleep well?" I asked them.

They both said yes. I looked down at Miss Kitty's purse. Smoochy Poo was peeking out at me. I stuck my finger in the vent, and she licked it. She was starting to like me. Tannya came over and stuck her finger in too, but Smoochy backed up and growled.

"Smoochy! You know me! Stop growling like you ain't never seen me before. Ya know, if you were a nice dog I might sneak you a treat from the kitchen. But you ain't getting no treat now."

"Did someone say treats from the kitchen?" Marv asked from the window.

"Marv!" Tannya scolded. "Quit harassing the patrons."

"Does anyone need anything?" Tannya asked.

Val and Miss Kitty hadn't eaten yet so they ordered a meal and some coffee.

I ordered a juice and a caramel roll. I figured the stress from yesterday should've pre-burned those calories. Tannya got the food out to the guests in the back booth, and then came over and stood by us. "Does anyone have any thoughts on what we should do now?"

"I think we should find a buyer and get the cash for the treasure and split it," Miss Kitty said.

"I agree!" Tannya said with way too much enthusiasm.

"We can't," Val reasoned. "They're stolen goods. We'd get thrown in jail for that. Trust me, I know."

"So, what then? We control this right now. Only the bad guys know we have the treasure and they want it back. And it's no good to us," I said.

"Maybe we should use it as a bargaining chip to get Jodi released," Val offered.

We all rolled our eyes in unison.

"Come on, you guys. I know you all hate her, but I also know you are good people. I'm willing to bet that all of you said a prayer for her last night," she said with raised eyebrows and tight lips.

We all exchanged glances. Miss Kitty and Tannya looked down like they were guilty. Then they all looked at me.

"What? I didn't sleep much last night. I was busy thinking about other stuff. She was the last thing on my mind," I said.

"Liar," Val said. She was half right. I could care less about Jodi, but I didn't want my life or property to have anything to do with her getting hurt.

I stuck my tongue out at her.

"So, what now, we just wait for them to show again?" Miss Kitty asked.

"Yeah. How do we know where they are?" Val asked. "Was there any action on the ship last night?"

Yes, yes there was. "No, I didn't see anything and the house was dark this morning too. I think the ship's slowly sinking, though. I swear it looks like it's tipping slightly to one side."

"It probably is," Val said. "They tried to fix it, but I knew it wouldn't hold."

"Well, Tannya talked to them from her phone earlier. Don't you have their number still?" Miss Kitty asked.

"Only Captain Morgan's, but he's still in jail. I'm sure Rex took his phone when he booked him."

The bells on the door rang as Rex came in—in uniform and with business on his face. "Good morning, ladies. I'm glad you're all here."

We all smiled and returned the greeting. We spun around on our bar stools to face him when he came in.

"Have any of you heard from the guys involved?" he asked.

We shook our heads.

"No visits, no calls . . . nothing?"

"No," I said. "They said we had twelve hours yesterday and that was eleven hours ago. They just said they'd contact us."

"We were just discussing our options," Tannya said.

"Options? So you *do* have the missing treasure?" Rex asked with a very serious look.

"I . . . ah . . . umm. What?"

"When I questioned Rick and John, they said you stole treasure from them. Did you?"

Tannya looked at us, not knowing what she should answer.

Val finally spoke up. "Yes, we did. That's how you win the game. This is Live Action Role-Playing, and the theme for this one is pirates. Tannya here was going to join their team and contributed treasure to their collection. Then they decided not to let her join and continued on without her, so, as the third acting LARP group in this play, we stole that back, and some of Wayde's, too. We were trying to win the game. I think they're just mad we won."

Rex squinted at her and then at the rest of us. "I hope you realize this is no longer a game. They're holding a young woman captive, against her will. Game or not, that's illegal. Jodi Vagerna is not a part of any game."

"Do you know anything on Jodi's whereabouts yet?" I asked.

"No. And Rick and John are not being helpful either. They claim to have no idea where Butch took Jodi, or what he plans to do with her."

"Butch? So that must be Flying Dutchman's real name," Miss Kitty mused.

"Yes. I'd imagine he wants to make a trade, the treasure for Jodi."

We all nodded. "When he contacts you, and it sounds like he will shortly, I want to know about it. I *will* be there when anything further happens." He started to turn to leave, then looked at us again. "That's an order," he said and then walked out.

"Boy, he was in a mood," I said.

"Yeah, he's really upset by this," Val said. "I feel bad."

"Me too," Miss Kitty said.

"ORDER UP!" Marv yelled from the kitchen. Tannya got our food and set it in front of us, then went to the other two tables and refilled coffee mugs. When she was done she sat next to us.

"I can't believe Wayde's been sitting on four million dollars. Why wouldn't he leave the country?" Val said between bites.

"I don't know. Maybe he was waiting for his mom to pass, and then got too wrapped up in the ship to leave. He's a nice guy," Val said, looking a bit heartbroken.

"He killed Mike. He's a murderer," I reminded her.

"I know. I hate knowing that. The guy I knew would have never done that to anyone."

"You didn't truly know him. He did it. He said he did. Whatever you're feeling for him right now you need to ignore, because it was all based on a lie," I told her.

She put her fork down and was having a hard time finishing the bite in her mouth. "I know," she said in tears. "I just miss him. I miss the guy I thought he was. I feel like I lost a good friend."

I leaned over and put an arm around her. "It's okay, Aunt Val. We're going to get through this mess together. We'll find you a man who's good and honest."

"Yeah, and not one who kills people," Tannya said and reached out and rubbed her arm.

We all looked at her funny. "I mean . . . well . . . I'm not good at mushy talk. But I feel bad. You deserve better than that. He's a jerk."

Just then the bells on the door jingled and in walked Wayde and Scooter.

27

Wayde and Scooter both wore jeans, sweatshirts, and baseball hats. "Morning, ladies," Wayde said. "I thought I might find you here." We all turned on our stools again to face them. "Did you ladies bring my stuff with you?"

No one answered. I wasn't ready for this. I'd thought we'd meet somewhere and make an exchange for Jodi. But these two weren't even *with* Butch. They were against him. That just caused more issues. "Well? Where are my things? Just hand them over, and we'll be on our way," he demanded.

"We don't have it with us," Val said.

"Where is it?" Scooter asked.

"Where's Jodi?" I asked.

"Who?" Wayde asked.

"Jodi, the girl from the raft," Scooter told him.

"Oh, I don't know!" Wayde said with a shrug.

"Well, Butch took her last night and she hasn't been seen since, and he wants the treasure too," Miss Kitty announced.

"Sorry, boys. Until you find Butch and Jodi, there'll be no treasure," I said. "We need to ensure her safety and release before we give anything back to you."

"Well, we don't know where they are. What are we supposed to do about it?" Wayde said with palms up.

"I don't know. But we're waiting here until we get further instructions from Butch and we know Jodi's alive and unharmed."

"Cut the shit," Wayde said.

"No, Wayde, *you* cut the shit. Your entire life has been a lie," Val snapped. Then she turned away from him on her stool. He looked surprised by her words. I was pretty sure I could see a hint of empathy in his eyes.

"Look, we can't give you the treasure right now. We have it in a secure spot until you're able to talk to Butch and Jodi. When you talk to him, give us a call, and we'll meet you for an exchange. And if we hear from him first, we'll do the same for you. You and Val have each other's numbers, so we'll wait until one of us hears from him," I said and spun around on my stool.

I looked straight ahead and could see Marv's head in the window. He gave me an approving nod and wink. I hid my smile. It felt good being the boss.

"Hey, Scooter!" Marv said with a wave.

"Hey, Marv!" Scooter answered. Tannya shot Marv a look and pointed at him warningly.

They stood there for a moment before anyone said anything. "If neither of us hears from him by noon, the deal's off. I'll find you and I WILL get my things back. The game's over. At noon, this ends." He turned to the door and left. Scooter followed.

"Asshole," Val muttered and then looked back at her food.

"I certainly hope that Butch calls soon. What the hell are we going to do at noon if he doesn't?" Tannya asked.

"He'll call," Miss Kitty said. "He wants the treasure."

The other waitress came walking out from the back hall. She was tying on her apron. "Good morning," she said to Tannya.

"Hey, girl. I've got some stuff I need to take care of today. Do you think you can hold down the fort if I cut out now?"

"Sure, go ahead. It's never too busy anyway. You go and have fun!" she said with a big smile.

"Thanks, I'll close out my tables before I go," Tannya told her and then walked away. We all finished eating and paid Tannya. We decided to go back to Miss Kitty's house to wait. Wayde could easily come to my house, but hopefully he didn't know where Miss Kitty lived. We felt we'd be safer there.

Tannya rode with me, leaving her car at Morning Glory since I'd have to come past there on my way home again anyway. Aunt Val rode with Miss Kitty. Her car and things were still at Miss Kitty's house.

Inside the house Miss Kitty got us all bottled water and put some snacks out on the island counter we'd gathered around. We talked a bit about Miss Kitty's plans to renovate the mansion. She didn't need to, though. Everything was less than nine years old and still very tasteful and modern looking. She said she was bored with it and wanted to change some things to help erase the memory of when her husband lived there. They had divorced last year when she found out he'd been cheating on her. He was also in trouble for drugs and involved in the death of a young woman who overdosed. He was in jail, and the house was hers. She had lots of money, so she didn't care about the expense.

The doorbell rang. We all jumped. Miss Kitty hopped up and down and clapped her hands. "Eeeek!"

She took off to the door after we all exchanged glances. She returned with a small box and a grin. Quickly she tore it open and pulled out a black hoody zip-up sweater embroidered with "GUN POWDER GERTIE." "Just as I promised," she said.

"Ah! Thanks so much! I love it!" Val said and gave her a hug. She threw it on over her shirt.

Tannya's phone rang. We got still. She pulled it out of her pocket.

"Hello?" she said and put it on speaker.

"Tannya, or should I say Captain Tight Ass?"

"This is she," Tannya said, tipping her chin in to the air and puffing out her chest.

"This is Flying Ductchman—" the speaker started.

"You mean Butch?" she snapped.

Silence. Miss Kitty fist bumped Tannya. Val raised an eyebrow.

"Look, Butch, I know why you're calling."

"Good, then let's make this easy. Leave the treasure outside of the house your friend owns on the lake, and we'll pick it up. Then this is all over and if you want you can claim the win."

"Screw you, Butch. First of all, you ain't in charge here. I am. Secondly, we wanna know where Jodi is. Let me talk to her so I know she's okay."

"Oh, I see. NOW you care about her?"

"No, we don't. But we do want her released, unharmed. We don't want her life to have any link to ours after today. And, well, if you harm her in any way this could come back on us since we were involved in the game too."

"All right, we'll trade."

"Let me talk to her. Put her on the phone," Tannya said and looked at us. We all nodded to let her know she was doing a good job.

"Fine." There was some rustling on his end. Then we heard him tell her to say hello.

". . . hello?" Jodi said, sounding weak.

"Are you okay? Did he hurt you at all?"

"No, he hasn't hurt me, but he won't let me go!" she said angrily.

There was more rustling, and then Butch came back on the line. "There, see, she's fine. Now I want the treasure. RIGHT NOW! I don't have time for these games."

"Well, we have an interesting situation," Tannya told him calmly. "Wayde and Scooter also want the treasure. So you three can figure that out at the meeting site. We'll return the treasure to you three. In return we want Jodi, unharmed. Meet us at the corner of County Roads 12 and 9 in thirty minutes. No guns, no games. There's an old farmhouse there. Pull off the road back by the red barn. We'll meet you there," she said. Then she got a huge grin on her face and said, "This message will self-destruct in three seconds . . . BOOM!" she yelled in to the phone and hung up. She set the phone down and busted out laughing.

Tannya was doubled over, laughing so hard she could hardly breathe and couldn't catch her breath. "I've always wanted to say that! HA HA HA!" she was laughing at her own, sad joke. It was contagious and made all of us start up. She started to collect herself and was wiping her tears away. We were all laughing hard at her. The joke wasn't that funny, but her laugh sure was. We finished our waters and drove in two cars to my house to collect the treasure. I thought it would be a good idea to call Rex and let him know the plan.

"Hey," he answered.

"Hi. I thought I'd let you know we have a bit of a plan." I wasn't really sure where to start.

"Okay . . ."

"So it turns out we do have some treasure . . . that we hid . . ."

He sighed. "And?"

"And, well, we're going to give it back and get Jodi for it in a trade."

"You know where Jodi is?" Ugh, I hated his worried tone.

"Yeah, but more importantly, I know where Butch, Wayde, and Scooter Potter are going to be in about a half-hour."

"Great job, Sara! Where are you meeting them?" he asked eagerly.

"At the old farm house on the corner of County 12 and 9. Tannya told them to meet us at the red barn."

"When?"

"In twenty-five minutes."

"Okay, I'll be out there with back-up and we'll stay out of sight until the exchange is made. Then you girls need to get out of the way, because we'll be making arrests. Just give them the treasure and work with them. They just want to get out of town, so I think they'll fully cooperate with you. It should be quick."

"Okay, sounds good. I'll text you when we get close."

"So where did you hide the treasure?"

"Um . . . in a safe place."

"Uh huh . . . okay, call me in a bit."

When we got to my place, Derek was there. "Hello," he said to us from his seat at the kitchen table. He was reading the paper and had a coffee and box of caramel rolls in front of him. "I think you're right, Sara. The ship's sinking."

"NO!" I said and rushed with the girls to the window. The ship was still above water but noticeably tipping to the back left side. "Bummer. I kind of liked the ship," I said sadly. At first I'd thought it was annoying and sort of an eyesore, but now I was used to it, and I liked the excitement of having it out there. Plus, it made a great conversation piece.

"That's so sad," Val said.

"Maybe we can have someone fix it," Miss Kitty offered.

"Can we keep it?" Tannya asked. We all turned our heads to her. "Seriously! Wayde's probably going to jail, so what's he need it for? If we fix it, maybe it can be ours."

We were all quietly pondering the idea until Buzz Kill joined in the conversation. "Ladies," Derek said, "You can't just take it over. It's sinking. Fixing that would take the service of a skilled marine engineer. We don't have any around here. It would cost a ton, and the boat wasn't skillfully built in the first place. Plus, you have to get it in off the water at summer's end and store it somewhere."

Everyone got quiet and until Derek changed the subject. "So what are you ladies up to now? What brings you by?"

"We're picking up the treasure and trading it for Jodi in about twenty minutes," Val blurted out.

"What? Where? Did you talk to Rex about this?" Derek asked standing.

"I called him a minute ago. He's on his way with back-up and is going to hide out until we make the exchange. Then we'll get out of the way so they can make arrests," I told him.

"And he's okay with this?" Derek asked me, with concerned eyes.

"I didn't give him a choice. I told him what was going on and the plan we'd made. He'll be there to watch over us."

"Well, that's nice of him," he said sarcastically. "Look, Sara, I'm not okay with you being used as bait. That hasn't gone well in the past. I'm not going to let it happen again."

"Well, lucky for you," my evil twin started, "you're not in charge. You don't need to be there, and you don't need to be involved."

"Sara."

"What, Derek? This isn't your jurisdiction, remember?" I said and stomped off to the laundry closet. I got a glance at Aunt Val's face as I passed by her. She looked surprised. Maybe I had been too harsh. I was just tired of being bossed around. No matter what I did, someone wasn't going to like it.

"Sara," he said, following me to the end of the hall. He took my arm gently and turned me to face him. "What's up with you lately? I'm concerned about your safety, but you don't seem to care about anyone but yourself," he said in almost a whisper. "I didn't drive over here for the weekend to be treated like this." His eyes were full of hurt. Hurt that I knew I had caused. I didn't mean to be mad at him. I was just mad that all of the shit going on had to do with his rotten ex. I just wanted her out of my life, *our* life.

"If you go, I'm coming with you," he told me and walked away.

"Fine. Sorry. We'll leave in five minutes." It was a half-assed apology, but I wasn't very good at them, so that's all he got.

"Fine," he said and walked into our room. I opened up the hall closet and the girls came around the corner.

"Girl, you're in a mood. He didn't deserve that," Tannya said. I looked at her and nodded. I was disappointed in myself too. And leave it to Tannya to tell me exactly what she thought. I loved her for that, but some days I didn't need the reminder.

"I know," I said quietly and went to work on the treasure. There were a lot of little packages. "I'll go get some garbage bags," I said and walked away.

After I shook the bag open, the girls piled in the packages from the washer. I tied that one off and got a second and third bag for the rest. The third bag was only half-full. "I have more in my room. I'll get them," I said and opened the door.

Derek was pulling on a sweatshirt. I caught a glimpse of his gun in his holster underneath it. It gave me the chills. I caught his eye but didn't mention seeing it. I took the bag to the closet and grabbed the packages from under my sweaters. Then we walked back out to the entryway. We slipped on our jackets and piled back in the vehicles. I had the three bags in the back of the Jeep.

Derek rode with me in the Jeep, and Val and Tannya rode with Miss Kitty. We pulled in the driveway of the old farmhouse and parked so we were backed up to the barn. There was a rotten, half-collapsed house to our right, and a wooden shed about the same size as the barn to the left, but that one had a sliding door that faced the driveway. Miss Kitty backed in next to us. I didn't see Rex, so I texted him.

Here.

He texted back: *We're behind the shed. Two cars, me and Johnson.*
Derek is with me, going to stay in the back of the Jeep.
Good.

We waited what felt like forever, and then up the county road we could see Butch in his truck, and Wayde and Scooter in the rusty truck behind them. Derek climbed in the back of my Jeep, behind the tinted windows. He didn't want to be seen. I exited the Jeep, and the girls met me in front of Miss Kitty's car. "We may as well get the bags out now," Val said.

Derek ducked down as we opened the hatch and got the treasure out. We set it in front of Miss Kitty's car and waited as they pulled up. Butch came up the driveway first. He pulled past us, made a U-turn and then parked right in front of our vehicles. We were trapped. I wondered if he'd done that on purpose. Wayde and Scooter parked behind him.

They opened the doors to the vehicles, and I could see that Jodi was in the backseat of the pickup truck. Her hands still looked tied behind her. Butch stepped out, and then Wayde and Scooter. They walked around the vehicle and faced us. No one said a word. Butch and Wayde crossed their arms over their chests and leaned back on the truck. Scooter noticed them and copied their attitude.

We stood all in a row on our side, Miss Kitty closest to the barn, then Aunt Val, Tannya, and me. I was closest to the Jeep. The treasure was in a pile in between Tannya and me. We were all in a tight row slightly in front of it.

"Good morning, ladies," Butch said. It was so strange to hear his normal voice and see him in normal clothes. He was clean shaven this morning, too. He looked nothing like he did a day ago. I guess that was probably smart on his end. "Well, I guess we'll load up the treasure and you can have your friend back."

"She's no friend of ours," Tannya said then spit on the ground and crossed her arms over her chest.

Everyone looked at her with surprise. I was trying to hold back my laughter. Man, she had a lot of guts. Scooter tipped his head in surprised approval at her remark. He looked proud.

Wayde answered back, "Well, she's not our friend, either. You wanted her, and now you get her."

"Fine, let her out," Tannya said.

"Actually we'll load the treasure first. Then we'll let her out."

Butch and Wayde looked at each other. The look gave me chills and suddenly made me feel very unsafe. I took a few steps back. And tripped over the treasure bags.

When I fell, all hell broke loose. Tannya turned to help me. At that very moment, Butch reached out and grabbed her by the hair and pulled her to him, simultaneously pulling a gun out of his pants and put it to her head.

"We don't want no trouble. We just want what's ours. When we get it and you get the girl, we'll be on our way," Wayde yelled.

I was still on the ground. I noticed Derek under the Jeep. He was on his belly and crossed his lips with a finger. Then he moved his hand to tell me to get back.

I moved my legs to get to a position from which I could actually stand. Butch noticed me and said, "Stay on the ground!" I froze.

I hoped that Rex was calling for more back-up. How in the world could he and Johnson—actually, I hadn't even seen Johnson yet—hold off these crazy pirates? And now they had a hostage, too.

"You two, put the bags in the bed of my truck!" Wayde said to Miss Kitty and Val.

They looked at him in disbelief.

"The keys are in my pocket!" Butch said. "You, come and get them out," he told Val, who was the closest. Val slowly walked towards him and reached her hand out towards his pocket. She made eye contact with me. She was telling me something with her eyes but I didn't know what. Then, watching her body language, I figured it out.

She positioned herself behind the side of Tannya, who was closest to me. Butch was turning his hip out to help her reach the keys and in turn he was turning further away from me. I took that as an opportunity and rolled as fast as I could under the Jeep and out the other side next to Derek.

"I can't find . . . there they are," Val said extra loud, which helped cover the sound of the gravel when I moved.

Derek mouthed, "Stay here and stay down." I nodded.

"Now put it all in the bed," Butch ordered.

"Actually," Wayde said. "You can put it in my pick-up."

I caught Derek rolling his eyes and mouthing a swear word.

All I could see were feet. I bet the faces were really good right now.

"No, *mine*," Butch said. "We'll leave here and figure out the split later, like we agreed."

"Actually," Wayde said, "the plans have changed a bit."

"Yes, they have," Scooter's voice said. I heard Tannya and Val gasp. Judging by in newfound confidence in his voice I was sure he'd just pulled a gun, too.

"Drop the guns!" Rex yelled, coming alongside the barn where Butch and Wayde could see him.

Derek moved to the back of the Jeep behind the driver's side back tire. He peeked around and then quickly pulled his head back. He mouthed that Scooter had a gun.

"Scooter, you fool! You have NOT changed," Tannya said.

"Shut up," Butch said to her. "Put the treasure my truck, and, Wayde, if you'd like, you can leave here with me. That way we know it's secure."

"Fuck you, Butch. I'm in charge. This is my treasure! You quit when the stakes got big, remember?"

"I had a family, a wife, and a kid on the way! Stealing and drugs were not the path I wanted then. I was happy to get out. But that all changed when I found out you killed Mike. Mike was like a brother to me. You took his life! And for what, a measly treasure? And now you think you're going to take it all and get away with it again? I spent the last three years of my life looking for you. And that cost me my family!"

"So what? What now?" Wayde asked.

"So, now, I walk out of here with the blood-treasure, and you go down with the ship," Butch said. "You stupid son of a bitch!"

With the bad guys distracted, I quietly crawled to the front of the Jeep and peeked. Butch was still holding Tannya with a gun to her head and blocking my view of everything except Miss Kitty and Val. I scampered across the opening and hid behind the front bumper of Butch's truck. I made it to the other side of the truck. I went to the back door.

From my knees, I reached up and slowly, silently opened the door while they argued. I cracked it open and made eye contact with Jodi. She was tied but not gagged. She looked like hell.

I put my fingers over my lips. I whispered, "Turn around. I'll untie your hands."

The rope was fat, so it was easy. Her wrists were red and bloody. I felt a slight pang of pity for her. Then I pushed the door open just a little further so she could come out. But when I did, it made a squeak.

I froze. So did Jodi. She was halfway out the door, and there was no question that the rest of the people had heard the squeak.

"What the hell?" Butch said. His face suddenly appeared in the passenger window.

"Run!" I yelled. I grabbed Jodi's hand, yanked her from the truck and ran with her towards the barn.

I could see Rex waving us towards him. I noticed another cop in the hay loft door above. He had shoved the barrel of a rifle out the doorway.

We got to the barn with Rex and Johnson covering us. No one dared shoot. Butch knew he'd go down instantly if he fired a shot at us. and Wayde and Scooter didn't really care one way or another whether Jodi was free. They knew Butch's bargaining chip was out of commission. I scrambled to the side wall, where I saw a broken board. I could see out of the little opening. Wayde grinned.

"All right, girls, now that your friend—"

"She's not our friend!" Tannya yelled.

"Fine, whatever, now that she's gone, you gotta hold up your end of the bargain. Load up that treasure."

Miss Kitty and Val hesitated.

"NOW, or your friend here gets it!" Butch yelled, shoving the barrel of his gun into Tannya's head.

Miss Kitty and Val moved toward the treasure while Wayde kept his gun pointed at the barn. Rex couldn't do a whole lot without risking the lives of the somewhat-innocent parties.

The girls tossed the treasure bags into the backseat of the truck and glared at the wannabe pirates.

"Are you happy now?" Val asked. I thought I heard the catch of a sob in her voice.

"Yup," said Wayde. "See you ladies never!"

"Scooter, face down on the ground! Drop the guns! Drop them now!" Rex said, slowly walking toward the men.

I wondered whether the girls were still in the line of fire, but I could see that Val and Miss Kitty had run and ducked down behind her car. Derek was still behind the Jeep, and Scooter was standing with his hands in the air.

Wayde and Butch both had their guns pointed at the barn. They were talking quietly to each other. Then suddenly Butch shoved Tannya hard to the ground. She crawled quickly away and hid behind the Jeep. I was so relieved.

Amid shots from Rex and Johnson, Butch got in the driver's seat and started the engine. The officers managed to shoot out at least one of the tires, and glass shattered as they hit the driver's side window and windshield. Wayde got in the passenger's seat. Scooter jumped up and climbed in the back. As the truck drove away, Wayde shot out a tire on Miss Kitty's car and my Jeep. Asshole.

As the truck sped away, despite at least one of their tires now being completely flat, Rex and Johnson and Derek kept firing. The back window shattered. They ran out of bullets as the truck squealed down the county road.

I could hear Rex on his shoulder CB calling dispatch. "You okay?" He asked Jodi and me. We both said yes. Then he and Johnson, who'd just jumped down the ladder from the hay loft, took off running to their squad cars parked behind the barn.

Rex sped away down the drive and took a left after them. I thought it was strange they headed back towards Nisswa and not the other way, towards the interstate.

Miss Kitty, Val, Tannya, and Derek started walking towards us. Jodi and I walked side-by-side. I looked over at Jodi, who was rubbing her wrists. Her face had changed. She wasn't the evil bitch I was used to seeing. She was a scared, hurt, little girl. She was on the verge of tears.

My heart and head were pounding from the excitement. I felt bad for her. She'd been through a lot, and no one here liked her. I reached out and slung one arm around her. As soon as I touched her, she stopped in her tracks, turned her body towards me and wrapped herself around me. Ugh!

I let her. It was an awkward moment. I patted her on the back a couple times and then pulled away before she was ready. I'd had all I could take. The faces on Val, Tannya, Derek, and Miss Kitty as they approached were a mix of surprise, disapproval, and sympathy. Jodi wiped her face on her dirty shirt. Derek approached and came over and hugged me long and hard. I felt like sticking my tongue out at Jodi, but I didn't.

"I told you to stay put," he whispered in my ear.

"I know, but someone had to help her," I said.

"You're brave. Stupid, but brave," he said. Then he kissed me. Tannya shoved him aside.

"I need a hug too!"

"Are you okay?" I asked her. "Were you scared?"

"Nah, I was fine. I'm pretty pissed, but I wasn't scared."

Derek stepped closer to Jodi. "Are you okay?" he asked her. She nodded.

"Where did they keep you last night?" Derek asked her

"I'm not sure. A campground of some sort. There were cabins. We stayed in a cabin. He didn't hurt me or anything, but I was scared. He fed me, but wouldn't let me shower. And he handcuffed me at night so I couldn't sneak out."

"Do you know what his plans are now?" Derek asked her.

"No, he was talking to someone on the phone saying he was going to make the captain go down with the ship and steal the blood-treasure back."

We all shook our heads.

"He was talking about a wife and kids, but it sounds like she left him a while ago for another man and took his daughter with her. He drinks a lot and was snorting crack last night."

"So, someone out there knows his plan," Derek pointed out.

Jodi nodded. "Whoever was on the phone."

There was a moment of silence and then Tannya asked, "So, Jodi, what brought you to town?"

28

We all stared at Jodi waiting for her answer. She just stared at the ground, the tears rolling down her cheeks. I was torn between high-fiving Tannya, giving Jodi the middle finger, and walking away. I kicked my evil twin in the ribs and walked away.

Derek got out his cell phone and patched through to the Nisswa police department.

An hour later the tow truck finally arrived and changed out both of our tires and we were on our way. Unlike Butch, I didn't want to ruin my wheel. I brought Tannya back to Morning Glory and her car, and then stopped by Jodi's car and dropped her off.

"You need to go to the police station in town. They're going to need a statement from you," Derek told her.

She nodded. "Where is it?"

Derek gave her directions. Surprisingly, she still had her car keys in her pocket. She stepped out and went to Derek's window. I looked over at her. "Sara," she started. "I'm . . . sorry . . ." tears fell down her cheeks again and she stepped away. She turned back again. "I'm sorry, Derek." She didn't look up from the ground when she said it. He didn't say anything back to her.

I didn't acknowledge her either. I stared straight ahead. Then I put the Jeep in drive and drove off. Derek reached over and patted my leg. "You're a good person," he told me.

I shook my head. "No I'm not."

"Yes, you are."

I let out a sigh. "I just never want to see her again, Derek. Do you understand?" I glanced at him. "I can't deal with her anymore."

"I know." He paused and looked out the window. "I don't think you will after this."

I turned my eyes to my rearview mirror. Miss Kitty and Tannya were following behind me. I could see they were stopped next to Jodi's car. Tannya was saying something to her, and it looked like Jodi had just noticed the cannonball and smashed window.

We drove towards my house in silence. Right before I turned into my driveway, my phone rang. I looked at the caller ID. Rex.

"Hello?"

"Where are your pontoon keys?" he asked urgently.

"Ummm, in the house I think. Why?" I asked.

"I need to get out to the ship! Where in the house?"

"I'm pulling in now. I'll look."

"I'm in your house," he said quickly.

"Oh, look in my jacket hanging there. They might be in the pocket," I told him as I pulled in. His squad car was parked by the house, lights still on. Johnson's was next to him. Miss Kitty pulled in behind me, and then Tannya did the same.

"I'm here," I said and hung up.

"Rex needs the pontoon," I told Derek as we exited.

Rex came tearing past us to the pontoon. "It doesn't go very fast!" I yelled at his back. "The cannon slows it way down."

"Derek, Johnson, girls, come on!" he yelled and waved to follow him.

We ran after him without question. "I have to get out to the ship! Help me get the cannon off!"

We all jogged over there. Johnson, who was mid-thirties and built strong, tall and lean, got there right after Rex. "Johnson and Derek, grab the back. Tannya and Sara, come grab the front," Rex ordered.

Val and Miss Kitty moved the broken junk off the dock to clear a path. "We have to move it to land. It'll be too heavy for my dock," I told them.

On three we all lifted and moved the cannon to shore. It was really heavy. We were all panting and red-faced. Good thing Miss Kitty ordered the small one!

"Derek," Rex said, shoving the key into the ignition, "County will be here with a boat soon. Will you show them the landing and help them out?"

"Sure thing." Derek untied the pontoon and gave it a shove.

Johnson jumped on board and sat in the front. "Thanks, Sara," he said and the two officers pulled away.

I looked to the ship. It was even more tilted now, though still far from sinking.

"What's going on now?" I asked.

"I don't know," Derek said. "The truck the boys were in is parked at Wayde's, though, and the rowboat is back at the ship."

They'd had at least a half-hour head start by this point. They must have gone back to the ship after they sped away.

"Why would they go back to the ship?" I asked.

"They're like sitting ducks out there," Val said. "They have no way to escape."

"Let's go in and watch from the window," I suggested. The sky was blue and the sun had a few hours of light left but it was still a bit chilly.

Once inside, we all slipped our shoes off and rushed to the patio door. I pulled open the blinds. Derek and Miss Kitty grabbed the two pairs of binoculars from the table and looked out. I could see Rex and Johnson getting close in the pontoon. They pulled up to the ladder and looked like they we tying the pontoon up.

Johnson drew his gun and aimed up at the ship's upper deck while Rex climbed up. Once there, he pulled a gun and pointed it across the boat. Johnson started up the ladder.

On deck in the far corner, which we could see now that the ship was tipped towards us, were the three men.

"What the hell?" Derek asked quietly.

"Oh, my God!" Miss Kitty said.

"What?"

"Tell us!"

"Let me see." Tannya, Val and I were all eager to see. It was hard to make out what exactly was going on without the aid of binoculars.

"It looks like Butch has Wayde and Scooter tied up?" Derek said, adjusting the focus.

"Really?" Tannya said and covered her mouth. She hugged Val. "Why?"

"Rex and Johnson are on deck now!" Miss Kitty informed us. "They both have their guns drawn and are talking to Butch."

"This is not good," Derek said. "They're tied up together, back to back in folding chairs, and there's a gas can lying on its side nearby."

"Doesn't Scooter's shirt and pant leg look wet?" Miss Kitty asked. "Is that gas or blood?"

My heart was racing and I could see Tannya tearing up. Val still had one arm around Tannya. Val covered her mouth with her free hand.

"I can't tell," Derek said. "Damn it, where's County with the back-up and the boat?"

I went to the living room and pulled the curtains back. I didn't see anyone yet.

"Sara, call 911 and tell them to patch you through to Nisswa dispatch. Tell them what we see," Derek said. I pulled my phone out and dialed. I watched him as he handed the binoculars to me and pulled his gun out of his pants. As he walked to the bedroom, he dropped the empty clip out of it into his hand.

Dispatch answered, and I told them what I saw. The dispatcher put me on hold but told me not to hang up. Derek came back out with his hands busy behind him. He was putting the gun back in his pants. He must have reloaded.

I pointed to the window. "Here comes County with the boat. Derek ran outside. He was waving them to the dock area. I watched while I was on hold as they launched the boat. They left the trailer in the water and took off. Derek stayed on shore, and I was grateful for that.

"It's getting bad. They look panicky!" Miss Kitty said.

I went over to the window and watched. I had the binoculars in one hand and the phone in the other. Dispatch came back on and said, "County should be there. Do you see them?"

"Yes, they're here. The boat's in, and they're headed to the ship."

"Oh, fuck!" Miss Kitty said.

On the deck I could see Butch with something small in his hand, which he held out. Rex and Johnson were both yelling and still aiming their guns. Derek came back through the door.

County had a small boat with a big motor, so it took them seconds to get to the ship. The two county officers were pulled up by the pontoon. It looked like they were tying up to it.

"He's got a lighter!" Miss Kitty said panicked.

"Oh, God," I said under my breath. I spoke to dispatch, "Butch has a lighter, and we're pretty sure he's dumped gas on two guys and the boat."

"He's crazy!" Miss Kitty said.

"I can't look," Val said and walked into the living room. Tannya followed her.

"Shiiit! I'm mad at him but I don't want him hurt!" Tannya cried. She sat down by Aunt Val and leaned her head on her shoulder. The tension was incredible. My breathing and heartrate were up like I'd just gone for a run. I looked with sympathy at Val and Tannya.

"Oh, God," Derek said. The way he said it gave me the chills. "Hurry, shoot him! WHY DON'T THEY SHOOT HIM?" Derek screamed at the window in frustration. "Fucking redneck cops! Just shoot the bastard!"

"HOLY FUUUCK!" Miss Kitty screamed. Pepper stood up and barked.

Something caught my eye at that same moment. I looked out the glass door. There were huge flames on deck. The ship was a blaze of orange!

29

My breath was completely sucked from my body. My shoulders sank with the weight of what I'd just witnessed.

"Oh, my God, send more help! He burned them!" I screamed into the phone. Then I set it on the table. I didn't hang up, but I didn't know what to do! I was panicking.

"Fuck!" Derek yelled and snatched the binoculars from my hand. I wasn't using them anyway.

"I think Rex fired! I think Butch was hit! Where the hell is he?" Miss Kitty asked with a shaky voice.

Tannya and Val stood up, side by side, and stared at me with big bulging eyes. They both had their hands over their mouths, shaking their heads in disbelief. I ran over to them and tried to wrap my arms around them, but Tannya melted to the ground and started bawling and Aunt Val pulled back.

"No," she said sternly. "No." She marched to the window and grabbed the binoculars from Miss Kitty's hands. Derek stepped in front of her view and fought the binoculars out of her grip.

"I'm sorry," he said and hugged her. He pulled her towards the living room and sat her on the couch.

I looked out to the ship and saw someone from County throwing a fire extinguisher up to Rex, who was leaning over the edge.

"Fuck, I wish I could do something!" Derek said angrily. I saw County digging around in my pontoon. I had a large fire extinguisher in the storage under the steering wheel. I watched as they found it and threw it up to Johnson. Rex was spraying the area, and Johnson joined him. The flames were getting smaller, and I could see Scooter and Wayde. They were hunched over in the chairs and very still. The smoke was swirling around them.

I looked over to the left and noticed Butch in the water swimming towards Wayde's house. "Derek, look!" I pointed. The county officers seemed concerned with the ship. One of them was racing up the ladder with a big first-aid bag strapped on his back. The other was standing on my pontoon talking into his CB. "Go get him!" I said to Derek.

Derek looked through the binoculars and found Butch in the water. "He's swimming back to the truck!" he said, handing me the binoculars. He kissed me quickly on the cheek, grabbed my phone and keys from the table and ran out the door.

"I can't believe he did that!" Miss Kitty cried with her hand on her chest. "Do you think they're okay?"

"I don't know," I answered quietly. "I don't know."

I stood and watched in horror. I felt so helpless. I had no way to get there and help. There was *nothing* I could do. It was the most horrible feeling. Miss Kitty and I again turned to the window. Side by side, we watched the red and orange flames. I heard sirens in the distance. I went to the living room window and looked. An ambulance and a fire truck were coming into my driveway.

I threw on my coat and ran out there. The ambulance driver rolled down the window and I ran over to him. "They're on the ship," I said, pointing in that direction. "The only two boats are out there. There are two burn victims. I'm not sure if they're still alive or not," I told him. "It was a big fire. I think Butch poured gas on them," I said shaking my head.

He radioed dispatch and told them to have the county boat come and pick them up. A minute later the boat started and buzzed over. The fire truck pulled up nice and close. The lights were flashing on all the emergency vehicles in my yard, giving it an eerie feeling.

The fire truck driver came over to the ambulance driver and his partner. They spoke briefly as they got two boards out of the back and two big bags. They also had a defibrillator bag and an oxygen tank. They rushed over to the county boat pulled up to my dock. The two EMTs jumped on, and they flew back over to the ship. The fire truck stood by but was as helpless as I was. Across the lake I saw Derek's Jeep towards the back of the driveway, but no Derek or Butch. I rushed back to the house.

When I opened the door, all three girls were sitting on the couch, squished together and crying softly. I felt awful. Val and Tannya were in such a horrible situation. I'd been there, and I knew how hard it was.

I hustled through the room, used the binoculars and looked around the property for Derek. I couldn't see him. I looked on land and then in the water for Butch.

There he was! He was still swimming. He was almost to shore. I frantically moved the binoculars around, searching for Derek. "Where are you?" I said aloud. Finally I caught a glimpse of him behind the front fender of the truck. Butch was just coming out of the water. He climbed to his feet, soaking wet. It looked like he'd lost his shoes, jacket, and pants during the swim. He had to be exhausted. He grabbed his arm and looked at his shoulder. I could see that he had been hit, but it must have just scraped by him. The wound was small and didn't seem to slow him down much. He slowly and weakly made his way towards his truck. He stopped in his tracks suddenly and looked up.

Derek was behind the truck with his gun drawn. I couldn't tell what they were saying to each other, but Butch put his hands up in surrender then slowly laid face down on the ground. Derek carefully approached him and then knelt on his back and tied his hands. I couldn't tell with what exactly, but it looked thick.

I watched as Derek used my phone to call someone. I scanned back over to the ship. The men had Scooter secured to a body board and were slowly lowering him by a rope down to the pontoon. The two county officers got him on the pontoon and set the board on the floor between the front two seats. I looked back to the ship deck. The men carried Wayde on the other board and tied up the end of the rope, that they'd just pulled up from the pontoon, to the board.

Meanwhile the county officer got in his boat and pulled it around to the front of the pontoon. He tied it to the rope ladder and jumped back on the pontoon just in time to grab Wayde. It seemed to take forever, but finally the two county officers carried his board to the sundeck and placed him up on it.

Then the two EMTs scurried down the rope. One of the county officers drove my pontoon back towards us. The county boat was left tied to the ship.

I ran outside, and with a nod from the fireman, got in the ambulance and backed it up to the dock. I left it running and opened the rear doors for them. The fireman got out and stood alongside me, ready to help.

I heard more sirens and looked over to the driveway. The fireman told me that it should be another ambulance since there was only room for one stretcher inside each.

It arrived just in time. They carried Scooter to one and loaded him in. I caught a glimpse of him. He looked really bad. His whole body was burned. His pants were almost completely gone and his shoes were mostly gone, too. Everywhere I looked his skin was black. I gasped at the sight and covered my mouth. I got a whiff of the smell of his burnt flesh and turned around and threw up. After I wiped my mouth off, I stood there and stared as they got the stretcher onto the wheeled cart and loaded into the back. Scooter's eyes were open, but I didn't notice them move or blink. His face was badly burned. He wasn't even recognizable.

The EMT rushed in and closed the doors. The driver jumped in and took off down the driveway. I glanced to the house and noticed all the girls in the window. As that ambulance left, they turned their eyes to me. I covered my mouth and turned away from them.

The fireman and the county officer were already carrying Wayde off the dock to the other ambulance. The two loaded him quickly in the back and left. He looked the same as Scooter, every inch of his body burned, only small charred pieces of clothing left. They loaded him in the second ambulance and off they went. I felt horrible for them both. I couldn't imagine the pain they were in. I doubted either would survive. I was surprised they weren't already in body bags.

The fireman gave the county officer a huge fire extinguisher to take with him back to the ship and then stayed with me as the county officer drove the pontoon away.

I looked over to Wayde's property. Derek, Butch, and the Jeep were gone.

My phone rang, I pulled it out of my pocket. It was Derek. "Hello?"

"Go into the police car. Look in the glove compartment and trunk for extra handcuffs. Get them out for me. I'll be there in a sec."

I ran over to Rex's police car and checked the glove box and found a pair. I opened the back door, too, and waited for Derek. A few seconds later he pulled into the driveway and parked by the squad car. I ran over to him and handed him the cuffs. He had Butch turn in the back seat and cuffed him before he removed the seatbelt he'd tied him with. Then he got him out.

Butch still looked exhausted as he maneuvered himself out of the Jeep. He caught my eye. I was stunned. It was hard to look at him, knowing what he'd done to Scooter and Wayde. I glared. He winked back at me. He was pure evil. It made me think I was lucky, and so was Jodi, that we weren't hurt. And to think, he did all this to avenge the murder of his friend? My evil side wanted to spit on him, but I fought it and just looked away. He'd get what he deserved—a life sentence, hopefully.

Derek shoved him into the back of the squad car and slammed the door shut. "Holy hell!" he said with a sigh and wrapped his arms around me. I cried into his shoulder for a few minutes. I felt so weak and helpless. Everyone was hurting, and I could do nothing to fix it. Poor Val and Tannya, they were going to be emotional basket cases. I knew how they felt. You loved men, then hated them, and wanted them to be okay but not in your life . . . this was going to suck for them.

Derek was holding me with one arm and calling Rex on the phone with the other hand.

"Rex, Derek here. I have Butch detained. He's in your squad. Yes. Will do."

I pulled away from Derek and told him, "I'll be in the house."

"I need to stay by the car," he answered. "I'll be in later."

I looked back to the ship. The fire on the deck seemed to be getting worse again. I'd thought the flames were out, but apparently not. The county officer was walking around spraying what he could but it wasn't helping. I watched from my patio for a moment.

When the extinguisher was empty, Rex and the county officer went down the ladder and returned to the boat and pontoon. When I saw them start back to my dock, I headed into the house.

Inside, Tannya and Val were both crying, as was Miss Kitty. They looked at me when I opened the door.

"Were they alive?" Val asked sadly between sobs.

Tears came to me too. "I think so, but they looked really bad," I told them. "I don't know if they'll make it."

We cried and talked sadly about what a horrible day this was. And about how evil Butch was, and how what we had thought was a neat game was actually a horrible cover-up to theft and a revenge plot.

"I'm sorry," Val said. "This is all my fault."

"No it isn't!" I assured her.

"It's *my* fault," Tannya said. "*I* was the one who wanted to start a LARP and get in on the action. I shouldn't have done that."

"I shouldn't have gotten so excited about it and bought all the shirts and boat decals and the cannon . . ." Miss Kitty said, hanging her head.

"For the record, we're all adults, and each of us chose to be involved," I said. "I don't know about anyone else, but I feel the cannon was worth it, even if it was only for the hole in Vagina's car." They all smiled slightly.

I glanced out the window and noticed the county officers were loading their boat up on the trailer. Rex and Derek were tying up the pontoon. They all stopped and looked in the direction of the ship. I walked to the patio door and looked, too.

It was glowing orange. There was no way to save it now. The fire was wrapping around the side and front and reaching high into the sky. The girls got up and joined me at the window.

"Well *there's* something you don't see every day," Miss Kitty said.

We watched from the glass door as about a third of it burned. Then it quickly sank to the bottom of lake.

Lake Hawsawneekee would never be the same. Now scuba divers from all over would come to tour the sunken pirate ship of northern Minnesota. It would be a legend in this town for generations to come. The story would change from person to person and year to year. New details would be added and some would be omitted, but the story of pirates on the lake would live on, especially in this small town.

Dang it, I was going to make the paper again. I had a lot of explaining to do to Joan about the cannon fuses I borrowed.

30

I took a deep breath and turned to Tannya. She had to be hurting the most. Scooter was her ex, but that was because of the drugs. Now he was clean, so up until earlier today I thought Tannya still had feelings for him. It was hard to tell what she might be feeling, because we were also held at gun point by his associate. He'd made a bad choice to partner with Wayde, but he was in a difficult situation too. I'm not sure how I would feel if I were her.

I locked eyes with her. "Is there anything I can do? Do you want to go to the hospital?" I asked her.

She thought about it for a moment and then nodded.

"Okay," I said and slung an arm over her shoulder. "Do you too?" I asked Val. She nodded as well.

Miss Kitty walked past us quickly and grabbed her shoes. "I'm coming, too. I want to be here for my friends," she said. I again wondered if we were the first friends she'd ever had.

The fire truck and county truck and boat trailer were gone. Derek came to the door as we were getting our shoes and coats. He looked at me with concern in his eyes. "Tannya and Val would like to go to the hospital," I told him.

"Okay, I'll come with too. Rex would like to see you for a second," Derek told me.

I walked out with the girls. Tannya loaded into the Jeep—I figured she'd come back for her car later—and Val into Miss Kitty's car, as I met up with Rex at his squad car. Butch was still sitting in the back. I glared at him.

"Hey," Rex said in his soft, sexy voice. He was covered in soot from the fire, and he smelled of smoke. I was amazed at how calm he was in the midst of all that had gone on in the last couple hours. "You okay?"

I nodded and looked down. "Val and Tannya want to go to the hospital," I told him.

"HOSPITAL? If he were any kind of captain he would've went down with his ship!" Butch yelled from the back. Rex slammed his door shut.

"Sorry. Don't listen to him." I saw Rex's jaw clench as he said it. "They took them to St. Joseph's in Brainerd. I'm going to need statements from you guys as soon as possible."

"Okay."

"No later than tomorrow noon. Tonight would be best. Let them know that for me," he requested.

"Sure."

"Thanks for your help with all of this. I think we should get you trained and maybe give you a badge and gun." He smiled slightly.

"Yeah, right."

"I'm going to get this jerk processed. You guys better hurry if they want to see them. If they make it, they'll probably fly them to the Cities where there's a better burn unit."

"Okay. Thanks, I'll talk to you soon," I said and rushed to the Jeep.

Rex turned back to his squad car. I waited for Derek to jump in the Jeep, and then we drove to the hospital in Brainerd. Miss Kitty followed in her car. We talked on the way there. I asked Tannya how she was feeling. She was totally lost and didn't know what to feel. She was a mess of angry, sad, hurt, and concerned. Derek looked at me sympathetically. I'm sure that's exactly how I'd sounded when I first met him.

We got to the hospital and parked in the emergency lot. We walked in as a group and went to the admissions counter. I explained that we were friends of Wayde and Scooter, had been at the scene and wanted to know if they were okay and if we could see them.

"One moment," the nurse said and checked her computer.

We anxiously waited. I watched her eyes dart around on the screen and her eyebrows squeeze together a few times.

"Okay," she said with a sigh. "Have a seat. I'll be right back." She disappeared through the door behind her. The older woman in the next cubicle smiled sympathetically. We looked around the waiting area and took seats in the far corner. No one said anything.

After a few minutes, the check-in nurse came out accompanied by a woman in surgical garb, including booties, a cap, and an apron. She approached us quickly.

"Hello," she said, "I'm Doctor Barnes." She sat on the edge of the coffee table in front of us. "You're the friends of Wayde Johnson and Scooter Potter?" she asked.

We nodded.

"Do they have any family or next of kin in the area?" *Oh, boy, no one uses "next of kin" unless . . .*

"I'm Scooter Potter's ex-wife. I'm able to contact his family," Tannya spoke up.

"And I'm Wayde's . . . girlfriend," Val said. "He doesn't have any family," she said sadly.

The doctor nodded and looked at the floor. Then she inhaled deeply and told us, "I regret to inform you that Wayde passed away en route to the hospital. I'm so sorry."

Val leaned over and put her head on my shoulder. I wrapped an arm around her. "And Mr. Potter, is in critical condition. His burns are the worst we've seen. We're trying to stabilize him for air transport to Hennepin County Medical Center in the Cities. They have an excellent burn unit there where he can get the help he needs."

"Can I see him before he goes?" Tannya asked eagerly.

"Umm," she said. "Let me see where they're at."

"I just want to say good bye," Tannya said sadly.

A few moments later the doctor pushed open the door and waved for Tannya to come with her. Tannya rushed to her. I watched them head down the hall together until the swinging doors blocked my sight.

I held on to Val. She silently cried. When she was still and relaxed and not sobbing anymore, Derek got up and brought us all coffees. We thanked him. I heard the thumping of a helicopter above us. "I hope she got to see him," I said.

Miss Kitty was pretty quiet. She reached out and rubbed Aunt Val's arm. "I'm sorry," she told her. "I know you cared about Wayde deeply." Val nodded.

A moment later I could hear the helicopter take off again. Just then Tannya appeared in the doorway. We all stood.

"I saw hi . . . hi . . . him," she sobbed. She was carrying a handful of tissues. "He looked bad. Real bad," she told us and then shook and caught her breath again, between sobs. She looked at me with pain in her eyes. "I told him I still loved him. I don't think he could hear me though," she told me.

"Of course he heard you. He knows you were there. That'll mean everything to him," I assured her and gave her a big hug.

"His burns were bad. His ear was gone," she said and starting crying harder again. I squeezed her tighter. "He still heard you, Tannya, and he knows you came," I repeated.

What a horrible sight. I saw it when he came off the water, but I couldn't imagine what that same sight would do to me if it were someone I'd loved. The image was burned into my head and hers too, I was sure.

The nurse from the cubicle came over and got some information from Val and Tannya.

After they were finished we drove back to my house. It was kind of sad driving into my yard and not having the ship on the water. The lake looked empty without *Poseidon's Zebra Mussel* floating on it.

I dropped Derek off, and then the four of us went to the police station and gave our statements. It was dark and we were tired, but we wanted to get it done so we didn't have to go through all the emotions again tomorrow.

Rex took our statements, and we all stayed in the room together. He had different questions for me, because of the time I spent alone in the woods with Butch and the fact that the whole thing took place in my backyard. He questioned Tannya and Val on the relationships that they'd had with Scooter and Wayde. It was hard for them to relive parts of it.

The week had started out so great. We were excited and having fun, and I'd found my dream shoes, but then again there was my head, ankle, the kidnapping, Jodi, the fire, the ship sinking and Wayde's death, and Scooter . . . the week had gone downhill pretty fast.

After our statements were taken, I went to Morning Glory and picked up two large take-and-bake pizzas and headed home. I invited everyone back for dinner. They accepted.

At home Derek had the oven warmed up. We ate a few bites but no one had much of an appetite. Miss Kitty said she was going to head home, and invited Val to join her. Val agreed to stay there again.

At the door she told me, "I called your parents and gave them the shortened version of what happened. They said they're going to be here about noon tomorrow. I'll be back over here by then to see them, too."

"Okay. I love you, Aunt Val. Get some sleep. I'll see you in the morning," I said and gave her a long hug.

I hugged Miss Kitty too and shut the door behind them.

Tannya was ready to go home too. I invited her to stay so she didn't have to be alone, but she wanted the peace and quiet. I hugged her and locked up behind her. It was after 11:00 p.m. by the time they'd left.

I went straight to bed and slept through the night. The day and the events had completely worn me out.

31

I woke up to my phone ringing. I ran to the kitchen to get it.
"Hello?"
"Hey, Sara, it's Kat. I'm calling from West's phone. Mine apparently doesn't work this far out in the sticks." *CRAP! I forgot they were coming today.* "We'll be there in about an hour."
"Great, can't wait," I lied. "I have a really good pizza for us for lunch. Sorry, nothing too fancy. It's been a crazy week around here."
"Pizza sounds perfect. Thanks. We'll see you soon."

I set the phone down and looked at the time. It was 10:45. How the heck did I sleep so late? I went to the hall and shouted to Derek that we'd have company in an hour. My parents were always early, so maybe less than that.

I quickly showered and dressed. Then I did a quick hair and make-up routine and went to the living room to dust. If I didn't, my mom would as soon as she got here.

I called Tannya to make sure she was okay. She said she was just getting up and had called HCMC. Scooter had died. He had just passed just a few minutes before her call. She told me that she needed to make some phone calls and just wanted some time alone. I invited her over, but she said she just wanted to bake cookies, and eat them and watch movies. I understood and told her I'd check in with her later and to call me if she wanted company. I told her again how sorry I was. She thanked me and hung up.

A few minutes later, my parents knocked. I let them in. They were greeted by Pepper. Aunt Val walked in just a few seconds later. We all hugged and then moved to the kitchen table. My mom had brought a bag of snacks and two homemade apple pies with her. I poured some snacks into bowls, and we all gathered around the table.

A minute later there was another knock at the door. I got up and welcomed my long-lost BFF Kat and her boyfriend, West. I gave them a quick tour and ended it in the kitchen. After introducing West to everyone, we joined them at the table. Derek brought an extra folding chair from the closet and helped me get beverages for everyone.

"All right, Sara and Val, tell me what the heck went on!" my mom demanded. "What's all this about a pirate ship, and a fire, and bad men, and treasure, and Chicago gangs . . . what else was there?" she asked my dad.

He shrugged.

"Okay, well, it all started with the pirate ship and Aunt Val calling to get bailed out of jail," Derek said with a smirk.

Everyone was staring at me and Val, who was sitting on my left.

"Ha, ha . . . funny story . . ." I started.

An hour later, Val and I were done with the story. I finished with the news of Scooter's passing this morning. We were all saddened by that, but Val toasted to the wellbeing of everyone else and that she was lucky to have so many good friends and family. I stood to put the pizza in the oven, and heard another knock at the door. I had no idea who else would be coming over today.

Everyone was quiet in the kitchen. I opened the door to Rex and Officer Johnson.

"Hi, come on in," I said and stepped aside. They were in their uniforms. Rex had worked a lot of overtime this week, and his eyes showed it.

"We didn't formally meet, Sara," Johnson said, I shook his hand.

Derek got up and shook hands, too. "How's it going, Rex? Jeff?"

"Oh, it's been better. I tell ya, if it's not one thing it's another," Rex said with a sigh, and gave me a strange look. I turned towards the kitchen, and he and Derek followed.

When they got into the kitchen, I introduced Rex and Jeff to Kat and West, and Jeff to my mom and dad. They shook hands with everyone.

"So, Officer, it's sounds like you had a busy week, too. Sara was just filling us in," my mom said.

"Yes, it was very busy," Rex said with a half-smile.

"I just can't believe it. Pirate ships and treasures. I bet you haven't seen that in this little town before," Dad said.

"I haven't, and the details just keep coming. That's actually why I'm here. Can I talk to you a minute?" Rex asked, turning to me.

"Sure," I said.

"Wait, we want to hear the juicy details too," Kat said with a wink.

"Yeah, tell all of us. We're intrigued," Mom said.

Rex inhaled deeply and nodded to Jeff. "Sara, I have a search warrant for the property," Johnson said handing me a piece of paper.

"For what exactly?" Derek asked stepping to my side and taking the paper. He looked at it while Jeff talked.

"For stolen property. It's believed that Sara has some property stolen from a woman by the name of Milly Larson, here in Nisswa."

SHIT!

"Sara?" my mom snapped with a parental tone.

Derek lowered the paper and looked at me with raised eyebrows. "Louis Vuittons. Really, Sara?"

I looked around the room. My mom and dad looked concerned, and West looked confused. Val and Kat had huge, excited eyes and smiles.

I looked back to Derek and Rex . . . and Jeff, who now had cuffs in his hands.

"Ha ha . . . funny story . . ." I said.

The End

www.danellehelget.com   Facebook—Danelle Helget